the
Sisterhood

ALSO BY A. J. GRAINGER

Captive

the
Sisterhood

✦

A. J. GRAINGER

SIMON & SCHUSTER BFYR

New York London Toronto Sydney New Delhi

SIMON & SCHUSTER BFYR

An imprint of Simon & Schuster Children's Publishing Division

1230 Avenue of the Americas, New York, New York 10020

This book is a work of fiction. Any references to historical events, real people, or real places are used fictitiously. Other names, characters, places, and events are products of the author's imagination, and any resemblance to actual events or places or persons, living or dead, is entirely coincidental.

Text copyright © 2018 by A. J. Grainger

Jacket photograph copyright © 2019 by WIN-Initiative

First published in Great Britain in 2018 by Simon & Schuster UK, Ltd.

SIMON & SCHUSTER BFYR is a trademark of Simon & Schuster, Inc.

For information about special discounts for bulk purchases, please contact Simon & Schuster Special Sales at 1-866-506-1949 or business@simonandschuster.com.

The Simon & Schuster Speakers Bureau can bring authors to your live event. For more information or to book an event, contact the Simon & Schuster Speakers Bureau at 1-866-248-3049 or visit our website at www.simonspeakers.com.

Book design by Krista Vossen

The text for this book was set in Dante.

Manufactured in the United States of America

First Edition

10 9 8 7 6 5 4 3 2 1

Library of Congress Cataloging-in-Publication Data

Names: Grainger, A. J. (Annalie J.) author.

Title: The Sisterhood / A.J. Grainger.

Description: First edition. | New York : Simon & Schuster Books for Young Readers, [2018] | "First published in Great Britain in 2018 by Simon & Schuster UK, Ltd." | Summary: While searching for her missing sister, seventeen-year-old Lil nearly runs into Seven, a girl trying to escape flames that tore through the compound of the Sisterhood of the Light—and something worse.

Identifiers: LCCN 2018004987 | ISBN 9781481429061 (hardcover : alk. paper) | ISBN 9781481429078 (pbk. : alk. paper) | ISBN 9781481429085 (eBook)

Subjects: | CYAC: Runaways—Fiction. | Cults—Fiction. | Sisters—Fiction. | Wales—Fiction.

Classification: LCC PZ7.1.G72 Sis 2019 | DDC [Fic]—dc23

LC record available at https://lccn.loc.gov/2018004987

For Naomi

Only in the Brightness shall we find
Light for all, for all eternity.

—THE BOOK

A t the center of the clearing, the Sun burned strongly,
its fiery fingertips slashing at the dark midnight sky.
Around it danced the sixteen members of the Sisterhood.
Their brightly colored dresses—the red chiffon, the
purple velvet, and the green taffeta—swirled wide, so that
the forest became gyrating flame. Brilliance's chest tightened at the sight, heart beating fast like the wings of an
insect trapped in a jar as the sisters raised their voices in
the Light's saying:

"I dance with the fire in my heart, in my soul, in my
veins. I dance until it rises up for me. I dance into the
Brightness. Into the Light. Into the Light."

Brilliance stared deep into the fire. She loved the way it
moved like liquid, undulating in shapes and colors. She loved
to lose herself in the Light's power as the flame became a part
of her: its pulse her pulse, its breath her breath. The power and
the beauty, the two sides of a knife.

The air hung heavy tonight with a coming storm, like

a thick coat in high summer. Somewhere nearby an owl hooted, and Brilliance jumped. Its cry had sounded almost human and in pain. Then the high priestess's voice cut across the clearing. Her hood was thrown back to reveal flaming red hair crowned with white flowers that glinted in the firelight. Her eyes were as blue as the deepest part of the ocean. The symbol of the Light—a yellow sun—was painted on her cheek. "The Brightness," she cried. "The Brightness is coming and it's going to save us all."

Excitement tore through Brilliance.

"The Light's Gift will show us the way," the high priestess said.

Brilliance's sisters began to move toward the fire, faces hidden by their cloaks, and the Light burned inside Brilliance, as red and bright as a flame.

CHAPTER ONE

Lil sat back in her chair and read the words she'd typed into the status update on the Find Mella website: "We love you, Mella. We miss you. We're here for you whenever you're ready." The message had been the same every day since Mella had gone missing—134 days. Lil added the sign-off: "Love, Mum and Mouse." Mella was the only one who still used Lil's childhood nickname. Ironic, now that Lil was over six feet tall.

Lil glanced at the rest of the page. There were a few new likes for the picture she'd uploaded last night of her and Mella at the beach last summer. The photo was just so Mella. She had one arm flung around Lil, and the other out wide, and she was smiling. A stupid pair of star-shaped, sparkly sunglasses were perched on her freckled nose. They were a child's pair, won playing an arcade game earlier that day. Mella had refused to take them off, and Lil had to admit that their bright-green color complemented her sister's pale-pink skin, flushed almost bronze after a summer of sunbathing. By contrast, Lil was blue white, pale as ice, made bluer because she was thrown into shadow by Mella's outstretched arm. She was smiling, though—not broadly like Mella, but a half upturn of the corner of her mouth. A half smile. By comparison to Mella, everything Lil did seemed to be at half pace. Not in a bad way. It was just that Mella did everything at warp speed, at 1,000 percent, and like the brightest star in the sky, she threw everything around her into shadow. But the light that a star emitted was a long-ago memory of what once was. It had died out years ago. The thought stung, and Lil clicked out of the photo quickly, not wanting to think about death and Mella in the same sentence.

She logged into her e-mail. There wasn't much in there. They'd had so many messages on this site in the early days—when the story had been on local news and radio—but they had mostly dwindled to nothing now. "No fresh leads," was what the police said. There hadn't been a single sighting in over two and a half months. Lil knew what the police thought that meant, but she would not . . . she could not believe that. Her sister was alive and they were going to find her. Even if it took the rest of Lil's life.

Erin had sent a new message. She had been Mella's best friend at school. She wrote every now and then. It was really nice of her. She and Mella hadn't even been that close in the end. Mella had lost touch with a lot of her friends from high school when she started college, then lost touch with most of them when she began going out with Cai. Mella was like that. She just moved on from things. Unlike Lil, who had been friends with Rhia since she moved to Wales from London when she was nine, although just recently maybe Rhia wasn't such a good example of Lil's loyalty. Lil didn't want to think about that now.

Instead she read Erin's message:

> Lil—hey! How's it going? Haven't checked
> in for a while, so I thought I'd e-mail. Any
> news? Dumb question, I know. You'd tell
> me if there was, right? God, I want there
> to be news. . . . I went up to the river
> yesterday—you know, by Haven's Field?
> I don't know why, I just wanted to see it.
> Probably sounds weird. You remember
> how she used to draw up there? Those
> damn trees! The ones she thought looked
> like women dancing? God, that girl could
> be crazy sometimes. Anyway. I'm rambling.
> Call me, won't you? Even if there's no
> news. It'd be nice to hear your voice.
> Take care, Lil.
> Call me! Call me! CALL ME!
> E
> XOX

Lil typed a quick reply:

> Hi, Erin! Thanks for checking in. No news
> on Mella. I'll let you know as soon as I hear
> anything. And I'll try to call you soon. Hope
> everything's good with you.
> Love, Lil xx

Lil wouldn't call. Erin was lovely, but it was too painful to talk about Mella. It hurt having to tell people that they still had absolutely no idea where she was.

After clicking send on the e-mail to Erin, Lil turned her laptop off. She had planned to upload some more photos onto the Find Mella website—she liked to keep the page fresh—but she'd lost energy today. Instead she looked out the window. The rain was properly coming down now, and the wind was howling around the house like it wanted to take it down, brick by brick. Even in a torrential downpour, the Welsh countryside was beautiful. There was something so amazing about the way it just rolled on and on. Lil had loved it the second they'd arrived. Mella less so. She'd missed the buzz of London.

Lil stared out into the storm for a long time. She missed Mella so intensely it was a physical ache. Sometimes in the morning when she woke up, there would be a second before she remembered that Mella was gone, and then the realization would rush in like an icy blast, and it would be like losing her all over again.

Lil had real trouble sleeping now, and the doctor had prescribed some sleeping pills because she was so tired she couldn't concentrate at school. She'd taken them and enjoyed blissful deep sleep, her dreams full of Mella: burying their granddad in the sand at the beach; driving into Old Porthpridd with the windows open, singing as loudly as they could to the radio; her, Mella, and Rhia eating chips in the rain, kicking their legs against the harbor wall.

After one week Lil had stopped taking the pills. Why

should she have a peaceful night when who knew where Mella was? Who knew what she was doing, whom she was with, if she was even still alive? Lil cut off that last thought with a gasp. Mella was alive. Mella was coming home. Lil had to believe that or else . . . She couldn't even consider the alternative.

Lil's clock radio beeped the hour. "This is Capital FM Cymru, and the time is one o'clock on Saturday, the eighth of July. Flood warnings are in place across much of North Wales this afternoon as unseasonably bad storms continue to batter the country—"

Lil jerked out of her chair and turned the volume down. She had to meet Kiran at the kayaking clubhouse in an hour, and she was going to be late if she didn't get a move on. She tugged her long hair, dyed unicorn purple this week—Lil's natural color was as close to mouse as you could get without actually being one—back into a ponytail. She was going kayaking, so there was no point showering, but after a quick sniff of her armpits, she sprayed another long blast of deodorant into each one. Then she pulled on her goat T-shirt—the one Mella had bought her a few birthdays ago, the one with the words "Here's looking at you, kid" and a picture of a fluffy baby goat on it—and took her gray tracksuit bottoms from the drawer.

Extra, extra, extra long for the vertically gifted, Mouse, she heard her sister saying. Even after four and a half months, Lil couldn't get her sister's voice out of her head. Not that she wanted to.

Her mum called from downstairs as she was pulling her red hoodie on. "Lilian! I'm going now."

"Coming," Lil shouted back. She grabbed her beaten-up white Converse trainers and bag and headed down the stairs to join her mum in the kitchen.

"Maybe I shouldn't go," her mum said. She was standing by the sink, and in the gloom, with her long, dark curly hair tucked behind her ears, she looked so much like Mella that Lil had to hold on to the doorframe and take a deep breath.

Lil flicked on the light and the mirage faded to reveal her mum: face pale and drawn, dark eyes ringed with bags. Lil wasn't sure her mum had slept since Mella left. Her mum's face was more lined too, and grew more so every morning, as though each day that Mella was missing was inked onto her skin.

"You should go, Mum. You deserve a treat," Lil said as she crossed the kitchen to the bread bin. Lil's mum was going to Chester to see an old college friend from her music academy. It was as far as Mum had gone since Mella left. Her mum needed to do this. Lil needed her mum to do this.

"It's a long way," her mum said. Despite being Welsh-born, her mum always spoke English to Lil. She had spoken English to Lil's granddad, too, although he'd always responded in Welsh.

Lil took out a slice of bread. It was moldy; so was the second piece. The third looked all right. She shoved the other two to the bottom of the pack, so her mum wouldn't notice. Her mum had been struggling to keep on top of stuff since Mella disappeared. Not that she should be solely responsible for the shopping. It was just kind of hard to get about here without a car, what with being in the middle of a field in the middle of three other fields, on the top of a mountain. Things would be easier when Lil turned seventeen and passed her driving test. But that wasn't until next February, and Lil hoped Mella would be home by then. She woke every morning hoping today would be the day that Mella came back.

Her mum was speaking again. ". . . there was an accident on the A55, near Brynford, earlier. Traffic jam, they said, on the radio. And the rain . . ."

"It's Wales," Lil said with a smile. "It always rains. It'll stop. Eventually." *Hopefully.*

"I don't like leaving you," her mum said.

"I'll be fine. And you can call me. It's only for one afternoon."

"Sandi wants to go for dinner afterward too, but . . ."

"You should stay for dinner."

"Really? Well, maybe . . . I don't know . . . if you think I should. Do I look all right? I didn't know what to wear. Maybe I should have gone for jeans. Do I look like I'm about to give a concert?" She sighed. "I look like I'm about to give a concert, don't I?" She was wearing a white shirt and black skirt and Nain's peacock broach. It was the outfit she used to wear for recitals, but still.

"You look great." Lil smiled and said gently, "Seriously, just go already. You'll be late."

"Okay." Still her mum didn't move. "I just . . . I don't know if it's a good idea. What if she comes back and there's no one here? You know what she's like. So hot-headed, she'll be off again before we know it." Her mum sat down at the kitchen table.

Lil sat down opposite her and took one of her mum's hands in hers. Delicate with long fingers, they'd once been her mum's most beautiful feature. She'd had them insured when she'd trained as a pianist at the Royal Academy of Music in London. It was where she'd met their father, although by some bizarre coincidence he'd grown up in Wales too, only a couple of villages away from where Lil's grandparents, Taid and Nain, lived. Now her mum's hands were chapped and red. The moisturizer Lil had bought her for Christmas was still in its wrapper in the bathroom.

She held her mum's hand softly but firmly, like she would a creature that might startle and run at a sudden movement. Her mum never used to be this fragile. She used to be kind of angry, especially about the things she cared about. Like the lack of music education in schools. That was her big topic. "Why is everything about maths these days?" she'd rant. "Art and music are just as important!" She and Mella were so similar like that, both passionate about certain things, and both of them would argue their point with anyone, even if the person didn't argue back or didn't care. Lil's mum had once had a full-on rant at the postman for putting a political leaflet through their letterbox. "Do I look like I'd vote for *them*?" she'd demanded, even though the postman clearly didn't care and was only doing his job.

Mum didn't seem to bother so much about stuff like that anymore. Or about anything very much, except Mella.

"You think I should go?" her mum asked quietly. Even her voice had changed. It was rougher somehow, like even saying words was an effort now.

"I do," Lil said. What was the point of her mum staying locked up in the house? It was driving her crazy and it wasn't making Mella any more likely to come home.

"Okay. But only because you asked me to."

Lil held back a sigh. If her mum went anywhere these days, it was always "because Lil wanted me to." If she made any decisions, it was "because Lil said so." It was as if her mother had handed over her entire life into Lil's keeping. After what had happened with Mella, she was too scared to say anything, in case she upset Lil and she disappeared too.

Her mum stood up then. "Right, looks like I'm going." She took her lipstick out of her bag, pulled the lid off, and then looked at it for a long while, as though she'd forgotten what to do with it. Finally she put it back in her bag, unused. Then she zipped up the handbag. "Your aunt called earlier. Said she'd drop by after her shift. Oh, if you get a chance to speak to her before then, can you ask her to pick up some supplies? Milk and that. Some more bread, probably. Whatever you want, really. Didn't get a chance to go to the shop, so there's not much in."

As if on cue, the toaster beeped and Lil's toast popped up. There was clearly no butter to go on it, and definitely no jam. Lil pressed the lever a couple of times before managing to catch the toast. She juggled it in her hands over to the plate. Mella used to jab a knife right into the toaster and skewer the toast out. "You worry too much, little Mouse," she'd say when Lil squeaked at her about possible electrocution.

"I love you," her mum said, tugging on her coat. "So much." Her mum said this every day now. Lil couldn't remember her ever saying it much before Mella left. She probably hadn't thought she needed to. There was such raw need in her mother's eyes these days. It hurt to look at her. All the love she felt for both her daughters was concentrated into just Lil now. It was kind of scary. Lil didn't know what to do with all that love.

"I love you, too, Mum," Lil said. It didn't sound like enough.

"I wish you'd come with me," Mum said.

Lil screwed up her nose and then tried to hide it.

Her mum smiled. It was watery. "Okay, well, I'll be back by six. I don't fancy the meal, so I'll come straight back. Sandi'll understand." She shouldered her handbag. "Be safe today, Lil. And call me. Or I'll call you. We'll call each other."

"Mum . . ."

"I'm going."

It took her mum another ten minutes to leave the house. First she wanted to check that her phone was fully charged, and then she couldn't find her car keys—which turned out to be at the bottom of her handbag. But finally, finally, she went, and after another brief hesitation—"Would you look at the weather!"—she was gone.

Lil waved her off from the shelter of the porch with a sense of relief. It was like someone had taken a rubber band off her lungs, and a little of the tightness that had been inside her eased. It was hard being positive all the time. Hope could be painful, especially other people's. Especially her mum's. It was so fragile. You had to be careful not to damage it.

Lil shoved the last bite of toast into her mouth. She chewed quickly because it was—*yuck*—cold, not to mention questionably moldy, and she went into the hall. When she stooped down to pick up her rucksack, she couldn't help but flick a glance down the corridor behind her. Taid and Nain's house was old—part of it had been built in the seventeenth century. Bits had been added on over the years, meaning that it was long and sprawling, with a narrow hallway that ran the length of it, from the front door to the back. There were no windows along the hallway, so it was always dark.

Mella had been convinced it was haunted. "A house this old? That many people living and dying here? It has to be, right?" she'd say. Lil said that she was being ridiculous. Still, sometimes Lil got a funny feeling about the place. It wasn't helped by the back door, which had never fit properly and banged in windy weather. People weren't as particular about locking their doors around here as they were in London, and a couple of times it had worked loose and swung wide open.

Shrugging off the thought of ghosts—*What nonsense*—she dragged on her coat and headed outside.

Lil's bike was resting up against the wall of the house, just beyond the porch. In the past her mum would have nagged her to move it before it turned to rust. Now it was just another thing her mum barely noticed. The helmet was hanging off the handlebars. It was full of water. She tipped it out and then checked the bike's wheels (not too flat), gave a quick squeeze of the brakes (all good), and hopped on. The wind nearly blew her straight off again. She had to drop her foot hard to the ground to stop the bike from toppling over.

She glanced at Taid's green VW Beetle. Her mum had promised to insure her on it as soon as she passed her test. Lil would rather be insured on her mum's little Renault, but she knew Mella would kill her for such sacrilege (and Taid would turn in his grave). They had both loved this car. Mella said driving it was like being in a sixties movie, although why that was a good thing, Lil had never established. Mella was a terrible driver. Whenever they were in the car together, Lil closed her eyes and prayed to all the gods she could name that they wouldn't die.

"*Take it, take it,*" she could hear Mella say, as though right in her ear.

"I don't know how to drive it," Lil said, as Mella blew a raspberry.

Mella would have taken the car. It wouldn't have bothered her that she had no license or that the insurance had lapsed. But Lil wasn't Mella.

She set her teeth and mounted the bike again, then pedaled hard up the drive and turned right onto the narrow road beyond. The house was halfway up a mountain, and it was downhill for two miles to the main road at the bottom. You went left for the kayaking club, which sat on the river, and right for Old Porthpridd, the nearest village, if you could call it one. It had a café, a newsagent's, and a bike shop. "Is this it?" Mella had asked. Lil was not into shopping, not like Mella, but even she'd been disappointed. It had taken a while to get used to the fact that it was forty miles to Caerwen and the closest proper shops. "And two hundred miles to any decent ones," Mella always said. They'd been here seven years, but Mella had never stopped missing London. "I'm getting out of here, Mouse," she'd say. "The first chance I get. And I'm never ever, ever, ever coming back." Lil hadn't taken her seriously. Hadn't considered how long "never ever, ever, ever" really was.

With the wind slapping her cheeks raw and threatening to tear her from the bike, it was going to be a struggle to get anywhere today. Her body was already rigid with cold. After a while she realized her muscles were aching, and she forced a deep breath out of her lungs and drew her shoulders down away from her ears. The wind ripped into her again and her shoulders shot back up, tense and hunched. It was an effort to keep the bike upright.

She only had to make it down to the river. Kiran would give her a lift back. He would have picked her up, too, if he hadn't had to drop his little twin brothers off at their science club. But Lil wondered again why she was even bothering going. Mella had been the kayaker. Lil was just pretending. Before Mella went missing, Lil had mostly just hung out in the café at the kayaking place, waiting for her to finish up. Then after Mella left, Lil went there to pretend that Mella was out kayaking and would be back any second. It was stupid, but for whole seconds at a time Lil could convince herself that Mella was about to walk in like she used to, curly hair tamed in a long French plait down her back, unpeeling her wet suit. "Why, Mouse," she'd say. "Fancy meeting you here! And, yes, I don't mind if I do have a hot chocolate. Sure is nice of you to offer."

It was in the café that Lil had met Kiran, in May. She was finishing a hot chocolate, doing her usual pretense of waiting for Mella and bracing herself for the long cycle ride home, when a super-tall (taller even than her) guy walked in. And amazingly that wasn't the first thing she noticed about him, because he seemed to have fallen into a pot of neon paint. His T-shirt was lime green and his trainers were tangerine orange. More amazing than that was he didn't look ridiculous. Just bright and happy. And like he didn't give a damn what anyone else thought of him. Lil liked that, so she smiled, brighter than she had in a long while, and he smiled back.

"Hi," he said with his Birmingham accent. "You here for the induction?"

Lil had never been interested in kayaking, but there was something about the way this guy asked that made her want to try it. Not because he was cute, although he was: with his brown skin, deeper-than-deep-brown eyes, and caterpillar eyebrows that were a facial expression all on their own. He had stubble, too, that curved around his full lips.

So she'd done the induction, much to Gavan's surprise. He ran the kayak club with his partner, Jon, and had been on Lil about doing a course ever since Mella went missing. "It might do you some good. Get a bit of fresh air in your lungs."

Cai—Mella's boyfriend and one of the instructors at the club—had been surprised too, and Lil had loved that, because she hated the thought of Cai knowing anything—*anything*—about her. She still wanted to gouge his internal organs out with a blunt instrument for what he'd done to Mella.

The wind whipped around her again, bringing her back to the present and nearly knocking her over. She ducked her head against it, which meant she wasn't looking where she was going. When she took the next bend, she didn't see the girl lying motionless in the middle of the road until she was almost on top of her.

Chapter Two

Lil swerved sharply. The bike's wheels skidded on the wet tarmac. She tried to brake but got no traction. She was heading for the wall, topped with barbed wire. Hitting that was going to hurt, so Lil did the only thing she could think of. She threw herself off, landing on the grassy shoulder with a bone-shaking jolt as her bike crunched into the wall. The impact took her breath away, but she hobbled to her feet as quickly as she could. The girl hadn't moved, and something darker than water stained the tarmac around her. Lil took a steadying breath and then went over to her.

Close up, the girl was a mess. Lil guessed she must be about fourteen, thirteen maybe. Her eyes were closed and she wasn't moving. Her face was pale and bruised, blood coming from a cut to her head. And her feet—*Oh my God, her feet!* Above her thin pumps they were caked with mud, and her ankles were lacerated with cuts. There were scratches on her wrists, too, visible under the long sleeves of her white tunic. The wind whipped about her, making her long hair dance.

The sight of her chilled Lil, but she fought back the anxiety and crouched down. "Hi," she said. "Hello? Are you okay?" With shaking fingers she touched the girl's shoulder. It was icy cold through the thin fabric of her dress. Lil shivered and nearly snatched her hand back. "Can you hear me?" she asked softly.

There was no response, and Lil's anxiety rose. Was she . . . was she *dead*? *This can't be happening.* Lil thought she might faint. The world seemed far away suddenly, the faint sun filtering through the trees, creating patterns of light and dark on the wet tarmac. Even the wind seemed to quiet for a moment. Then, there was a noise behind her, and Lil snapped around to see a flock of birds rising up from the steep wooded bank. One cawed loudly, and the sound cut through to Lil. She blinked and her vision cleared. At the same time something seemed to switch on in her brain: A power cable finally connected to the main circuit board. What the hell was she doing? She needed to call 999 immediately. This girl needed help.

Lil's backpack lay where she'd dropped it on the side of the road, her phone inside. It took a moment to open it, and then she couldn't find her phone. *Where is it? Where is it?* As she rifled through the bag—a book, chips, a sweater—she cast an anxious look at the girl, who still hadn't moved.

Her fingers closed around the rectangle of metal, but relief became horror when she tugged the phone free and saw the cracked screen. It must have gotten smashed during the fall. Nothing that Lil did could get it working again. Almost crying with frustration, she threw the phone back in her bag.

What was she going to do now? They were in the middle of *nowhere*. No one drove on this road. There were only about two cars a day, and that included her mum's. The nearest village was miles away. It would take Lil over an hour to walk there. And then what? There was no doctor's office and certainly no hospital. And what would she do with the girl? She couldn't just leave her here, lying in the middle of the road.

Her panic sharpened, but then a thought cut through her mounting dread: first-aid training. Gavan didn't let anyone put so much as a pinkie in the river before doing a full-on first-aid course. But could Lil remember it? Why hadn't she paid more attention? Because it had been more fun to mess around with Kiran, and she'd never thought she'd have to use it. What if she did it wrong? Could you make someone worse?

Lil gave herself a stern talking-to. What were her options? Stand about and have a nervous breakdown while a girl lay—*Do not think "dying"*—or try to help the best she could. Lil took what she hoped was a steadying breath and crossed back over to the girl.

"Check for responsiveness by talking to the patient," Gavan had said.

"Hello," Lil said, and amazingly her voice sounded calm. It gave her confidence. "Hello," she said again. "My name's Lil. I'm here to help you. Open your eyes if you can hear me." That's what Gavan had told them to do: "You want to get the patient responding to you. The smallest gesture to show they are conscious." *The patient.* It sounded so cold and remote. Nothing like the reality of someone lying unconscious in front of you, covered in blood.

Lil wished she'd not panicked so much at first. She could have done this already. A terrifying thought came to her. What if the girl had been alive, but had died because Lil hadn't reacted quickly enough? The idea was too overwhelming and Lil pushed it aside as best she could.

When the girl didn't respond to her voice, Lil touched her shoulder again, more firmly this time, and shook it. Her skin was cold and wet, and her bones were tiny. It was like touching a baby bird. She didn't react to Lil's touch at all, so Lil tilted her head back as tenderly as she could, one hand on her forehead and two fingers under her pointed chin, to make sure her airway was clear. Her neck looked exposed like that, and it brought home to Lil even more how vulnerable she was, and how fragile. But there didn't seem to be any obstruction in her throat, and she was breathing. *Thank God.*

Lil's movements were less flustered now. She was shocked at how she instinctively seemed to know what to do. She started to move the girl into the recovery position. She barely weighed anything; her arms were so skinny.

Lil sat back on her heels, assessing what to do next. Rainwater seeped through her tracksuit bottoms. She took off her coat and draped it over the girl. The girl was wet through; her thin dress was no protection at all from the storm. Lil felt a lurch of compassion for her, a desire to help, no matter what.

She'd have to go home and call the ambulance from there. Perhaps she could use her broken bike to create a barricade or an obstacle in the road, slowing down any vehicle that might come past. It wasn't ideal, but Lil honestly didn't know what else to do, and the chances of a car coming down this road were remote anyway. Despite the girl's small size, Lil didn't think she'd be able to carry her, and besides, you weren't supposed to move someone, were you? Gavan had definitely said that could make a person worse. Or was it worse to leave her lying in the middle of the road? Perhaps Lil should drag her closer to the shoulder?

No, Lil decided. She'd leave her here rather than risk causing more damage, although the thought of the girl being alone made Lil's insides twist. But she could run pretty fast. She reckoned she could be home in less than five minutes. She was getting to her feet, still scared but more rational now that she had a plan, when the girl's eyelids flickered open. Large dark-brown eyes, bloodshot with tiredness, stared up at her.

In biology they'd watched a documentary of a lion chasing a zebra. At the moment that the lion brought it down with a giant paw, the camera zoomed in on the zebra's face. Foaming at the mouth, lips drawn back in a silent scream, and eyes wide and terrified—exactly like this girl's.

Fear scoured Lil, and for a moment she was speechless. She pulled herself together. "H-hi," she stammered, voice shaky, from fear or cold or both. "Hi! Are you okay? . . ." She trailed off. It was obvious this girl was anything but all right.

The girl didn't answer. Her gaze flitted from Lil's face to the trees that clung to the steep slope on one side of the road, their thick roots spread out like spiderwebs. They were strung together tightly, so you couldn't see between them. Rainwater gushed down the bank, making the mud run like a river. Lil couldn't tell what the girl was looking at up on the ridge. It was almost impossible to make out anything, like someone had taken a huge eraser and rubbed everything out, leaving only smudges. And it was so quiet. Even the storm seemed to have stilled, and there was only the *drip-drip* of the rain off the leaves. It was as if the world were drawing a breath before . . . Before what?

Calm down, Lil told herself. But there was a charge in the air, and Lil felt a sudden, desperate urge to get inside, where it was safe. *Safe?* Lil was caught off guard by that thought. Safe from what? She was less than a mile from her home. Nothing ever happened here, and yet she couldn't shake the instinct that was building inside her, growing stronger every moment. *Run*, it said. *Run now.*

"Are you okay?" Lil asked again, like a broken record, but she couldn't think of anything else to say. "What are you doing out here? What happened to you?"

The girl didn't answer. She had paled further, and her eyes were even wilder and darker. She looked ready to bolt, and Lil didn't know what to do. "It's okay," Lil said, as softly as she could. "I'll help you. What's your name?

I'm Lil. It's okay. It's okay," Lil repeated, as if saying it enough times would make it true. "I live just up there. You can come back to my house and we can call someone. Someone who'll help you."

"No, no. Call no one." The girl shook her head, drawing back from Lil, her limbs scrunching up under her, like a small animal ready to crawl back into its hole. She looked even younger suddenly, no more than nine or ten.

Lil felt panicky again. "We can't stay out here. You're hurt, and it's raining." *Not safe*, her brain screamed at her. *Run. Run. Get away.* "Come with me," she said. "I'll help you."

The girl shook her head even more vigorously.

Then, without any warning, a shaft of sunlight broke through the thick clouds overhead, catching Lil full in the face, blinding her, and making the dark world glitter in an almost magical glow. It disappeared as quickly as it had appeared.

Lil blinked in the fresh gloom, and then her eyes widened in amazement at how the girl's expression changed. The terror retreated from her features, and she even smiled. "You will help me," she said quietly but with absolute assurance.

"Yes . . . yeah," Lil said, although she had no idea what had made this girl suddenly change her mind. She looked upward, as though the explanation might be there, but all she could see was the sky, heavy with dark rain clouds, hiding the brief sun.

CHAPTER THREE

Shivering and bent over against the wind and rain, Lil and the girl struggled back to the house. Lil tried to ask where she had come from and her name, but she just shook her head and wouldn't answer, so Lil gave up and concentrated on getting them home. The girl was exhausted and obviously in pain. It was clearly taking her a lot of energy to put one foot in front of the other. She made it only a few steps on her own before needing to lean heavily on Lil. There'd be time for questions later.

The rain was growing stronger, so Lil took her hoodie off as well and wrapped it around the girl's shoulders, ignoring her protests. She still had Lil's coat on. "You need them more than I do. You can go into shock when you've been injured." Lil didn't know if that was true, but it sounded convincing. She'd left her bike and backpack behind. She'd come back for them later.

Lil's unease and sense of being watched intensified on the journey back. The emptiness of the countryside pressed in on her with each step, and it was an enormous relief to reach the driveway to her house. She was glad to shut and lock the front door behind them. The familiarity of home settled around her like a hug.

Lil led the girl into the living room and helped her onto the sofa, then ran to the kitchen to get her some water. The girl was trembling so hard—from cold or fear, it was hard to tell—that Lil had to help her hold the glass to her lips. She managed only a couple of sips. Lil set the glass on the coffee table and then grabbed a few of the snuggly blankets that always hung over the back of the sofa and tucked them around her.

"Thank you," she murmured.

Lil gave what she hoped was a reassuring smile. She bent down to turn on the gas fire. Soon a warm glow filled the room, and Lil's tension dissipated. *Home. Safe.*

The girl, however, was still wound up tight as a coil. Her eyes darted about the room, not settling on anything for long. She jumped when Lil asked, "Are you all right here for a minute? Try to keep warm. I'm going to call an ambulance for you."

"No!" the girl cried, her voice snapping out like a whip. "No! No ambulance. No . . . no police. No one!"

"But you're hurt. Badly hurt. Your head's still bleeding. There was this kid at my primary school, fell over in the playground, hit his head. Everyone thought he was fine, then the next day he was dead. . . ." Lil trailed off. She always talked too much when she was nervous, and there was something about the way this girl stared, like she was looking right down inside you. It made Lil uncomfortable.

"You can't tell anyone I'm here," the girl said. "Please. Please!"

"But—"

"*Please!*" Her voice cracked, emotion bursting out like a firework.

It scared Lil. She remembered the hunted look in the girl's eyes earlier. "I think you need help. Proper help—" she began.

The girl cut her off. "If you call someone, I'll leave." She pushed the blankets off and put one shaky foot on the floor. Her face blanched as she tried to stand. Lil leaped to steady her. The girl flinched as Lil caught her arm.

"Okay," Lil said. "I won't call anyone. I promise. Just please don't go. You're not well enough. Stay here and I'll try to help you." She couldn't risk this girl running off, not in this weather and not with her injuries. "Just . . . just sit down. Rest. I'll get some bandages for your head. Does it hurt? We've probably got acetaminophen." Bandages and acetaminophen didn't feel like enough. The girl could barely stand. Her hair was a mess of blood and mud. She most likely had a concussion.

After settling the girl back on the sofa, Lil dashed upstairs to get supplies. She was reluctant to leave her alone for long. Lil ran their conversation over in her mind. Calling for help was the sensible thing to do. Sabrina, her aunt, was a police officer. She would know exactly how to protect and care for this girl. Lil could use the telephone in her mum's bedroom. The girl wouldn't even know. Lil weighed her decision. Rationally it made sense, and yet she balked at the idea of going back on her word. It felt wrong. *Check her injuries*, Lil told herself, *then work on persuading her to accept real help.*

Lil grabbed some towels from the airing cupboard, and bandages from the cabinet in the main bathroom. Even though it was only midafternoon, the storm had turned the sky dark purple, and the bulb was out on the landing, so everything upstairs was in shadow. Lil's earlier anxiety returned, and once again she had the sense of being watched. She was being silly, letting her imagination run away with her. This was her home; there was nothing bad here. Still, Lil only just resisted the urge to run down the shadowy stairs and back into the brightly lit living room.

When she entered, the girl was drawing the curtains, shutting out the dark sky and barren landscape. "The mountain was staring," she said.

Despite the odd choice of words, Lil knew what she meant. She had always loved the view from that room, but today it was oppressive, the way the desolate landscape crept up to the window, like it was trying to get in. It didn't help that there were no other houses for almost four miles.

Resisting the urge to turn the latch on the door, Lil sat beside the girl on the sofa. "How are you feeling?" she asked.

The girl stared at Lil a long moment, as if registering her words. When she didn't answer, Lil said, "Your head's still bleeding. I've got all this stuff, but I don't know. . . ." Lil dropped everything on the sofa cushions. The supplies looked pathetic now. She picked up a towel. "Maybe wrap yourself in that as well, so you don't get any colder. I can get you some dry clothes after we clean you up a bit."

The girl took the towel and put it over her knees. There was more color in her face. She picked up the bottle of antiseptic and stared at it as if she'd never seen anything like it before. After a minute, she placed it down and began to wad some cotton pads to hold against her head to stem the bleeding.

"Let me," Lil said, although she'd never been good with blood. "I can sort it. You just get warm."

"You are cold also."

"I'm all right. Honest." Lil went around the sofa to reach the girl's head more easily. A wave of nausea washed over her as she saw how matted with blood the girl's hair was. *Don't be pathetic. And don't you dare faint.* Taking deep breaths in through her mouth, Lil poured antiseptic onto a cotton pad. "This might sting." The girl flinched slightly but made no sound. "So," Lil said as she cleaned the cut, relieved to see that it was long but shallow, and less bad than the amount of blood suggested, "will you at least tell me your name?"

The girl hesitated a long time. Finally she said, "Alice. My name is Alice."

"Hi, Alice. I'm Lil." She had finished with the antiseptic and replaced the lid. "I've cleaned it up as best I can, but you should see a doctor."

"I have no need of further care," Alice said. She murmured something else, which Lil missed, then she raised her left palm up to the ceiling, and Lil caught sight of a mark, like a burn, running along the underside of her arm. Seeing Lil looking, Alice yanked her sleeve down quickly, her expression a mix of fierce defensiveness and terror.

Lil was too scared to ask any questions, in case Alice got even more spooked, so she said nothing, just silently gathered up the bloodied cotton pads and spare bandages.

Alice watched her warily, head tilted to one side, and then suddenly, she said, in a voice earnest and full of passion, "I thank you for offering me aid. 'Help your troubled sister,' saith the Light, 'and you shall receive my blessing and protection.'"

"Help your troubled sister," saith
the Light, "and you shall receive my
blessing and protection."

—THE BOOK

✴

Despite the rain, all of the sisters had gathered outside to welcome the newcomer. It was always a celebration when a girl was brought out of the Dark, and a cheer went up as Moon brought the girl forward. She was round as the sun and apple cheeked, but Brilliance's eyes flitted over her only briefly before fixing, as they always did, on Moon. You rarely noticed anything but Moon. She was beautiful, incredibly so, like a Pre-Raphaelite heroine: something by Millais or Rossetti. Her colors were straight out of a paint pot: titanium-white skin, indigo eyes as pale as the early-morning sky, and cadmium-red hair. Brilliance always felt an urge to paint her, but no artist would ever capture Moon. And it wasn't only how she looked that made you stop. She was just *fascinating*—each movement was fluid as a brushstroke. Each word considered. When she spoke you wanted to listen; when she asked you for something, you wanted to give it. You couldn't put your finger on why. Charisma or personality that some people had. Brilliance's ex-boyfriend had had it too. It was alluring; it was dangerous.

Moon held the new girl protectively in the curve of her arm, and Brilliance felt a surge of envy as the memory of her own salvation flitted through her mind.

That guy had been hassling her for ages as she'd sat begging on the corner of the street, not taking no for an answer, until Moon had arrived and told him to "back off." She'd smiled at Brilliance the way she was smiling at the new girl now, like they were old friends. "I've been looking for you," she'd said. "Come on, everyone's waiting." She'd put a hand out to her, leading her away, out of the Dark and into the Light.

Something about Moon just made you feel less alone, less like the big idiot you were for leaving home with no plans and no money. And from the moment she met her, Brilliance had known she could trust her. Maybe it was just that she'd *needed* to trust her. Brilliance had been running on empty, with no money, no prospect of getting any, no food for days, and barely any sleep. Brilliance had been sleeping on the streets for weeks. The guy Moon had rescued her from had been the last in a long line of creeps.

Brilliance had felt a spark of fear when she first arrived at the Sisterhood. She and Moon had driven all night, arriving at dawn, and in the harsh morning light, Brilliance wondered if she'd been mad to come all this way with a woman she'd only just met. There was something unnatural about Moon's extreme beauty. Her eyes glittered almost too bright in the rising sun, like the underside of a knife. Brilliance felt afraid, but it was too late by then. She was miles from anywhere; Moon's arm circled around her as she led her from the car. So Brilliance had let herself go—because what other choice did she have? She never regretted it. Coming here had been like coming home.

Moon was introducing the new girl to the rest of the sisters, moving along the line of them. Her arm was still tight around her, holding her close.

Another sister for the Light.

CHAPTER FOUR

"'Help your troubled sister,' saith the Light, 'and you shall receive my blessing and protection.'" That was what Alice had said. What did it mean? It sounded like some kind of blessing, a religious thing maybe. . . . Lil pondered the words as she threw the dirty cotton pads into the kitchen bin.

And where had Alice come from? Something bad had obviously happened to her. That cut on her head. That burn. Why was she so afraid? It had seemed like she was looking for someone in the trees on the side of the road. No, more like she was hiding from someone and was afraid they'd found her. Lil wondered again if she should call her aunt, and again decided to leave it for the minute. Alice's injuries weren't as bad as they'd first appeared, and Lil didn't want to risk her running away. That would be more dangerous than not calling the authorities immediately, surely. She'd talk to Alice once she had a chance to rest and see if she could convince her to get proper help.

After washing her hands in the kitchen sink, Lil went

back into the living room. Alice had fallen asleep sitting up, her head drooping down onto her chest, like a child, and Lil felt a rush of protection. She went over and eased a cushion under Alice's head, sliding her gently down the sofa so she was resting more comfortably. Then she tucked the blankets around her tightly. As she did so, Lil remembered how Mella had lain under these blankets a couple of winters ago when she got the flu. Mella. Where was she right now? Was she out of the rain? Was it even raining wherever she was? Lil hoped, more than anything, that someone was looking after her and at that thought, she piled another blanket on top of Alice.

A knock on the front door made her start, and she hurried over to the window to see who it was. Kiran. *Kiran.* Dressed as brightly as usual: luminous green rainproof jacket, navy cargo pants, and yellow Adidas trainers. He stood huddled on the small porch to keep out of the rain. Lil had never been happier to see him.

"Lilian!" he said when she opened the front door. "I've been . . ." He broke off as he took in her sodden and muddy clothes. "What happened?"

"I fell off my bike."

"Are you okay?"

"I'm fine." Lil's voice sounded strained to her, unnatural, like an out-of-tune violin.

"Seriously, I wish you'd called." Kiran sounded really worried; his beautiful dark-brown eyes assessed her carefully. He'd driven all the way over here just to see if she was all right. He was so thoughtful. Lil wondered for a second if maybe it meant something . . . something more. Things with Kiran had been kind of charged recently, like there was a current between them, an energy that hadn't been there before. Was Kiran's worry part of the same thing? No, she cut the thought off, mentally shutting the door on it with a slam. She was being ridiculous. It was thoughts like this that were making stuff weird between her and Kiran.

"It's nothing. I'm fine."

"You're not. You're bleeding."

Her hand went automatically to her shoulder, where Alice's head had rested while they stumbled home. "It's not mine."

Kiran's eyebrows shot up. Kiran had the most expressive eyebrows of anyone ever. Most people could just raise their eyebrows (one or both), whereas Kiran's had a gamut of emotional responses.

Before he could say anything else, Lil took him by the hand and tugged him into the kitchen. She shut the door behind them and leaned against it, breathing a deep sigh. She hadn't realized how overwhelmed she felt until Kiran arrived. This slice of normality made everything even weirder. She felt uneasy and on edge. Something terrible had happened to Alice. Something that wasn't over. Lil knew that with absolute certainty. It was a sixth sense.

"Lil, what the hell is going on? You're freaking me out here." He was close to her, and he smelled of rain and dry coffee beans, which was what the kayak club always smelled of. Just being around Kiran made Lil happier in a way no one else could—not even her best friend, Rhiannon, these days. And the best thing was, Kiran had never even known Mella. There was no Before Lil for him. He didn't say things like: "Oh, Lil, you used to be . . ." There was only a Now Lil, and there was something comforting in that.

She tucked her wet hair behind her ears. "So . . . when I fell off my bike, I did it to avoid knocking into this girl."

"What girl?" Kiran asked.

"I don't know. She was just lying in the road. She'd fallen down the bank, I think, just along the road at the end of the drive."

"Whoa. Was she badly hurt?"

"She'd hit her head . . . and . . . and . . ." She trailed off. Something stopped her mentioning the burnlike mark on her arm. She didn't know why, but it felt secret somehow, like telling Kiran about it would be a betrayal.

Kiran didn't notice her half-finished sentence. "Did the ambulance get here okay in the storm?" he asked.

Such a simple question. Such an obvious thing, and yet Lil hadn't called for one. How could she explain why not? "I didn't . . . ," she said. She shuffled uncomfortably on the spot, rocking slightly on the balls of her feet. "The paramedics didn't come. I didn't call them. I brought her back here."

Kiran's eyebrows shot up to his hairline. "*What?* Why?"

Lil drew a deep breath and tried not to sound defensive . . . or guilty. But why should she feel guilty? Again she got that sense of something unspeakable having happened to Alice. A shameful secret that had now rubbed off on her.

"My phone broke," she said, trying to keep her voice steady, "when I fell off my bike. I didn't have any other options. I couldn't just leave her in the road! I was going to call as soon as we got back here, but then . . . then . . . she . . . she made me promise not to . . ." Lil trailed off again. She was rambling.

If Kiran thought what she'd done was crazy, he didn't say it. "Where is she now?"

"In the living room. Come on, I'll show you, but be gentle. She's terrified. She doesn't want anyone to know she's here."

They crossed the hallway.

"Head injuries can be—"

"Serious, I know," Lil interrupted. "She was unconscious when I found her, but she seemed all right when we got back. Well, not all right, but better, and the cut on her head wasn't as bad as I thought." Nausea turned Lil's stomach over as she realized what she was saying. "I've been really stupid. I just . . . I didn't know what to do! I think something bad's happened to her, K. Like, really, really bad. I should have called Sabrina, but I . . . if you'd seen her. . . I just felt like she needed someone she could trust. . . ."

Lil was struck again by a thought of Mella. If Mella were scared and injured and begged a stranger to help without telling anyone, Lil would want that person to do it immediately and unconditionally. She wouldn't want them to go back on their word. She wouldn't want them to risk Mella running away again—and that thought tore through Lil. Because it was Lil's fault that Mella had gone and stayed gone. And Lil suddenly understood her reluctance to call the police and tell them about Alice. She'd failed Mella, and she couldn't fail this girl. She could not be responsible for another person going missing.

Lil pushed open the living room door.

The room beyond was empty.

"Hello?" Lil called. "I left her right here." The blankets were strewn across the sofa. Lil picked them up, as if Alice might be hidden underneath. "Where would she . . . ? Oh no. She must have heard me talking to you in the kitchen, or you knocking on the door, and thought I'd called someone. She thought you were the police! We *have* to find her." Lil went over to the windows and yanked back the curtains. The windows remained shut and bolted. She hadn't gone out that way.

"Okay, Lil, but I don't think she can have gone far. I mean—"

Lil cut him off, her panic spiraling out of control. "You don't get it! I *have* to find her! I promised I wouldn't tell anyone. She said she'd run if I did! I *promised*, Kiran!" Mella was slipping away. Lil was failing her sister again.

It felt like that game she and Mella had played when they were little: *If I make it to that lamppost before the next car goes past, I'll pass my French vocab test. If I hold my breath until that woman with a dog passes me, Mum will buy that new sweater for me. If I can look after this girl, help her, then Mella will come home.* It was ridiculous. Impossible. "Superstitious nonsense," Nain would have said, but it felt like hope, like control, like something that Lil did could finally make a difference.

Lil darted out into the hallway, pushing open each door. "Alice!" she called. "*Alice!* No one is going to hurt you. I promise. Please answer me!"

As Lil pulled the door to her granddad's old study shut, she felt a breeze on the back of her neck. The back door. It was never closed properly unless you bolted it at the top, and her mum must have forgotten this morning. It swung open at a gentle push from Lil. She stepped outside, the rain buffeting her. Lil cupped her hands around her mouth and shouted again.

Kiran came up behind her. "You think she went out there?"

"I don't know, I don't know."

"We can walk out—"

Lil held her hand up. "Hang on," she said. "I thought I heard . . ." Lil rushed past Kiran, back into the house. "She's upstairs. Come on."

She hurried up the stairs, shouting as she did so.

"Lil," Kiran called, coming up after her. "Calm down. Why are you getting so upset?"

Lil didn't answer. How could she explain why she was freaking out? Because this wasn't about Alice anymore. It was about her sister. They'd become mixed up in her head, and Lil didn't care how illogical that might be. To ensure Mella's safety, she needed to ensure this girl's.

All the doors on this floor were closed, and Lil began working through the rooms: her grandma's old sewing room, the guest room. Kiran was checking the bathroom. They were making a lot of noise. "Maybe we should go more quietly," Lil suggested. "We don't want to scare her worse than she is."

Kiran nodded. His hand was on the handle of the door to her mum's room. "Maybe you should look in here. It feels personal."

Lil nodded and pushed the door open. *Please let Alice be in here.* There was no one there. Disappointment swept over her. She cast only a fleeting glance around her mum's room. It was so messy these days. Another thing that had changed since Mella had gone. Her mum used to be so tidy. Now sheet music was piled up in corners; paperbacks, their spines broken, lay strewn across the floor; yesterday's coffee mug and the day before's (and the day before that's) sat in a row along the chest of drawers. Lil's eyes passed over the bright-red one, musical notes and the words "I might be crotchety" emblazoned on it in gold letters. A present from Mella.

Lil shut the door, trying not to linger on the mug or the photo of her mum, age sixteen, playing the piano at Konzerthaus Berlin, on tour with the National Youth Orchestra of Wales. Mella loved that photo. She was always saying that Mum should hang it in the living room. Sadness washed over Lil, but she pushed through it to search the rest of the rooms on the floor.

Alice wasn't in any of them. There was no way she could have gotten down the stairs without them seeing her, which meant there was only one room left to look in on this floor. Lil stood outside it, staring at the door handle like it might turn into a snake.

Kiran was beside her, steady and calm as always. "You want me to check it?"

"No," Lil said gently. "It's just a room."

Just a room. Hand on the door handle. *Just a room.* Turn the handle. *Just . . .* Push the door open. *A . . .* Step inside. *Room.*

It was Mella's room.

Everything was exactly as she'd left it the day she disappeared. After the police had done their searches and returned everything, Lil's mum had put it all back, piece by piece, like a jigsaw. Lil's mum came in here all the time: to dust, to vacuum, or just to sit on the bed. Lil never did. She couldn't bear it; it still smelled of Mella. Walking in here felt like she had just popped out for five minutes, not that she'd been gone four and a half long, agonizing months.

Sunshine-yellow drapes hung around her bed. The walls and ceiling were painted to look like a blue sky with wispy clouds. It had taken Lil and Mella a whole weekend to get it right. They had been going to do the same in Lil's room but hadn't gotten around to it. The wardrobe doors were covered in postcards, posters, magazine cuttings, and artwork, including a sketch Mella had done of their grandfather. Lil found it hard to look at Mella's stuff—when she did, she didn't know whether to cry or scream.

Where are you, Mella? Lil asked in her head. A conversation she'd been having with herself since that terrible morning when they discovered Mella gone.

Visiting the man in the moon, Mella replied.

The desk was littered with crystals and colored stones.

More hung from leather thongs around the mirror, and there was a string of brightly colored stones wrapped around the bed's headboard. Mella's latest obsession before she disappeared: healing crystals. Mella always fixated on some spiritual obsession. Before the crystals it was star signs, and before that, tarot readings. When Nain was alive, Mella had gone to church with her every Sunday for three months, before losing interest and buying a book on Buddhism. And then there had been one summer when all of Mella's decisions had been made based on the answers of a Magic 8 Ball.

Lil lifted up one of the crystals. It was small and the color of a duck's egg. The one next to it was pink—a rose quartz. Once, Mella had told Lil to "fill it with happy thoughts and positive energy." Lil had had no idea what she meant, but Mella had that desperate look in her eyes—the one she got when she hadn't slept for days—so Lil had brought the stone to her lips and whispered knock-knock jokes to it until Mella laughed, then she'd handed it back and said, "It's a happy quartz now." Lil found out later that rose quartz was supposed to lead to romance, as well as self-love and acceptance. The three things Mella craved more than anything else in the world. It hurt to acknowledge how damaged and vulnerable her sister was. It was agony to realize how little she'd done to help her. The last words Lil had said to her were seared into Lil's brain, scar tissue that would never heal.

Trying as best she could to push the painful memories away, Lil scanned the rest of the room. Mella was too present: in the bras, pants, tights, stripy socks, skirts, and Mella's favorite boots with the shiny steel toe caps, strewn across the desk and floor. The boots were at the same angles left by her feet as on the last day she stepped out of them. Lil had been surprised Mella left those boots.

Took your blue Converse, didn't I? Mella said in Lil's head. *Much more comfortable—and better for the sandy beaches in Australia.*

So you're in Australia?

Maybe. Maybe not. Keep on guessing, Mouse.

The bed was unmade too, duvet thrown back exactly as Mella had left it all those months ago—except it wasn't. It was a fabrication, created by Lil's mum. Just like the shoes.

Lil kept a perfect memory of Mella on that last morning, even though Lil hadn't seen her. Her eyes had been shut tight. She'd been too mad to look at her sister, but Mella had stood right over her bed. "Don't be angry, Mouse. Please."

Kiran touched Lil's hand. "Lil," he said gently. "Lil, she isn't in here."

Lil knew he meant Alice, but it was Mella she thought of; her throat was raw with tears.

"You okay?" Kiran asked.

Lil nodded. She gripped the door handle so tightly her knuckles went white. She let go and forced the air into her lungs, forced the misery back inside. "Yeah. Yeah. I'm fine, fine, yeah." It sounded unconvincing, even to her. "We need to find Alice." Then Lil pulled the door to Mella's bedroom shut so quickly she almost trapped her own fingers in it.

"She can't have just vanished," Kiran said. "Are you sure she didn't go out the back door?"

"No," Lil started, "but . . ." She hoped not. "Where else could she be?" As if in answer, there was a noise above them, the soft creaking of floorboards. They both looked up.

"Why would she go in the attic?" Kiran asked.

"Because it's quiet and away from everyone else." They were Mella's words, spoken so many times. That was where Mella had gone when "the darkness" descended. It was strange that Alice had unwittingly chosen Mella's refuge; again Lil was struck by a similarity between them. "She must be up there. She couldn't have crept past us, could she? I mean, she was completely silent like . . . like . . ."

"Like a ghost," Kiran finished.

Goose bumps popped up on Lil's arms. There was something unnerving, almost otherworldly, about Alice. It was nothing that she could put her finger on, but something about Alice made Lil nervous. She was being ridiculous, though. It was all in her head. She gave herself a mental shake and crossed the landing to the rickety ladder that led up into the attic. She and Mella had played up there a lot when they were younger, making a den out of old sheets. They found some of Nain's old clothes up there too and played dressing-up. Mella liked drawing up there as she got older, said it was peaceful and the light was good. There was a large window in the roof, and the attic was bright even on gray afternoons. Lil hadn't been up there since Mella left. *What if I get up there and Mella is sitting on the floor, legs crossed, charcoal in hand, sketching a self-portrait in the old dining room mirror—the one with the crack down one side?*

There was a noise up there: soft like the pad of feet. "Can you come after me, just in case . . ." Lil didn't finish the sentence. In case what? A small, frightened girl with a concussion attacked her? She shook her head and began to climb the ladder.

Lil poked her head up through the trapdoor. She spotted Alice straightaway. She sat under the large slanted window. Pale light trickled down over her. Her head was tilted back like Mella used to do when she was sunbathing.

"Hey," Lil said gently. "You scared me. Thought you'd run off."

"I needed the Light," the girl said.

"Light?" Lil asked, confused. A murky gray slopped down onto the floor from the skylight, casting long shadows in the attic. A light switch hung by Lil's head. She went to pull it, but Alice stopped her.

"Do not chase the Light away," she said.

Since they'd come into the attic, Kiran hung back, standing by the trapdoor, shielded by Lil. As he stepped forward, emerging from the gloom, Alice's eyes flicked to him. Her pupils dilated and her pale skin flushed deep pink. "Who's that?" she asked, wonder in her voice.

"Kiran," Lil said. "This is my friend Kiran. Alice, Kiran. Kiran, Alice."

"Hi," Kiran said, smiling lopsidedly, something he did when he was uncomfortable. He ruffled his hair, another nervous tic, and his expression said, *Why is she looking at me like that?*

Lil shook her head as if to respond, *I don't know.*

There was a long, awkward silence as Alice continued to gaze in awe at him. Did she fancy him? No, that wasn't it. Rhia's little sister had reacted the exact same way on seeing a giraffe for the first time. It was as if Alice had never seen a boy before—but that was impossible.

And the sisters shall live in one feminal
community, in union with the Light.

—THE BOOK

Brilliance led the new girl to the room at the end of
the first-floor corridor. The wind was battering the
windows all along the hall, and rain would be pouring in
through the cracks in the roof soon, but this room would
stay dry. It was the largest and grandest on the compound,
and it was where they always put the novices. It was important for them to have time to adjust and learn that such
earthly luxury was unnecessary in the Light. They stripped
the rest away at the Illumination so that they might enter
the Brightness pure and free.

The Brightness.

The thought sent a shiver of excitement through her.
The Illumination ceremony was hours away now. At sunset, tomorrow night. The new girl was lucky to have been
saved when she was; come tomorrow there would be no
sisters here to save her. They would all be resting in the
Light's eternal embrace.

When they got to the bedroom, Brilliance drew back

the heavy curtains. It was dark outside, the sky a slate gray, and the wind lashed at the trees hard enough to tear some of the weaker branches off. The driveway was littered with bits of tree and dead leaves. She turned away to check the room. There were only two beds in here, and again they were the better ones—with proper mattresses, pillows, and duvets. Many of the sisters slept on the floor with blankets bundled under them.

"This is the biggest room I've ever seen!" the girl said. Brilliance had not asked her name; sisters were discouraged from asking any questions about a novice's past. "So they feel safe," Moon had said. "We don't judge here. Whatever they did in the Darkness is irrelevant now they are in the Light." Besides, there was no point learning the girl's Dark name; she would take her true Light name if she stayed.

She sat on the bed nearest the window and was still taking in the size of the room. It was pretty impressive; Brilliance had to admit to still being awed by it.

The novice stopped her wide-eyed search of the room and said suspiciously, "What've I got to do to stay here?"

"You don't have to do anything," Brilliance said quickly. "The Light provides for all our needs." And for Brilliance it really did. The Light had changed, had brightened—she smiled at the pun—her life so much.

A frown crossed the girl's face. "Moon mentioned something about the Light before. . . . And that mark on your faces?"

Brilliance touched her cheek, where every morning

she painted the symbol of the Sisterhood, the yellow sun.

"I'm not sure . . . ," the novice said. "I don't know that I believe . . ."

"No one forces you to do anything you don't want." Brilliance smiled. The new ones were often wary of the Light at first, but they always came to it in the end. It was power and energy. It was what drew all the sisters together, and it was beautiful. When Brilliance imagined it, she saw sunshine through leaves or the sparkles of dust in a room.

"Oh, well, okay, I guess. So I don't have to, like, pay anything to stay here?"

Brilliance shook her head. She'd asked a similar question. She smiled at the memory; how ignorant she'd been before Moon instructed her in the true path.

"How long have you been here?" the novice asked.

"Long enough that I know the irrelevance of such questions." Brilliance smiled at the girl's perplexed face. She'd learn.

"And how long are you staying?" the girl pressed.

"Forever," Brilliance replied. "The Light's embrace is eternal."

"Oh."

"Why? Do you want to go home?"

The novice screwed up her face like she was solving a maths problem. "No, I mean"—she gave a half laugh that held no humor in it—"I reckon they're better off without me anyway." She ducked her head to avoid Brilliance's gaze and crossed to the window.

She didn't seem to notice the storm. She was too

preoccupied with the house. "Still can't get over the size of this place. Don't you guys get lost?" Her eyes darted in all directions. Then she frowned. "Wait," she said. She did another sweep of the courtyard, the driveway, and the garden, which was just visible behind the tall hedge. "There are no . . . where are the men?"

"There aren't any," Brilliance said.

"That's . . . isn't that weird?" the novice said.

"It is the way of the Light," said Brilliance. It was the answer Moon had given her, but at the time she'd also thought it strange and she'd been disappointed. She liked guys, and guys liked her. But then, hadn't that been half the trouble? Boyfriends had never worked out that great for her. Her hand went to her cheek; the bruise was a long-faded memory, but the blow that had caused it still felt fresh. "You need to find yourself in you before you can lose yourself in someone else," Moon had said. That was true. So true. Moon was like a walking quote book. Brilliance wanted to write them all down to look at later. Moon just said things in a way that made sense, that made you see everything so much more clearly.

CHAPTER FIVE

"We'll find out where she's from," Lil told Kiran in a hushed conversation in the hallway, while Alice got changed in the bathroom. Lil had cobbled together some of her mum's clean clothes. Alice's white dress was ruined. Mud-splattered, bloodstained, and torn. Even clean, it would not have been suitable for the weather. Yet another clue in the riddle that was Alice.

"We can't deal with this ourselves, Lil," Kiran said.

"I know, and we'll get help, but let's just try to talk to her first. If she won't say where she's from, maybe she'll tell us where she's going. She must have a plan."

"There's something seriously weird going on here. Did you see the way she was looking at me? And she's a mess."

"I bandaged her head," Lil said.

Kiran raised an eyebrow. "Three half-hour resuscitation sessions with Doreen"—Doreen was the dummy they used at the kayaking club—"did not prepare us for this. And it's not just her head, anyway. Lil, she needs help.

Proper help." He was always so rational, and he was right. Which was kind of annoying.

"If we can't get any information out of her, we'll get the police involved," Lil said. "But let's give it a go first. Okay?"

"I guess," he said. "And it does mean we'll have more to tell the police when we call them."

Lil was relieved that Kiran had agreed to wait it out a bit longer. Alice running at first sight of the police was too big a risk. Perhaps they could gain her trust and persuade her to accept help; that was better than forcing it on her when she was terrified and suspicious.

While Kiran went downstairs to phone his dad to say that he'd be back late, Lil hurried to her room to change. She was grateful to Kiran for sticking around, especially as he so obviously thought she was making the situation worse by keeping Alice a secret. Still, his presence was a comfort. It was good to have someone to talk to, and the uneasiness she'd felt since finding Alice had retreated since he arrived.

Once in her room, Lil crossed to her wardrobe and tugged it open. She hadn't changed clothes since finding Alice, and she was cold and wet. As she decided what to wear, there was a thud on the windowpane. She looked over to see a branch from the nearby tree thrash against the glass. The sky was a crimson slash, and rain poured from it as though from a wound, the wind as loud as an airplane. The sound reminded Lil of the fighter planes she'd seen once with her dad. It must have been at some sort of air show. Lil couldn't remember the details, only that she'd been scared and had buried her face in her dad's legs. She remembered feeling safe as he put his hand on her back. When had he decided to remove that protective hand permanently from their lives? When had he stopped caring whether they were safe or not? He was in Australia now. Working as a conductor for the Sydney orchestra and living with a woman Lil had never met.

Turning away from the window, she noticed one of Mella's sketchbooks on her desk. She'd been photographing it for the Find Mella website. She sat down and pulled it onto her lap.

Mella? she said in her head.

There was a brief pause, and then her sister answered. *Hey, Mouse. What's up?*

Where are you?

Guess.

Lil stretched out her legs and looked out the window again. *You're on the beach. You're drawing.*

What am I drawing?

A sketch of the beach. There's some boats out to sea, and nearer some kids are paddling—

Mella blew a raspberry.

Lil smiled. *Okay, okay, you're doing a life study of the cute boy lying on the sand next to you. . . .*

Ooh-la-la, that sounds better. And he looks over, sees the drawing, and is overwhelmed at my talent!

Sure, yeah, maybe . . . Lil trailed off. *Mella, come home, please. I'm scared you're—*

Don't say it. It isn't true if you don't say it.

Does that mean you're not?

I'm alive in your head.

That's not enough.

The image of her sister faded from her mind, replaced with the one on that last morning: "Are you awake? . . . Don't be angry, Mouse."

Lil switched on the desk lamp and flicked through Mella's sketchbook. The pictures were mostly of Cai.

Cai. Mella's boyfriend. Nineteen-year-old, in-a-band, lightly-tanned-skin, perfectly-wind-tousled-except-it-was-styled-in-the-bathroom-mirror-blond-surfer-hair, abs-you-could-stack-books-on, so-sexy-your-ovaries-ached Cai.

Cai was the first person they'd suspected when Mella went missing. The police questioned him for hours and searched his trailer but found nothing. He swore he hadn't spoken to her since the day before. Lil went around to his place countless times in those first few days, asking, then begging, him to tell the truth. He was largely silent at first and then angry. "I did nothing to her, all right? Nothing." Lil hadn't believed him then and she didn't believe him now. Cai knew something more about Mella's disappearance than he was letting on, but there was no way for Lil to prove it.

She'd never liked him, even in the beginning, before his utter-douche-bag credentials came to light; and she hadn't liked Mella around Cai. Mella met him at the kayaking club. He'd started working there just before Christmas, and Mella noticed him immediately. Mind you, it was hard not to notice Cai. "You know how some people just expect to be looked at?" Rhia once said of him. And it was true. Cai moved like he was auditioning for a part. No, he moved like he'd already gotten the part everyone else wanted.

Mella had liked plenty of guys before, but with Cai it was different. Mella looked at Cai like she couldn't look at anything else. It scared Lil, that intensity. It was a part of Mella she couldn't get to, and a part of her she didn't want Cai near because it was fragile.

There was a vulnerability to Mella. She wasn't shy or quiet or any of those things. In fact, she was loud, with a laugh you could hear three rooms away, and a sarcasm that could cut. But still, beneath her snark and her outlandish look-at-me clothes, she was sensitive, easily hurt, and overly self-critical. "Did I sound like an idiot when I said that?" she'd ask Lil. Or, "Do you think they liked me? Or were they just pretending?" Or, "God, I do such stupid things sometimes." And Cai, with his dark eyes, as dark as a shark's, was not gentle enough to care for Mella. From the moment she'd met him, Lil had known he would devour her sister, piece by piece, until there was nothing left.

"You don't know what it's like to be in love, that's all," Mella said when Lil expressed concerns about their relationship. "So what if we fight sometimes? We need each other. And love is hard, Lil. It makes you crazy, but if you love someone, you have to take the good and the bad. That's the deal."

At night Lil would hear her sister's voice pleading on the phone, "No, it wasn't like that. . . . You know I love you.

I barely even spoke to him. I'm sorry. Sorry. Sorry."

Sorry. Sorry. Sorry. On and on.

Mella was so intense, that was the trouble. If she did something, it was always with every bit of herself, until she found a new diversion and moved on. Like the horoscopes ("horror-scopes," Nain had called them), the crystals, and the tarot cards. Cai had been another addiction, one they all hoped would pass. Only it hadn't, and now Mella was gone.

Lil flipped through the rest of the sketchbook, until she came to the last sketch. The one of Lil and Mella, copied from a photograph that was in a frame on the sideboard in the kitchen. The likenesses were astonishing. Mella was incredibly talented. Mella's arm was around Lil, pulling her close as she stared down the camera. Lil stared—as always—at Mella.

Taid had taken the photo the day they arrived on the farm. "We need to mark this occasion," he'd said in Welsh, and their mum had quickly translated. It was the only photo of Mella left in the house. Her mum had taken the rest down shortly after Mella went missing. Said it hurt too much to look at them. Lil knew her mum kept the baby albums in her room, though, and was sure she spent hours flicking through them when she was alone.

Are you awake? . . . Don't be angry.

The memory burned and Lil shut the pad quickly and slid it across the desk, as though she could shut out the past, too.

Lil's room was at the back of the house and overlooked

the sprawling, messy yard. Taid hadn't been interested in growing flowers, and Lil's mum had soon forgotten about the few she'd planted after they moved in. Lil could just make out the rough edges of Nain's old vegetable patch. There was something moving out there in the gloom between the rotting wooden stakes that once held tomatoes and sunflowers. A fox? Badger? There was a burrow nearby.

Lil sat forward in her chair, peering out into the twilight. She gave a start when she caught a glimpse of a pale smudge with huge, dark eyes and a round mouth staring up at her from the yard below. Her fear was replaced by an embarrassed laugh when she realized it was only her reflection in the glass. *Idiot*, she told herself, and stood up to change. Dusky-gray jeans, purple socks pulled over the top, a blue-and-white stripy long-sleeved T-shirt, and the cable-knit sweater she'd swiped from her mum's wardrobe last week.

She was pulling the sweater over her head and wishing she could shower—she still felt cold and was, let's admit it, a little smelly—when there was a knock on the bedroom door. Lil turned to find Alice in the doorway. She'd rolled the tracksuit trousers up and pulled the drawstrings as tight as possible, but they were still massive on her. The sweatshirt swamped her too, stretching down over her hands, covering up the mark on her arm. Lil was struck again by how defenseless she was, and how small, framed in the doorway, the hallway light catching in her hair and making its wisps into downy feathers. Lil was reminded of a baby bird. Tenderness spread through her.

"Oh," Lil said gently. "You can't wear that. It's way too big. I'll find something else." Mella's stuff would fit better, but Lil couldn't bring herself to go back into Mella's room, and besides, she didn't want Alice wearing her clothes.

"It is vanity to care about the vessel." Alice was solemn, her tiny hands clasped before her. Lil wasn't sure she even understood what Alice said half the time. Like now, what vessel? It all sounded learned, like a quote. Lil's curiosity about her was increasing every second. Where had this girl come from? Everything about her—her clothes, her way of speaking, even her accent—was strange. If she'd emerged from the back of Nain's wardrobe, dressed in a fur coat and talking about the White Witch, Lil wouldn't have been that surprised.

Lil pulled a sweater from her chest of drawers. It had shrunk in the wash, so would probably just about fit Alice. "Here," she said, holding it out. "See if this is any better."

Alice's mouth dropped open and her hand reached out to touch the pile of clothes in the drawer. "These are all yours?" Astonishment and fascination filled her voice. "All your very own?"

"Yeah," Lil said. She shifted uncomfortably from foot to foot. She didn't have *that* many clothes. Alice should see Mella's wardrobe, or her mum's. "If there's anything you want instead, help yourself. They'll be too big, but . . ."

With a dignified and wounded air, Alice said, "A true

sister does not desire another's property." As though Lil had accused her of stealing.

Lil didn't know what to make of her. No teenager talked like that. Not even Addiena Thomas, and she was the smartest girl in Lil's year. "I just meant you're welcome to borrow anything you like from me. I want you to be comfortable while you're here."

"You mean share?" Alice clapped her hands happily. "To share is to radiate Light." She held her palm flat up to the ceiling. Her gestures were alien too. Then, more quietly, and sounding almost like a normal teenager, she added, "We shared our possessions at home."

It was the most regular sentence she'd said, and Lil pounced on it. "You have a big family, then?" she asked, feigning casualness. Her questions jostled inside her like bubbles in a Coke can, and she was desperate to let them all pour out. Alice was so reticent, though; if Lil wanted to learn anything, without scaring her off, she needed to go slowly. "You've got brothers, sisters?"

Alice's eyes narrowed, suspicious. "Why do you ask about the sisters?"

"Oh, er . . . no reason," Lil backtracked with a stammer. "Just that . . . you mentioned something about sisters before and then said you shared things. I did with my sister too. Share stuff, I mean." If sharing was your sister swiping your brand-new top before you had a chance to wear it and then never giving it back.

It freed up your wardrobe for more new stuff. I was doing you a favor, Mella said in Lil's head, a smile in her voice.

"She is your blood sister?" Alice inquired.

Blood sister? Again with the weirdness. "Er . . . yeah? I mean, we have the same parents."

Alice appeared disappointed. "Oh, yes. I see. It's not the same." She turned away, as though Lil had let her down.

"You don't have blood sisters?" Lil asked. Questioning Alice was like trying to catch snow; her answers melted at a touch.

"I call them sisters. You would not. We are not all from one source; like a river, we merge from many springs to flow as one."

Lil took a second to process what Alice meant. "So you . . . erm . . . have different dads? Or mums? Are some of you adopted?" Alice's home sounded very, very different from anything Lil had ever known. It was hard to find the right questions to ask.

"I don't know what that is." Alice scrunched up her nose. "A-dopted?" Alice said, putting an emphasis on the first syllable. "The word is unfamiliar to me."

Lil could feel her brow furrowing. How could Alice not know what "adopted" meant? And how was it possible that Lil only felt more perplexed the more answers she got?

As if sensing her confusion, Alice said, "We are not blood related—at least, not all of us—but we are sisters." A look of pain crossed her face then, and she closed her eyes briefly, as though to shut out a memory. At the same time she raised both palms up flat and said, "May the

Light shine upon them in all Her glory." When she opened her eyes, they glistened with tears.

"What's happened to you?" Lil asked softly. Alice seemed to have gone through so much, and while Lil didn't understand a lot of what she was saying, she couldn't help but feel for her.

Alice ducked her head. "I have said too much already. Thank you for inviting me into your home. I will not trouble you for long."

"But what's your plan?" Lil asked. "When I found you, where were you going?"

Alice didn't answer, and Lil sensed that the window of opportunity to ask her more had closed. Her face was wary again and uncertain. It cleared for a moment as her eyes fell on the bookcase that ran along one wall. "You have so many books," she cried.

"Yeah." Lil went to stand behind her. "Mostly kids' stuff. I don't read much of it now."

Alice pulled one out, a smile lighting up her face. "*Alice's Adventures in Wonderland*. I know this one."

Lil sat down next to her. "That was my sister's favorite. She loved the White Rabbit." She smiled as she realized, "Hey! You're called Alice too! Are you named after the book?"

"'A sister's name is her most sacred possession,'" Alice said sadly, and she stroked the book cover tenderly. "A friend told me this story. Before that, I knew of only one book." Alice picked up another book. It was *Winnie-the-Pooh*. Her smile widened. "Look at this funny little bear! What is this? A pig? A pig and a bear are friends?" Her eyes were oceans in her face, and she sounded so innocent that Lil couldn't help but laugh.

"Yeah, that's Piglet and Winnie-the-Pooh."

"Poo?" Alice said, screwing up her nose.

Lil laughed again. "'Pooh' with an *h*. Not 'poo' as in . . . well, 'poo' without an *h*."

"It's a strange name."

Lil nodded. "I'm sure there's a reason he's called that, but I don't know it."

Alice had opened the book and was turning the pages carefully, like each one was precious. She stroked the illustrations. "They are very beautiful. For children, yes? I would have loved this when I was a child." She paused and then said more quietly, "I didn't know it could be like this. The world."

Lil wasn't sure she understood what Alice was saying, but she felt sad anyway.

Alice laughed and turned the book around to show Lil the page. "Look," she said, "he's got his head stuck in a pot!"

Lil grinned. "Yeah, my dad always liked that drawing too. This was his book from when he was a kid. He read it to us when we were little."

"Where is your father now?" Alice asked quietly.

Lil looked down at her hands. "He left."

"I never knew my father. My mother abandoned us too when I was small. They are recreant now."

"What do you mean? Recreant?" Lil struggled to pronounce it.

"You don't know?" Alice asked, eyes wide in surprise. "How can you not know?" She shook her head. "It's not like I thought it would be out here. It's not like they said it was."

"Like who said it was?"

Alice shook her head again, as though the question didn't matter. She returned the book to the shelf and sat back on her heels. Misery clung to her like a blanket.

"I want to help you," Lil said, distraught. "Please. Just tell me what I can do."

Alice didn't answer; her sadness was replaced by another emotion, no less uncomfortable: fear.

"What?" Lil asked. "What's the matter?"

"We are being watched."

Lil's heart fluttered with fright. "What do you mean? Who's—"

Alice held a hand up, indicating for Lil to be quiet. Her gaze was riveted to the yard, right at the back, where the trees were tightest and the shadows longest.

"It's probably just a sheep," Lil said, trying and failing to sound reassuring. "They get out of their fields all the time. They're like Houdini or something, my *taid* said. . . ." Lil stopped talking. She was rambling and Alice had gone rigid with terror.

The hairs rose on the back of Lil's neck. Part of her wanted to pull her curtains across the window, but another part of her was afraid to. She had a vision of the gathering gloom pressing unseen against the glass pane like fingers, fumbling for the lock. She remembered playing What's the Time, Mister Wolf? as a kid. No one could move so long as you kept watching. But as soon as you turned your back . . . Prickles of sensation ran up and down Lil's back.

"Were you witnessed bringing me here?" Alice asked.

"No . . . no," Lil stammered. "I don't . . . I mean, there was no one around." She remembered the sense of being watched on the road. "Who are you hiding from, Alice?"

Then the outside security light flicked on, and Alice jumped. "What's that?"

"It's just the light. The yard light." It lit up the entire yard, beating back the darkness. "There's no one out there," Lil said, tugging the curtains closed. "No one for miles." Lil regretted saying that. It reminded her how isolated they were. "Alice, you need to start talking to me. Where are you from? What's happened to you? Everything you say is . . . well . . . odd. Sorry, that's rude, I know, but . . . it's like you don't live in Wales." *On Earth*, Lil added in her head.

"'Knowledge is the Dark's curse. Do not seek it out unless you are certain it leads into the Light.'"

"What? What does that mean? You talk in riddles! How can I help you if I don't—"

Alice whitened, cheeks burning crimson. "Please. Forgive me. I cannot give voice to these things." In a scared voice she whispered, "It is forbidden!"

"What is forbidden? Where are you from?" The words came out more screechy and old-hag than she'd intended, but she was incredibly frustrated. They were going around in circles! Lil drew a deep breath. "Okay," she said. "I get it, you can't answer my questions about your past, but tell me one thing. What are you going to do now? You must have been going *somewhere* when I found you. What were you doing out there in the rain? How did you get there?" Lil sucked in a breath and made herself stop talking. She hadn't meant to let her questions out in such a torrent.

Alice hesitated and then said, "When I left, I didn't have a plan, only to flee. I cannot go home. I can never go home." Her shoulders slumped as if under the weight of her misery, and the brightness of her brown eyes dimmed.

"Alice," Lil said softly, "I'm so sorry." She touched Alice's shoulder gently. She didn't know what else to say.

Alice gave her a weak smile.

There was a knock on the door and Kiran's head appeared around it. "All right?" he said, glancing from one to the other as though he could sense the tension in the room. He held out his phone. "Sabrina. She sounds panicked. Said she's been trying to call you for ages. I told her you broke your phone falling off your bike."

Lil gladly took the phone. Sabrina was exactly who she needed right now. And yet Alice had vehemently rejected any offer of help from the police. Lil didn't know what to do.

"Hi," she said.

"*Diolch i Dduw eich bod yn ddiogel.*" Sabrina's blast of

Welsh, and its normalness, came as though from a different world, but a comforting, familiar one.

Lil gripped the phone tighter to her, letting her aunt's warm concern and love seep through her. "Sorry I scared you. I'm okay, honest."

Am I? Lil glanced at Alice. This was too much to handle. She should tell her aunt everything that had happened. Sabrina would know what to do. But would Alice run?

Sabrina was talking. "Well, that's a relief. Can't believe you were out cycling, sweet pea. Don't you listen to the weather report?"

"We were supposed to be going kayaking."

"Kayaking! Lilian, we have had an entire month's rain in five hours. The river is going to burst any minute. Are you all right up there?"

"Yeah, but it's cold. Sabrina, there's something else I should tell you. . . . I . . ." Lil paused. She could sense both Kiran's and Alice's eyes on her. What should she do? If someone was after Alice, then she needed the police, social services, a hundred other things that Lil couldn't provide. Was keeping Alice's secret really the best way to help her? And yet doubt nagged at Lil.

She couldn't talk with them both staring at her. She went out into the hall, still torn. In the end Lil was saved from having to make a decision because Sabrina said, "Hang on." Then when she spoke again, it was to someone else, her voice muffled like she had her hand over the phone. "Tell the Fischers they don't have a choice. . . . Yes. . . . Yes. All right, I'll tell them myself." Then she was back, loud in Lil's ear: "I have to go. It's chaos down here. And this damn rain just won't stop. Stay put, okay, sweetie? Hopefully the rain'll stop soon. I'll tell your mum you're all right—she's gone to Chester today, right? Heaven knows how she made it in the storm. And I'll speak to Kiran's dad. Much better for you and Kiran to keep out of the storm for the moment. I'll call again later. Get up to you tonight if I can."

"But . . ."

Sabrina was gone.

Lil held the phone, already regretting not telling her aunt about Alice. Should she call back? No, Sabrina had sounded busy. She'd leave it for now. They would just have to deal with it. She went back into her bedroom and handed the phone to Kiran.

"What did she say?" he asked.

"That it's raining." Lil grinned, feigning lightness as she felt anything but.

Kiran laughed. "Good to know our police force are so observant. Anything else? They want us to stay here, don't they?"

Lil nodded. "Until the storm passes."

"And . . ." Kiran jerked his head in the direction of Alice. It wasn't exactly subtle.

Alice didn't notice him, though. She stared intently at Lil, desperate to know too.

"I didn't say anything," Lil didn't add that she had wanted to but never got a chance.

Relief passed over Alice's face. "They told me the world was untrustworthy, but you are not."

Unease squirmed inside Lil. As if to confirm the dread growing in her gut, the outside light flicked off, plunging the backyard into an impenetrable gloom again.

Beware the world beyond the gates of
the Light; Darkness there lurks.

—THE BOOK

It had been four full moons since Brilliance relinquished
the name given to her in Darkness and took her Light
name.

It was beautiful and pure, and Brilliance loved it. She
smiled to herself as she crossed the courtyard beside the
house and went out into the surrounding wood, heading
for the cliff top. It was raining hard, water pooling in the
branches and then dripping down her neck, and the wind
was like a wild thing, tearing around her. She was glad of
the cloak that each sister wore, but what she wouldn't have
done for her parka right about now. But that was a part of
her old life. "A sister dresses for the Light, identical to her
sisters, so that we may all be equal in the glory."

In the distance she could hear voices. Even in the
storm the sisters were felling the trees that would
become the wood for the Sun's fire at the Illumination
ceremony tomorrow night. Everyone was excited about
it. The Illumination was an annual event, the death of

one sun and the beginning of another, but this year's ceremony was to be extra special. As a Beta, Brilliance didn't know everything about it, but the sisters couldn't talk about it without smiling, even Dazzle. "Can you believe it's nearly the Brightness?" she said, eyes wide. "The B-r-i-g-h-t-n-e-s-s." She emphasized each letter.

"A total consummation with the Light," Moon had said of the Brightness. "A rebirth for every one of us."

Rebirth. New beginning.

New her.

That sounded good to Brilliance. A fresh start, that's why they were all here.

She pulled her hood down farther over her eyes as she cut down the path that led to the cliff top, careful not to slip on the mud. She loved this wood. Its trees were epic, with their wide, wide branches, like arms hugging the sky.

The commune was surrounded on three sides by high walls and on the fourth by a wood that led to a cliff with a sheer drop to the sea. It was empty and quiet here.

Brilliance had hated the remoteness of her former home. Nothing but miles of space and thoughts. Here, though, she didn't mind it. There were so many women. Sixteen members in all. You were never truly alone, always had someone to chat with. It was good. It was nice. Even after only a few months, it felt like . . . it felt like a place she might belong.

Brilliance was happier here than she had ever imagined possible. "How did you know?" she'd asked Moon only days after her arrival. *That I was searching for this place*, she'd meant, only there was no need to explain. The high priestess had understood immediately. She always seemed to understand, instinctively and easily. A gift from the Light? Or just her own special self? Either way, it didn't matter.

"I knew you were the Light's daughter the second I saw you," Moon had said. "You will find the peace you seek here, sister."

Brilliance had been looking for the Sisterhood her whole life without even knowing it. Desperately searching for something beyond herself, something that knotted her frayed edges together, made her whole, gave her a purpose. "There has to be more than just eating and sleeping and drinking and boys and schoolwork and then work and finally dying," she'd said to one of the other sisters, an Alpha called Luster, who'd been assigned to help her settle in. "Doesn't there? Something bigger than us? Some reason that we are all here on this planet. Some reason *I'm* here."

"I'm sure you will find it with us," Luster had said with a smile.

She had. This. Was. It. This Light. This escape from Darkness.

The only cloud on her horizon was her family. She couldn't think about them without feeling bad. But she couldn't go back. To leave would be to lose the peace this place gave her, and she could never do that. She could not go back to the Darkness of her old life, her old self, her old name.

I'm happy now. She sent the message out on the wings of a bird. *I'm safe. Be happy for me. I'm going to be okay.*

Chapter Six

Leaving Alice curled up on the end of Lil's bed reading, Kiran and Lil went downstairs to get something to eat. Lil was starving. She'd lost all track of time, and she hadn't eaten since that toast, which now felt like a lifetime ago.

The kitchen was colder than normal, and dark. Even with the overhead light on, the shadows stretched long across the room, and the windows were black mirrors that reflected Lil back at herself. She imagined the light spilling out down the driveway and shining like a beacon across the mountain. Anyone out there could follow that light right here. That made her uncomfortable, and she quickly dragged the curtains closed, shutting out the dark, stormy evening.

When she turned around, Kiran was rummaging through the fridge, pulling out what few supplies they had. Lil hoped the storm wouldn't last too long, or they'd have to start eating grubs to survive. "You guys were up there a long time. Did she tell you anything? About what's happened to her?" Kiran asked.

Lil shook her head. "Not much. She refused to answer lots of stuff, and when she did, well . . ."—Lil gave a half shrug—"not a lot of things made sense. Not to me, anyway."

Lil didn't know what to make of Alice. She should have told Sabrina what was going on. She was realizing with a steadily increasing dread that they should have called for help ages ago. Everything had gotten out of hand. She had that sensation of being at the highest point of a roller coaster, just the second before the car you're in plunges down the first loop and there's no way to stop the ride, even if you want to get off.

She should call Sabrina back, but a part of her still hesitated. She didn't want to go back on her promise to Alice. She was scared she'd leave.

"Look, can we just not talk about Alice for a bit? I feel . . . I don't know. . . ." She needed a few moments to try not to think about how badly she was handling all of this. "Do you want a cup of tea?" she asked, pushing her thoughts to the back of her mind for a minute. *Just while I calm down. Just a moment to think.*

Kiran eyed her a second, and she thought he was going to push her, but "Do you have any tea?" was all he said.

Lil loved him for that. It was crazy not to talk about the elephant—or in this case, girl—in the room, but she just needed to process. Her mind was racing. "Probably not. How do you feel about hot water?"

"That as a beverage of choice, it's very underrated." He waggled an eyebrow.

Warmth rushed over Lil and she suddenly felt an urge to

hug him. Being with Kiran felt so wonderfully normal. It pushed out all the weird freakiness about Alice's appearance, her way of speaking, and Lil's irrational sense that there was someone watching them, waiting for them, out in the dark.

"Cai was there this morning," Kiran said, breaking into her thoughts. "At the kayak club."

Lil grimaced. "Yuck. I'm almost glad I fell off my bike. Did he say anything?"

"No, too busy chatting up some brunette."

Lil winced. She hadn't expected Cai to stay faithful to her sister—hell, he'd barely stayed faithful when Mella was still here—but the way he flirted with anything that was female and had a pulse made her sick. He'd done it almost the second Mella was gone. And he'd been so unhelpful in their search for her: "Dunno when I last saw her." "Dunno what we talked about." "Dunno where she might go." "Dunno why." "Dunno, dunno, dunno" was his response to everything. He was a grade-one douche bag.

Lil didn't want to think about Cai now, or ever, and instead rummaged in the cupboard to look for tea bags, finding a few tucked in the back. Once she'd made the tea, she carried the steaming mugs over to the table, saying, "There's no milk. Sorry." She sat down. "What did your dad say about you staying here?"

"Not much. It's better I'm here than out driving in the storm."

"Yeah," Lil agreed. That made sense. "Will the twins be scared? Because of the storm?"

"Are you kidding? They'll have set up some kind of tracking equipment to measure the speed of the wind, and they'll have Dad outside with a ruler, measuring the depth of the water."

"We had to do that for school once. Rhia and me. We were supposed to take recordings of how much rainwater had fallen every day for a month. We couldn't be bothered to do it, though, so we made the results up. We got confused and put meters instead of millimeters on the results table, so we reported that it had rained sixty-five meters in a month."

Kiran laughed, and Lil felt the familiar twang of guilt that she got whenever she thought of Rhiannon these days. Kiran didn't know that she and Rhia weren't speaking. No, it wasn't that they *weren't* speaking. That made it sound active. It was more just a passive moving apart. Kiran was in the year above, so he just assumed that she hung out with Rhia in lessons and at lunch and on the weekends, when she wasn't with him or endlessly, *endlessly* checking the Find Mella website and calling the police for updates.

She didn't know exactly what had happened between her and Rhia. Lil had pulling away from Rhia for a while, unconsciously at first, ever since Mella left, or maybe even before that. Rhia had three sisters and a mum and dad who actually liked being married to each other, rather than barely being able to tolerate occupying the same room, and the whole family was so close. Doing stuff together all the time and enjoying it. Rhia's mum made Lil welcome every time she went over, but it hurt, seeing them happy, laughing, joking, getting on so well. It made Lil's own family seem even more inadequate . . . and Lil couldn't bear it. She hated herself for feeling like that, until in the end it was just easier not to go around. And then that came to not talking in the evenings. And finally, to making excuses not to sit with Rhia at lunch.

It was easier with Kiran. His family was almost as dysfunctional as Lil's. That made Lil worried, too—*Am I the kind of person who can only be friends with someone if they are miserable?* But Kiran wasn't miserable. He was a 90-watt bulb, making everything around him brighter.

The truth was, Lil had changed; the second she realized that this time Mella wasn't just hiding out, that she'd really gone, the old Lil disintegrated, to be replaced by a new, quieter, shier, more anxious one. She looked back at the stuff she used to care about—schoolwork, the cute boy in year ten, whether the spot on her nose would be gone by Rhia's birthday party—and she felt embarrassed. None of that stuff mattered, not one little tiny bit. She was angry with stupid, naive Lil, sweating the trivial, but also protective of her, like she was a child. That poor thing hadn't known what was coming. She would give anything now if her biggest worries were what lip gloss she should wear on Saturday or what sweater she should buy.

Kiran bent over the sink to add some cold water to his tea. "Too hot." Lil made a *Poor baby* face and he smiled, but he was watching her closely.

Unlike most regular-size humans, Kiran was taller than her. That was one of the things she liked about him: less neck crooking when he was around. The bad thing was his tendency to catch her eye the way no one else was able to, and to hold her gaze, like he was doing now. She ducked her head and he ducked his, following her.

"What?" she said.

"Don't know." Kiran shrugged. "You look different today."

"Different how?"

"I don't know." He smiled. "Maybe it's the wet hair."

"À la drowned rat. Thanks!" She reached forward to punch him playfully on the arm. He caught her fingers and a charge went through Lil. She tugged her hand out of his quickly. This was Kiran, *friend* Kiran.

Sure, Mouse, and I'm the queen of France, Mella chimed in her head. *Now you must obey my every command. I demand a crown of marzipan and a throne of chocolate. Or I'll chop off your head.*

Shut up, Lil said feebly.

Mella cackled, and the sound of it hurt, because it wasn't real. Just a memory, and every day Mella faded a little more from Lil's mind.

"Maybe there are some biscuits in the other cupboard," she said, moving away from him. Right now she didn't have time for anything other than finding her sister.

When she checked the cupboard, Lil turned back to find Kiran sitting at the kitchen table. He held up a chunk of cheese. He must have found it in the fridge earlier. "Does mold count as one of your five-a-day?"

And whatever weirdness there had been between them disappeared.

After turning on the oven and putting the french fries that she'd found in the freezer in to cook, she dropped back into a chair and wrapped her hands around her tea. The mug was pink with blue flowers, and the words on it said: "I'm smiling because you're my sister. I'm laughing because you can't do anything about it." Mella had bought it for her the Christmas before last. She thought it was hysterical. Mella had a very odd sense of humor sometimes.

As though waiting for the right time, Kiran studied her for a long moment, then said, "We kind of have to talk about this, Lil. We can't just ignore it. . . ."

Lil's stomach twisted. She'd messed up; she should have told Sabrina. "I know. . . ."

"So . . . ?" He raised an eyebrow. "What did she tell you? Alice."

Lil drew in a fractured breath and filled Kiran in quickly on everything she'd learned about Alice: the sisters-but-not-blood-sisters and about her not being able to go home. "She talks so strangely. I don't get half of what she says. Do you know what 'recreant' means?"

"No idea. I don't even know how you spell it."

Lil went and got the dictionary from the top shelf of the dresser. Her mum kept it there for the Saturday crossword puzzle, not that she did them much anymore. After stroking off a layer of dust and a dead fly, she flicked to the R section. It took a moment, but then: "There . . . 'recreant.'" She read the meaning aloud. "'Adjective. Unfaithful to a belief; apostate. Noun. A person who is unfaithful to a belief; an apostate.'"

"'Unfaithful to a belief'?" Kiran repeated. "Like a religious one?"

"I guess," Lil said. A picture formed in her mind: ill-defined and as nebulous as a cloud but growing all the time. "Recreant," "light," "glory," "sisters," "forbidden" . . . they were all words associated with religion, weren't they? "So she came from somewhere religious?" Lil said, thinking aloud. "A church? No. . . . Her family was religious?" She sighed. "She's scared, Kiran. What are we going to do?"

They exchanged a look.

"We are so out of our depth here, Lils."

"I know." Lil put her hand over her face. She'd placed Kiran into a bad and possibly dangerous situation, and for what? "I'm sorry. I just . . . it's . . ." Lil took a deep breath. It was hard to say this, but she felt she owed it to Kiran to explain. "I didn't with Mella. . . . I wasn't . . ."

I let her down, she wanted to say, but she couldn't. How would Kiran respond? She couldn't bear him to look at her differently when he knew how selfish she'd been, how she hadn't helped Mella when she needed her most. And that was the reason she wanted to help Alice and the real reason she hadn't told Sabrina about her. When Alice had said she would leave if Lil told anyone, she'd gotten scared. She didn't want to be responsible for someone else disappearing.

"I want to make it right for Alice," Lil said. Then, after a deep breath, she added quietly, "I didn't with Mella."

She was afraid to look at Kiran, but when she did, understanding filled his eyes with a soft warmth, making their brown seem even richer. And Lil wondered why she hadn't told him her fears immediately. How could she have doubted that he would get exactly what she was feeling? Or if not get it, just accept it, respect it. Because he was Kiran. He always got her. Always.

CHAPTER SEVEN

Once the fries were cooked, Lil piled them on a plate and added it to the tray of the other stuff they'd found, and carried it upstairs. Alice stared at the food curiously.

"Sorry, it's not much," Lil said.

Kiran began wolfing down the fries, dunking four or five in the ketchup in one go and shoving them into his mouth. "What?" he asked, mouth full, when Lil gave him a look. "I'm hungry!"

Lil rolled her eyes with a smile. She leaned over and separated the fries into two piles. "Yours," she said to Kiran, "and ours."

"Yours is bigger."

"Because there are *two* of us." She gestured at Alice to eat. Alice had been staring at Kiran in a mix of wonder and disgust. "Don't mind the piggy here," Lil said, "but I would eat quickly. I'm not sure how long I can defend your pile."

Alice hesitated and then picked up a fry, turning it around and around in her hand, looking at it from every angle.

"Do you want salt with it?" Lil asked.

Alice didn't answer. She tilted her head and squinted at the fry. Then she held it to her lips, and her tongue poked out to lick the end of it. After another lick she bit off the tiniest amount. Confusion turned to pleasure on her face, and she took another, larger bite. Then she smiled. "Good," she said, "it's good."

"You've never had fries before?" Kiran asked.

Alice shook her head solemnly.

"Try them with ketchup," Lil urged. Where had Alice come from that she had never eaten fries before? Maybe her family was super healthy, but surely she'd have heard of them. Seen them. At school, if nothing else.

"They're better with mayonnaise," Kiran said. "Bet you don't know what that is either." He grinned.

Alice narrowed her eyes, offended. "We have only what the Light sees fit to provide."

Lil kicked Kiran and gave him a *Shut up* look. "He didn't mean anything by it. We're just trying to understand. It seems like it's pretty different for you at home."

Alice paused midbite and then swallowed slowly. "Yes, everything is new and strange to me here."

"But some stuff must be the same, right?" Lil pressed. "Like . . . like . . ." She hesitated, trying to find common ground. "Like school! Where do you go to school?"

"I don't go to school. The sisters govern our education."

"*The* sisters" not "*my.*" Alice definitely wasn't talking about siblings, Lil was certain of it. She exchanged a glance with Kiran. Nuns were known as sisters. Could Alice have come from a convent? Or maybe an orphanage? Didn't the Catholic Church sometimes look after orphaned children?

"Who are the sisters?" Lil asked quietly. "Are they who you're running from?"

For a second Lil thought that Alice wasn't going to answer. Then she said, "It's hard to explain in a way you'll understand. I . . ." She drew in a deep breath, as though it was hard for her to speak. "While you were downstairs, I asked the Light for guidance. She said I can trust you. That I *should* trust you." In a hushed breath she added, "I lied to you before, when I said my name was Alice. My true name, my Light name, is not Alice. It's Seven."

"Seven?" Lil repeated, shocked, although not by the fact that Seven had lied about her identity. "As in the number seven?"

Seven nodded. "Yes, I was born on the seventh hour of the seventh day of the seventh month."

Kiran whistled. "What are the chances of that?"

Seven looked at him as if he might be a bit stupid. "It is prophecy. My birth was predetermined by the Light."

"Oh," he said. "Right. I . . . see." He raised an eyebrow at Lil, who shook her head at him. She didn't want Seven to think they were laughing at her or communicating silently about her. She knew what a big deal it was for Seven to tell them anything about herself.

"Telling you my name is a sign of my trust. To name things is to own them."

A shiver went over Lil at the idea that just naming something gave you power over it. It gave a tiny but frightening glimpse into the place Seven had come from, and Lil realized that she'd been kidding herself, thinking that she and Kiran could handle this. The thought was like a light turning on, and suddenly she could see everything clearly. It didn't matter what Seven wanted, or what Lil had promised. Something terrible had happened to Seven.

"I'm calling Sabrina," she said, her voice strong and assured. She was doing the right thing. "I get that you're scared," she told Seven firmly but not unkindly, "but I wouldn't be helping you if I didn't do this. You can trust my aunt. She's great; she'll know what to do."

Her phone was broken, so she used Kiran's, but there was something wrong with it. The phone wasn't connecting. She pulled it away from her ear. There were four bars, but it wasn't working. "I'll try the landline," she said, handing it back to Kiran. "Maybe the storm's interfering with the reception."

"But that wasn't working earlier. Sabrina couldn't—" Kiran said.

"I'm sure it'll be fine now," Lil said. *Dear God, please let it be fine now.* She went out into the corridor. It was dark, inkiness spilling down the stairs, so that it was almost impossible to make out the hallway below.

As she crossed the landing, the sky lit up with a blinding flash, and a second or two later there was a loud clap of thunder. Rain followed, slamming into the house at an angle, so it hit the windowpanes hard. The sound of it did something to Lil. Her nerves had been stretched too tight, an elastic band pulled taut, since she'd found Seven on the road, and now they snapped.

She took the stairs two at a time, energy coursing through her. At the bottom she flicked on the light switch, filling the house with beautiful, normal electricity and pushing back the darkness and her own growing fear. Her relief was immense.

She moved quietly toward the landline, scared for some reason to make any noise. She could hear the low murmur of voices coming from her bedroom: Kiran's a soft mumble, Seven's shriller, panicked. Lil wondered if Seven might follow her, try to stop her, but she didn't. Perhaps Kiran had convinced her it was a good idea, or perhaps Seven was secretly relieved that Lil was getting help.

Other than the sound of the storm, everything inside the house was quiet. They were so isolated here. Lil had never worried about it before. She viewed the countryside as a friendly place, with the sheep and the hills. Now that isolation squeezed in on her, making her small and afraid. She remembered the burnlike mark on Seven's arm. Had someone hurt her deliberately? Why? What reason would anyone have to hurt someone as vulnerable and innocent as Seven?

She pressed the talk button on phone. There was no dial tone. She punched the redial button. Nothing. The line was dead.

"Kiran!" she said; her voice came out croaky and loud in the near-silent house. For some reason the sound of it spooked her.

She whipped around quickly, as if checking whether her voice had drawn anyone out. The hall was still empty. The light didn't seem so bright now, or so comforting. Rather than shout for him again, she dashed back upstairs, the phone still in her hand.

Lil dropped the house phone onto her bed in frustration. "It's not working." There was another clap of thunder overhead. She sank down onto the bed.. "The lines must be down because of the storm."

Lil had procrastinated, and now the chance to call Sabrina was gone. If they wanted her, they'd have to venture out into the storm by themselves, and the roads around here were dangerous enough on a good day. For the moment they were stuck here, alone.

Kiran came up behind her and Lil jumped. God, she was so on edge.

"You all right?" he asked quietly.

"I don't know what to do," she said.

"There's nothing we can do for now. I don't fancy driving in this, unless we have to."

Lil nodded. He was only voicing what she'd already thought.

"We'll have to wait it out." Kiran sounded resigned but not angry or resentful. That was one of the best things about him. He got on with things as they were, didn't apportion blame or wish things different.

Lil glanced at Seven. She was pretending to read a book, but Lil could tell she was listening. She went over and crouched down in front of her. "I'm really trying to do the right thing here." Lil drew a deep breath.

Seven jutted her chin out. "I do not need the authorities. The Light will protect me, as is Her will."

"It hasn't done a great job of it so far. Look at you!" Lil snapped, and instantly regretted it, but Seven was unfazed.

"The Light has not forsaken me. She brought me here, to you."

Lil gave a long sigh. "I guess. Not that I've done anything to help you."

"You have!" Seven cried, clapping her small hands together. "You've done so much. I am a stranger, but you took me in, even though you know nothing about me." Her large brown doe's eyes assessed Lil intently. "I was taught that people outside are not kind, but you are. It proves what I always believed: that the Light shines where She will and all are welcome in Her glory." She smiled gently. It was beautiful but fleeting.

After a moment she added, "I am sure your aunt is kind and good too, but sisters can't trust the police. They have destroyed us before. I cannot risk that happening again. And I cannot risk being taken back home. So long as I stay away, my sisters are safe. I will not endanger their home or their lives for my own."

"But—" Lil began.

Seven raised a hand. "That is my decision." Her tone left no room for doubt.

Lil acknowledged silently that it would be a waste of time and energy to ask anything more. "Maybe you should get some rest," she said. "You look exhausted."

Relief filled Seven's eyes. She was clearly so glad that Lil wasn't going to ask any more questions. "I am quite weary," she said.

That seemed like a massive understatement, given the deep-purple circles under her eyes and her pale, washed-out face.

Lil insisted Seven take her bed. Seven refused at first but finally fell gratefully into it. "I have never had my own bed," she said. "All to myself." She was asleep almost immediately.

CHAPTER EIGHT

It was too early for Kiran and Lil to go to bed, but they piled blankets and sleeping bags on the floor and snuggled down into them anyway. It was cold. Lil didn't see how she'd be able to sleep at all tonight. It wasn't just Seven. It was Mella. She always felt more anxious about her when it rained: *Let her be somewhere safe and dry. Let her come home.*

Recently the police had scaled back the search. Four and a half months was a long time for a young girl to be away. Lil knew what they were implying—that Mella was dead. But she wasn't. Lil knew she wasn't. She could feel it deep down inside: Mella was alive and she was coming home. They just had to keep searching, keep hoping.

She pulled the sleeping bag up to her ears and tried to switch off her brain. Kiran's voice broke the silence. "You're not going to throw up on me, are you?" he said.

It took Lil's brain a second to click to what he was talking about. She'd been so far away in her own head. Then she gave him a weak smile. He was trying to distract her, and she was grateful for it. "Once," she said. "That happened one time! I had too much vodka. Which was your fault! Plus, I've apologized, like, a thousand times."

"You can never apologize enough for vomiting in someone's hair."

"I didn't throw up in your hair. Your hair just happened to be there." She laughed and Kiran grinned wider. He had such a nice smile. It was kind of lopsided, but that made it even nicer. It was weird lying next to him like this. So close. Almost like they were in the same bed.

As Kiran moved about, getting comfortable, Lil lay perfectly still. It was something she'd perfected—this way, she found that even if she didn't sleep that much, which she never did these days, she didn't feel so tired the next day. She'd also gotten into the habit of focusing on her breathing: *In, out, in, out, in, out.*

The night was the worst time. It was when images of Mella and where she might be crowded her head, forcing everything else out. In the early days Lil thought she would go mad imagining all the terrible places Mella could be. In the daylight she could keep her visions under control, if she kept busy. But at night, when there was only the darkness, they rushed in on her all at once. She'd breathe in and out, in and out, focus on the way the oxygen came down into her lungs, the sound of her heart beating.

Nighttime was when she talked to her sister the most.

Mella? Lil said in her head now.

Yup!

Do you have somewhere to sleep tonight?

Of course! I'm warm and cozy and tucked up tight so the bedbugs don't bite.

Kiran had stopped moving and the house was completely silent.

Are you really safe, Mella?

An image of Mella on a street corner, wrapped in a ratty sleeping bag, popped into Lil's head. No . . . worse . . . lying beaten and . . . *No. Don't you dare even let that thought enter your head. Mella is fine. She's fine. She's coming home. She's coming home.*

"Lil." The sound of Lil's name in the darkness made her jump. It was just Kiran, though, of course.

She rolled over. "Yes."

"Are you asleep?" He shuffled his sleeping bag closer. In the darkness she could see the outline of him.

She smiled, grateful for the distraction, anything to stop her agonizing over Mella. "Yes," she said, "asleep and snoring at six thirty in the evening."

He grinned and propped himself up on one arm, and the sleeping bag slipped, revealing his right shoulder. His T-shirt had rucked up, showing the top of his arm. Lil had to admit that his bare arms were nice. His skin was a tawny brown and smooth as silk, and he had muscles. Not big ones—Lil hated that—but just a little definition. The perfect amount, actually. That must be due to all that kayaking. Lil wondered what it would be like to touch him. To run her hand over his skin. To trace the taut line of his muscle. Would it be as soft as it looked? Lil was grateful for the darkness as heat flared across her cheeks.

Ooh-la-la, Mella said in her head, and gave a wolf whistle.

Lil's blush deepened, and then she mentally shook herself. What was she doing? Why was she thinking like this? They were friends. Friends.

Sure, sure, Mella piped up. *You keep telling yourself that, Mouse.*

"You know," Kiran said, "your room is kinda creepy in the dark."

Lil laughed warmly, and probably more heartily than the comment warranted because it meant he had no idea what she had been thinking, and thank God for that. "Are you scared of the dark, Kiran?" she asked wryly.

"No! Course not. I'm far too rational for that."

Lil laughed again. "Mella hated the dark too," she said, settling onto her back and looking up at the ceiling. It was too distracting looking at Kiran while his shoulder was exposed like that. She kept wanting to touch it. Ugh. What was wrong with her? *Stop this right now*, she told herself. "It was worse when we first got here. It's just so dark. And so quiet. It's not like that in London. There's streetlights and always some noise, cars or whatever." Lil remembered how amazed she and Mella had been to see the stars. They'd seen stars before, of course, but not like this. As clear and sharp as a needle point.

"Yeah, it's the same in Birmingham. It took me ages to get used to it here." Kiran and his family had moved to Wales earlier in the year. He paused and then said quietly, hesitantly, "I didn't realize your sister's room would be like that. I thought . . . I mean, it's like she never left."

Lil didn't answer for a minute. They never spoke about Mella. Kiran helped her put up MISSING posters, but he never asked questions. Lil had told him about her being missing the third time they met. She'd spoken fast, and angrily for some reason, like he was going to challenge her. "And I put up posters in case anyone's seen her," she'd finished. "And so she knows that she can come home at any time." He'd nodded, thoughtful. "Makes sense," he'd said. "I'd do the same."

When she went to the kayaking club the next time, he'd put up a corkboard by the entrance. Above it was a sign that said: HELP US FIND MELLA LAVERTY. "I thought it could be good to have a place to put everything. I've put a place for sightings." He ran his hand through his hair awkwardly. "Is it all right? I mean, we can take it down if you hate it."

"It's perfect," Lil said. She wanted to hug him, because he hadn't run away and never spoken to her again, awkwardly shuffling past her, head down, whenever they bumped into each other. So many people Lil considered friends had done that. When people didn't know what to say, it was easiest to say nothing at all, to pretend nothing had happened. All the time Lil knew they were bubbling over with questions, though. *Why did she leave? What did you do? What didn't you do?* And the worst one of all: *How did you not know she was that unhappy?*

How did you not know? Lil asked herself that every day. It was the hardest one of all to answer, and the one filled with the most regret. If only she'd paid more attention, if only she'd been more patient, been there more for Mella, could she have stopped all this? Could she have stopped her running away?

"Sorry," Kiran said now. "I shouldn't have said that. . . ."

"Mum put everything back exactly the way it was after the police returned it. I hate it. It feels like she is still here, and every time I see it, I have to remind myself that she's not. But then, I'd hate it more if we'd packed everything up, because that would feel like . . . like she was . . . wasn't coming back."

"Dad packed up most of Mum's things a few months after she died. I went mad. 'Cause it meant she was gone—properly gone." Kiran's mum had died of a brain tumor eighteen months ago. He almost never spoke of it.

Lil didn't know what to say, so the silence stretched between them until finally Lil reached out and took Kiran's hand. The touch of Kiran's skin made Lil's heart speed up, and for just a moment, just a second, she let that feeling take over—fill up the emptiness and pain and ache of guilt that Mella's disappearance had left. Then the guilt resurfaced and she slid her fingers out of his. She couldn't afford to forget her sister for a second. Not a single instant.

"Did . . . did," she asked hesitantly, "you keep any of her stuff?"

"Bits and pieces. The books she wrote, of course." His mum had been a professor of astrophysics at the University of Birmingham and written three books on black holes and dark matter. Two of them were widely recognized as the best in their field, and all were long, with pages of densely packed type, made up of lengthy sentences of long words that Lil didn't understand. "Dad kept her wedding ring too. And the engagement one. And I kept this jade necklace that she always wore. It's shaped like an elephant. I loved it when I was a kid. Mum always said he came alive at night and would go on adventures. She'd tell me bedtime stories about him."

"Him?" Lil smiled.

"Yeah, he was called Eliffant." It meant "elephant" in Welsh. Kiran's mum was born in a village a few miles from Porthpridd. "Dad said he should have been Haathee, because they don't have elephants in Wales, only in India." Kiran's dad was born in Birmingham after Kiran's grandparents had emigrated from India.

Kiran drew a short breath. "Wow. I haven't thought about those stories in a long time." He sighed. "I guess it was just stuff. Not her, not really. It just felt weird having it go to someone else. Like now there's someone else wandering around in my mum's clothes, in her shoes. You know. Mind you, she would have hated the idea of Dad just chucking it away. 'Not more landfill, Dev!' she would have shouted. She hated waste. Her and my dad's mum had that in common. She never throws anything out. Her house in Birmingham is full of old junk. She would kill me if she heard me call it that! But she's even got a load of my dad's old rompers. And his baby teeth!"

"Ew!" Lil wrinkled her nose.

"Yeah! Gross, huh." Kiran hesitated and then said softly, "What was she like? Mella. You don't talk about her much."

"Talking about her doesn't change anything." That sounded more bitter than Lil had meant it to, and it wasn't true, either. "It's painful, remembering; even saying her name sometimes hurts. I think about her all the time."

Kiran nodded like he understood.

"She was loud." Lil smiled. "So loud. And funny. And this amazing artist. Seriously. Mells was so talented." She paused. She wanted to say that Mella was the best, because she was, but that wasn't the whole truth, not really, and Lil wanted to tell someone the truth. "Sometimes she just drove me crazy." The words tumbled out. "I just wanted one day, one occasion, you know, when it wasn't . . ." Lil caught herself. She'd been about to say *when it wasn't all about her.* Instead she said, "When things were quieter, when she wasn't crazy robot dancing and falling over and breaking her ankle."

"Did that really happen?" Kiran raised an eyebrow.

"Yes, my sixth birthday! On my seventh she started this tradition of making croissants, only she forgot about them and set fire to the kitchen. We needed to call the fire brigade." Lil laughed at the memory, but there was a tinge of something else to it. A stain that had grown over time.

Lil talked quickly. She didn't want to let that thought take up residence in her brain. "Then on my twelfth she got so drunk on peach schnapps that she threw up all over the hallway. And then on the morning after my sixteenth"—the sadness rushed in—"she left, and we haven't seen her since."

Lil gazed into the distance. Tears came so readily now that she didn't realize her eyes were full of them until the world fractured. "I shouldn't talk about her like this. She was great. Just . . ." She turned to Kiran. "Sometimes she was . . . she could be too much." How could she even think that? It made it sound like she'd wanted Mella gone, and she hadn't. She hadn't. Just sometimes for her to be a bit less Mella, but then . . . Mella was Mella. Lil sighed. "Hey, maybe if she'd been around that day in the kayaking club, she would have taken you kayaking and we wouldn't have met at all." Was that what Lil really thought? No. Yes. Maybe.

"We would have met. It was meant to be," Kiran said, the words so quiet they were barely a whisper, but they rolled around Lil's head as loud as a cry. Her heart rose up like a balloon to meet them, before it deflated again. Her head was too full of thoughts and she couldn't make sense of any of them.

Lil and Kiran lay in silence for a while.

"When Mum died," Kiran said, "that was it. It was over. At least you have hope. Right?"

Hope. The trouble with hope was you didn't know when it would be fulfilled, and that meant jumping every time the phone rang, or someone knocked on the door, or you saw a girl on the street with curly brown hair. Sometimes hope felt very close to despair, because despite fighting with everything you had to deny it, you couldn't help but wonder if maybe she wasn't coming home . . . if maybe something had happened to her.

Lil shut off that thought. "Yes," she said so suddenly that Kiran jumped. "Mella's coming home. Yes, definitely."

"Of course she is," Kiran said, and he looked at her pensively, not because he thought she was delusional, but because he somehow seemed to realize that she hadn't really been talking to him. He went to touch her hand and then hesitated. They both watched the hand travel toward Lil's and then stop. It hung there a moment and then dropped back to his side. Lil wasn't sure if she was relieved or disappointed.

"Things were bad for Mella at the end," Lil said after a minute. "I mean before she left. She and Mum were fighting. About Cai. About homework. Mella was in trouble. A lot. She'd never been great at school. But then at college it was like she just gave up, even with her art coursework. And I was so angry with her. She wouldn't let anyone help her."

"Hmm. Sounds like someone else I know," Kiran said.

"What do you mean?" Lil was surprised.

Kiran shifted uncomfortably. "Just that . . . sometimes you are kind of shut off."

"Shut off?"

"Distant. Like, I don't know. It's hard to talk to you."

Lil was hurt. Aside from Rhiannon, Kiran was her only confidant. "I don't mean to be difficult," she said.

"No!" Kiran said. "I'm saying this wrong. I mean you're

Lil: You're funny and smart and . . ." He ruffled his hair, something he always did when he was nervous or uncomfortable. "It's just you don't talk about stuff, like proper stuff, ever. If I bring anything up, you change the subject. And . . ." He paused. "Rhiannon says you don't talk to her much now either."

"You've been talking to Rhia about me?" Lil was annoyed, but mostly she was embarrassed. She'd been mean to Rhia, and Rhia deserved better. Selfishly, she didn't want Kiran to know about it.

"No. Just . . . I bumped into her the other week. She was in Porthpridd. I assumed you would be with her, but she said she didn't see you much now. Or at all, actually."

Lil fiddled with the zipper on her sleeping bag.

"It's none of my business," Kiran said. "I shouldn't have mentioned it."

The feelings warred inside Lil for a minute. She was defensive and hurt, but then she sighed. "It's hard to think about stuff. Talk about stuff. There's so much to do with the social media stuff for Mella, the Find Mella website has to be updated every day, and Mum needs me. I guess I don't have time to just hang out like I used to." But that wasn't the truth, not really.

After a long moment Lil said quietly, "I can't talk to Rhia. I want to, but I can't. Her family is so perfect. It makes mine seem . . . And then I get . . . embarrassed." *And angry, and jealous. And I hate myself for it, because do I really want someone else to be unhappy in order to make me feel better?*

Lil tugged at the zipper again, then looked up at Kiran.

"Me and Rhia are okay. We will be okay. I just need . . . Mella needs to come home and then everything will be fine." She had to turn away then because Kiran's eyes were too raw, as if reflecting Lil's own. It hurt too much to look at all that empathy. More than that, Kiran's eyes said, *What if she doesn't come home?* Lil wasn't ready to think about that yet. She would never be ready to think about that. Because Mella was definitely coming home. She had to.

"I have to be there for Mum," Lil said. "That's the most important thing. I have to keep it together for her."

"You're amazing," Kiran said softly. "I mean, I think you are. To stay strong and sane . . ."

Lil wondered if he would still think that if she told him she heard her sister's voice in her head.

"After Mum—" He was cut off by a noise from Seven, and they both looked over. Kiran half sat up to peer through the gloom.

"Is she awake?" Lil asked.

"Seven?" Kiran called. There was no response. "No, I don't think so." He settled back down in the sleeping bag and blankets. He didn't finish whatever he was going to say about his mum, and Lil didn't want to press him. He was so quiet and still that she was sure he'd fallen asleep.

Lil yawned but couldn't drop off. She stared at the ceiling a long time, listening to the silent house. She jolted when he spoke again and very quietly said, "The fact that I don't ask about Mella doesn't mean I don't care. I just figured you'd tell me if you wanted to." He turned toward her, his face so close that she could see the shadow of his eyelashes on his cheek and feel his warm breath on her neck. If she turned her own head, their lips would be touching. Heat coursed through Lil like a flame, because she wanted to turn her head, she wanted to kiss Kiran. *No, no, no. No. No.*

With an effort of will, she lay still, head flat on her own pillow, thinking icy thoughts to calm the heat coursing through her veins. "Good night, Kiran," she said softly, gently, but it came out like good-bye.

Beside her, Kiran let out a breath slowly, steadily, and it sounded like disappointment.

May the Light bring you peace.

—The Book

"Look at the flame," Moon commanded, her indigo eyes flickering in the firelight, her hair redder than ever.

All the sisters had gathered in the clearing in the woods, for the Refulgence, their nightly communion with the Light, at midnight, when the Dark was at its strongest. The shadows were long over the grass, but they were beaten back by the roaring bonfire. Brilliance could feel its heat on her face, and not just any heat, she thought with a thrill, the Light's heat. Moon kept the Sun's flame burning in an orb in her room, and it was transferred here every evening by Evanescence, the first Alpha, Moon's second-in-command. Then it was shared with the Sisterhood, so they might all be cleansed by it.

Tonight's communion was even more special. It was the last one before the Illumination.

"The Sun's flame is not fire, but water that soothes as it touches, cleansing you," Moon said, "freeing you from your pain, your fear, freeing you from yourself and from the Dark." She wore her red tunic tonight: red for the Light's intensity. Sleeves rolled up, arms stretched out, the fire catching in her hair and flickering on her white skin, she looked like a goddess. "Only when we are entirely without self can we be free," she went on. "It is only by stripping your soul to its barest state that you can enter the Brightness." Moon threw her arms up, voice carrying to the sky, driven up by the fingers of fire, smoke rising in tatters, and Brilliance was reminded of that Turner painting: the one of the burning ship.

"I want you to stare into the Sun's flame," Moon continued. "Imagine yourselves reaching out to touch it. Feel the flame's heat cleansing you, taking away your Darkness, leaving behind only Light, only happiness, only Brightness." Moon was as mesmerizing as the fire. "Breathe in. Take the Light inside you!"

Moon's voice was a crescendo now: as loud as a shout but also as gentle as a whisper. She caught Brilliance's eye and it seemed she was talking only to her. "Take the Light, my sister. Make it yours."

Brilliance breathed in. The smoke mixed with the headier smell of the incense burning in the seven stakes around them, and she felt herself slipping into the flame. Further and further, until its power surrounded her. The thousand thoughts pushing at her brain evaporated in its smoke. She drew another long breath and the flame became a part of her: Its pulse was her pulse; its breath was her breath as she drew in more of the cloying air into her lungs.

There was nothing but the Light. Not the Darkness. Not the smell of the rain after the earlier storm. Not the sound of the owl, or the fox sniffing in the undergrowth. Just Light. Pure, pure Light. Dancing in a kaleidoscope in front of her. Touching everything. The leaves, the branches, the grass, and farther, too. A shaft of it struck the bay. Brilliance could see more than ever before. She could see the whole world, and it was magnificent. And she was a part of it. A part of this Light. A part of this shining new world.

Slowly, many hours or maybe only seconds later, Brilliance began to come back to herself, as though waking from a deep sleep. She hung for a while in that moment between sleeping and waking, when everything was in perfect balance. She was aware of her toes, her fingers, how they connected to the muscles, to the tendons, how the blood flowed through her in an intricate maze of hidden veins. The peacefulness still clung to her. She could still remember the union of Light and Earth and self. She didn't want to shake that off yet, to swap its softness for the harsh edge of the world. Not yet.

She drew a deep breath, and somewhere nearby an owl hooted.

Brilliance felt at peace.

"May the Light always protect you," Moon said.

Brilliance opened her eyes, blinking, and the world was dark compared with the Light's fire. She wanted to go back immediately into that other place. That feeling, that beauty was a drug and she wanted more, more, *more*, and she didn't care what she must do to get it.

She walked back to the house in a daze, following the other sisters but barely concentrating, her mind still on fire with the Light. She was so out of it that it took her a moment to register the sounds of confusion up ahead. It was Moon's voice, raised in a shout, which finally brought her back to herself. She was surprised to see fear and horror on the faces of everyone around her.

"Wh-what's happened?" she asked, but no one answered. She followed their gaze to where Moon stood with Dazzle, the youngest of the sisters. Even from a distance Brilliance could see the panic in Dazzle's eyes.

"I . . . don't know," Dazzle said, shaking her head. "I don't know."

Moon's hand snapped out like a snake, gripping Dazzle's face tight; her nails dug crescent shapes into the girl's jaw. "Well, think," she said, shaking Dazzle as she spoke. Anger pooled like spittle in her words. "Think harder! When did you last see the Light's Gift? When *exactly*?"

The violence of it took Brilliance's breath away. She was too surprised to react.

Dazzle flinched in pain, but she forced the words out. "I . . . last night. . . ."

Moon turned her eyes on the rest of the group, and Brilliance shrank back from their glare. It was like being caught in a laser. "Have any of you seen her since then?" Moon's voice was almost unrecognizable and her face twisted into a mask of anger.

There was a general murmuring of no. Everyone looked at the ground. No one wanted to attract her attention.

"The . . . the gate . . . was open. The keys are gone." Dazzle's voice was barely a whisper.

Moon let go of Dazzle so quickly that she stumbled backward. One of the sisters, Luster, the Alpha who had been Brilliance's guide, caught her and steadied her.

Moon turned to Evanescence. "Find her," she screamed. "FIND HER *NOW!* Find *my gift!*" Her eyes were as black as the sea in a storm. Her words reverberated around the wood.

Chapter Nine

Mella was standing in Lil's bedroom, playing with one of the prisms on Lil's dream catcher.

"You're back!" Lil gasped.

Her sister turned slowly. She smiled, but despite being so happy to see Mella, Lil couldn't shake the feeling that something was wrong. Then Lil realized what it was. Lil's hair had changed color three times since Mella had left. Mella hadn't changed at all. Dark hair pulled back in a high ponytail. Candy-floss lip gloss. Pale-blue minidress with white polka dots, Lil's Converse trainers. She looked exactly the same as the last time Lil saw her, the night of Lil's sixteenth birthday. "You ignored me," Mella said. "I needed you and you ignored me."

Lil blinked, and when she opened her eyes again, her sister was gone. All that remained was a dark shadow on the carpet where she'd been standing.

Lil sat up, her face wet with tears. It was still night and the room was dark. Lil could just make out the shape of

Kiran lying next to her and Seven curled up under the bundle of blankets in her bed. She didn't know what had woken her until she heard the banging coming from downstairs.

"Wh-what?" Kiran asked groggily, rubbing his eyes and rolling over.

Realization flooded Lil's brain. "It's someone knocking on the front door." She flicked on the bedside lamp. "It's okay. It'll be my aunt. She must have decided to come up and check on us." She was glad. Her dream still clung to her, and she wanted to see her aunt's warm, loving face.

"At three a.m.?" Kiran asked, looking at his watch.

Sabrina must have been worried and driven out here to make sure they were okay. It was amazing that she'd made it in this weather, but Lil was just relieved they weren't on their own anymore. Then she glanced across at the spot where Seven had been sleeping. It was empty. Kiran noticed at the same time. Lil's bedroom door was open just enough for a tiny girl to squeeze out and into the hallway beyond.

There was another knock. They both jumped.

"It's my aunt," Lil said. Who else could it be? "Or maybe Seven went out for some fresh air and the door shut behind her." Even as Lil said it, she knew it was ridiculous. "She's gone, hasn't she?"

"Probably."

Lil swore under her breath. "We should have expected this. We're going to have to find her." Her heart sank at the thought of going out into the storm, but what choice did they have? Luckily, if Sabrina was here, searching in the dark would be a thousand times better with her. If it was Sabrina at the front door.

Mouse, Mella said, *I'm scared.*

Shh, Lil said back.

As Lil stepped into the hallway outside her room, the house seemed to breathe in around her, like something was pulling the walls tighter and smaller. There was another thwack on the front door. It turned Lil's insides over. She flicked on the lights in the hallway. There was a flash and then a pop. The lights went out. A blown fuse. Great. Perfect timing.

"There are candles in the kitchen," she said in Kiran's general direction, because it was too dark to see him. She heard him moving about and then saw a beam of light as he turned on the flashlight on his phone.

They went down the stairs together, Lil slightly ahead, Kiran holding his phone up so they could see the way. When they got to the front door, Lil peered through the glass. Usually you could make out the shape of the person beyond: fuzzy like a blurred photo. There was nothing out there now but darkness. "Seven?" Lil said. "Sabrina?" No answer. The uncomfortable feeling in the pit of her stomach growing, she opened the door.

There was no one there.

Lil went out onto the step and looked about, while Kiran shone the flashlight into the dark corners of the driveway. It only made them seem darker somehow. "That's so weird," she said. She was going to call out again, but that feeling came back, of not wanting to disturb something.

Her Wellington boots were in the hallway, and she pulled them on quickly, then went a little way down the drive. The wind was properly howling now, slapping her in the face and whirling her hair out behind her. She pulled her sweater more tightly around her. The driveway was dark, the sky a slice of blackness above it, apart from the silver orb of the moon.

Lil looked about. She felt prickly all over. The gravel driveway was empty and so was the lane beyond—or so she thought; it was full of dancing shadows. Lil had an urge to run back to the house. She almost jumped out of her skin when Kiran yelled her name. She looked over to find him gesticulating wildly. She jogged the three or four steps back to him.

"What?" she said. But before he could answer, she heard it. That thud. Again. And it wasn't coming from the front of the house. Had it never been coming from the front? Or perhaps whoever had been making that noise had moved around to the back?

Lil was icy cold, and it had nothing to do with the wind. Sabrina would never knock on the back door. You couldn't even get to the back door from the front of the house. There was a gate, but it was always locked. Otherwise, the only way to it was across the Merryns' fields, and that meant climbing several fences, and beyond that were miles of nothingness.

"Why would someone be at the back door?" Kiran asked.

"Seven could have gone out that way. Or maybe in the storm . . . Sabrina got stuck and had to. . ." Lil didn't bother to finish her sentence. It made no sense. She again had that prickly sensation of being watched. She really wished the lights hadn't gone out. The phone's flashlight barely penetrated the darkness.

"You want to answer it?" Kiran asked.

"Not really," Lil said.

"But it's got to be Sabrina or Seven, right? Or one of your neighbors."

"What neighbors?"

"Or someone who got lost?"

Kiran's suggestions were perfectly logical, but Lil doubted they applied, and why was the person just banging? Why not say something?

Lil went back into the house. She then shut and bolted the front door. Beyond the reach of Kiran's flashlight, the hallway was ink black, a dead space of nothingness. Anyone could be standing right beside her and she wouldn't even know. The hairs rose on the back of her neck again. She turned around sharply as there was another bang. And then in that instant she realized what the noise was. "The back door," she said. "We didn't bolt it properly when we went out earlier looking for Seven. It's blowing in the wind. Quick, get the candles from the kitchen and I'll go and lock it." Her voice echoed loudly in the empty house. There was an inky patch near the top of the stairs, as though someone was standing there. "Seven?" she said, her voice quieter.

There was no answer.

"There's no one up there." Kiran swung the torch upward. He was right. The stairs were as empty as they should be, but still, Lil couldn't shake the feeling . . .

She hung back by the kitchen door as Kiran rummaged through the cupboard under the sink. "You said there were candles in here?" he asked.

"Yeah, or maybe in one of the drawers." There was another thud. The sound of it brought the hairs up on the back of her neck. She wanted that door shut now. How long had it been open? Since yesterday afternoon? Since yesterday morning? Had someone gotten in? Fear washed over Lil like an icy shower. "Can I have your phone?" she asked Kiran as he emerged from the cupboard, candles and lighter in hand.

Once he'd lit a candle and handed the phone over, she set off down the hall.

"What?" he cried after her. "Wait! Lil."

But she didn't want to wait. She wanted to lock the back door. Right. Now.

When she got to the end of the hall, she found freezing-cold rain blowing in through the open doorway. The flashlight on Kiran's phone was pretty rubbish and only illuminated the doorframe. The door itself was just blackness, like a portal to another world. She wished she'd waited for Kiran. She could hear him moving about in the kitchen, presumably lighting more candles, and the sound was reassuring.

She swung the phone around, trying to assess what

had happened, and saw that the door had flung back with such force that one of the hinges had snapped. She drew a deep breath. It was just a door; it had blown open loads of times before. Seven had probably left it open when she went out. There was nothing to be afraid of. Lil gave herself a stern talking to and then reached forward. Her hand closed around the door handle and pulled. To no avail; the door was well and truly wedged. She didn't have the strength to move it at this angle. She'd have to go outside.

She took a deep breath and stepped out. The rain lashed her face and hair. Lil fumbled for a bit before she found the door handle. She tugged again. It gave much more quickly this time, so quickly, in fact, that when a gust of wind caught it, she was knocked off balance. Lil stumbled, Kiran's phone flying out of her hand as she landed bum-first in a puddle of icy water.

The door slammed shut.

It was total blackness now. The moon must have disappeared behind a cloud. It didn't even seem like there were any stars. Lil splashed around, desperately looking for the phone. The wind howled in her ears as loud as someone screaming. Then she heard it: a faint scratching over by the house, like fingernails clawing at a windowpane. She looked up, heart sounding a percussion in her head. Two eyes gleamed back at her.

Lil couldn't help herself. She screamed.

CHAPTER TEN

At the sound of her cry, the creature—Lil was sure now that it was a fox—bolted across the yard. Lil's breathing came out jagged and uneven. She struggled to get to her knees and then to stand as the icy water seeped through her tracksuit bottoms to her skin. Forcing herself to recover her nerves—*It's just a fox*—she splashed around again, trying to find Kiran's phone. When she couldn't, she shouted for him. She turned around quickly, with that lingering sense of someone watching her.

There was a patch of white glowing faintly by the tree line at the back of the yard. It seemed to float among the trees, fading in and out of view as the wind blew. It looked ghostly, and Lil shivered, feeling her heart begin to race.

"Seven?" she called. It was little more than a whisper, but the shape stopped moving, coalescing into patches of light and dark. "Seven, is that you?" Lil said again, louder this time and moved forward, hands stretched out in front, the darkness clawing at her. She blinked, and when she opened her eyes again, the white shape was gone.

The moon had come out from behind the trees, casting a bright glow across the whole yard, and there was Seven, standing by the fence. Relief ran over Lil like warm water, until she remembered that Seven was no longer wearing a white dress. The white shape she'd seen couldn't have been her. Fear almost took Lil's legs out from under her.

She whirled around quickly, looking everywhere for any sign of that white shadow. There was nothing, only her and Seven. Whatever else—whoever else—had been here was gone, or hiding. Lil's knees buckled at that thought, but she tried to reassure herself. It was a sheep, most likely. They were always getting loose, but doubt niggled at her. She'd seen no sheep today, and the neighboring farmer had probably put them indoors ahead of the storm. Heart thumping, Lil did one last rove of the yard and tried to force it from her mind.

She strode quickly toward Seven, keen to get them both inside as fast as possible. "What are you doing out here?"

Seven was staring up at the moon. "It is beautiful, isn't it?"

Lil barely glanced up. The moon didn't seem relevant at the moment. "Why did you leave like that? We didn't know where you were. We were worried about you."

"They said the moon did not shine as brightly out here, and the stars were different. If we ever left, we'd get lost and not find our way back. But the sky is just as radiant. The moon is just the same. It's the sun's opposite; it tethers her to the earth. We all have our opposite, our balancing force." She smiled at Lil, her eyes round and dark in the moonlight.

"What are you doing out here?" Lil asked again. She didn't want to get caught up in Seven's riddles. Understanding them was like trying to find the end in a tangled ball of wool. The more you looked, the more knotted up you got. "You can't just go wandering off in the middle of the night! I found you . . . I feel responsible for you now. If anything happened to you . . ."

Kiran appeared at the back door, candle in hand. "Everything all right?" he shouted.

"Come on," Lil said after waving at Kiran, "let's go inside. We'll sort it out. It'll be okay." She didn't even know what needed sorting out; it was just something to say. She started walking across the lawn.

Kiran was shouting about finding more candles, so she couldn't be certain, but she was pretty sure Seven said, "You don't know what I've done."

Lil hesitated a second, but Kiran was standing in the doorway with the light and she wanted to get inside and get warm, so she kept walking. When she reached him, Lil ducked against Kiran, wrapping her thawing fingers in his sweater. He brought his arm tight around her. She'd never held him like this. But it felt right. It felt good.

"And then there was light," Kiran said as Lil struck a match and brought the flame against the wick of the candle. Kiran had managed to find an extra whole pack of them in a kitchen drawer. The kitchen walls flickered with candlelight.

Lil felt immediately calmer; the fear she had felt earlier receded, thanks to the warmth of the room. She was less cold, too. She'd found a pair of clean tracksuit bottoms hanging on the kitchen radiator and changed into them in the larder, not wanting to go back upstairs in the dark. Sensation finally returned to her fingers.

She had good memories of this room. It was the best in the house, in her opinion. She and Mella had hung out here a lot, before Mella started spending all her time with Cai, of course. With the AGA stove, it was the warmest place to be. They would do their homework at the kitchen table. Or Lil would. Mella mainly painted intricate patterns on her nails and checked messages on her phone.

"Oh!" Lil said, the thought jogging her memory. "Kiran, I'm so sorry. I dropped your phone in the puddle. I'll buy you another one." Although with what money, she wasn't sure. "Or it might still work. I could go check."

"No," he said quickly. "Don't go out there again. Let's wait till it's light or see if we can sort the electricity. Then we can get that outside light working." He turned to Seven. "You all right?"

She sat at the kitchen table. The blanket Lil had draped around her hung loosely over her shoulders, which were hunched. Neck tucked in, she was like a tortoise retreating into its shell. The habitual fear was scored into the lines of her face, but this time it was mixed with something else. An expression Lil couldn't exactly read. Seven was staring at the photo of Mella and Lil that stood in a frame on the sideboard. "My sister," Lil said. "Mella." She gave a weak smile.

Seven looked at Lil and then back at the photo. "You don't look alike."

"No. Mella looks like my mum. I take after my dad."

Seven was staring at Lil like she was solving a crossword puzzle.

"What?" Lil asked.

Seven shook her head: *Nothing.* But she kept staring. It made Lil uncomfortable. She turned to Kiran. "Should we try to find the fuse box? I think it's probably in the cupboard under the stairs."

"Sure," he said. "We should check the home phone again too. They might have fixed the line."

Lil opened her mouth to say she doubted it, but her eyes fell on Seven, who was still staring at the photo of Mella. She got up and took it down from the cabinet, and was weighing it in her hand.

"Seven, what . . . ?" Lil asked.

"Mouse?" Seven's voice was unsteady.

Lil's breath caught in her throat. How did Seven know that name? No one called Lil that but Mella.

Her own disbelief was reflected in Seven's face. "I found you," she said breathily, "by the Light. I found you."

"You called me Mouse. How did you know that name? . . ." Lil trailed off. "What's going on?"

Seven came forward, placing the photo down on the

table, before clasping Lil's hands in hers. Lil shrank back slightly. Seven's gaze was so intense.

"I know your sister," Seven said. "She's the reason I came here. You're the reason I came here."

"I don't . . . what?" Lil stammered. "You know Mella? How . . . ? I don't understand." Her mouth formed the words, but they felt entirely disconnected from her brain, which felt like it was on fire. Seven *knew* Mella? Seven had *seen* Mella? That meant she was alive.

Of course I'm alive, said Mella's voice in Lil's head. *Rude!*

And Lil smiled, despite everything. Because after months of nothing, she had saved a girl in the road who somehow knew Mella. How was this possible? It was too much to take in. Lil felt overwhelmed—happy, yes, but overwhelmed.

Kiran put his arm around her shoulder in a hug that was more than a hug. It was like he'd grown twelve feet tall and twelve feet wide and he was wrapped around her and holding her. He smiled at her, and it said, *See, you were right! You knew she was all right.*

But they didn't know that. Lil's happiness became anxiety once more, because Seven was very far from okay, and if she knew Mella, then there was every chance Mella was in trouble too.

Lil took a deep breath. She was getting ahead of herself. "How do you know her?" she asked. "Where is she? Is she okay? Please, you have to tell me everything. Where's my sister? Where's Mella?"

CHAPTER ELEVEN

"Your sister is a member of the Sisterhood of the Light, like me. We are the chosen daughters of the Sun. She is our creator and our spirit guide. We call Her the Light and honor Her always." Seven's voice was hesitant and quiet. Every word she spoke was fragile, like the unfurling of a flower.

"What does that mean? The Sisterhood of the Light? How did Mella know about you?" Lil asked. She was scared of startling Seven into silence, but she couldn't hold back. There was so much she wanted to know and so much she needed to understand.

"Moon, our high priestess, goes out into the world and brings back the Light's daughters so that they may be saved by the Brightness."

"Light's daughters?" Kiran repeated. His eyebrows dipped into a near perfect V.

"Yes, those who belong to the Light but who have been born into Darkness."

"Darkness!" Lil repeated angrily. "Mella wasn't born in Darkness. She was happy here! She was loved. How can you say that? Who is this Moon to go around gathering up people who have homes and families who love them! Is that why she left us? Because of you guys?"

"Lil," Kiran said gently. "Let her explain."

Lil knew he was right, that getting cross with Seven wasn't going to help, but she didn't care, because it hurt to hear her and Mella's childhood condemned like that. What gave Moon the right to take her sister away?

"Your sister had already left home when Moon met her."

"Oh," Lil said, and then again, even sadder, when she realized the implications. "Oh." Moon hadn't forced Mella to leave.

So it was my fault, she said to Mella in her head.

There was a moment's silence, and then Mella said, very quietly, *You were kinda mean, Mouse.*

Lil's cheeks flushed with shame. She would regret that last conversation with Mella for the rest of her life.

"High Priestess Moon found your sister living on the streets."

"Sleeping rough?" Lil's heart twisted at the thought. *Oh, Mella, what happened to you?*

"She was afraid and alone, and Moon brought her home to us and to the Light."

"And that's where she is now? At your home? At this Sisterhood?" When Seven nodded, Lil asked, "Where is it?" Her heart was racing. This was the best, the only, lead they'd had in months. Lil wanted to run out of the house right then, get in Kiran's car, and drive until she found her sister.

"I don't know," Seven said.

Lil felt like a popped balloon, the hope of a second ago seeping out of her. "Why not? You came from there! This morning!"

"I've never left the compound before. I was scared. I just ran. . . . I don't know. . . ."

"Well, think!" Lil almost shouted. "Please. This is important!"

"Lil," Kiran said softly.

She rounded on him. "If Seven can tell us something, anything, then we'll find her. We can find Mella." To Seven she said, "Which way did you run? Here, I'll get a map. Maybe if you see it, you'll remember something."

"I get how important it is," Kiran said. "We both do," he added, looking at Seven, "but . . ."

He didn't need to finish. Seven had dipped her head, her back curved in misery. "I don't know the way," she said. "I'm sorry."

Lil drew in a deep breath. She didn't want to make Seven any unhappier than she already was. Perhaps they could try again later, when Seven was calmer. "Was she happy with you?" she asked instead. "This Moon helped her?" Her voice was still sharp; there were so many emotions coursing through her, and she was so frustrated that Seven couldn't tell them anything about where she'd come from.

"Moon gave her the Light," Seven said simply.

What did that mean? Lil exchanged a glance with Kiran, who gave a small shrug.

"I know you don't understand me," Seven said, and then she drew herself upright, as if preparing for something. "I want to talk to you. Now that I know you are Mouse, I believe I can fully trust you, but I have to be careful. The Darkness is tenacious, and I must be sure that I am keeping to the Light's path."

"The Darkness?" Kiran asked.

"The Light's opposing force," Seven replied. "Everything on Earth has its opposite: masculine, feminine; sun, moon; night and day; light and dark. Our high priestess's name is Moon to remind us of that. The Light is life, and creativity, and love, and all the good things. The Dark is fear and envy and hate. And misery. It can't ever be completely overcome, but its energy can be countered by the Light."

"And this . . . this is a set of beliefs?" Lil asked tentatively.

Seven nodded.

It sounded like some alternative religion, almost like a cult. Lil had heard about them, of course. There was one in Texas and another in France and one in the north of Spain somewhere, but they were stories. Things in newspapers and on TV that happened to other people. And the realization was a punch to the gut—in those stories the members had died; either they committed suicide or were killed. "You left the Sisterhood because you were in danger, right? Did . . . did someone try to hurt you?" Lil remembered what a state Seven had been in when she found her and that burn on her arm. "How? What did they do?"

Seven shook her head and wouldn't speak, but her blanched face, her wild, haunted expression, was the only answer Lil needed.

"Did someone hurt Mella the way they hurt you?" Lil asked. She was terrified to hear the answer.

"I don't think they have hurt her," Seven said. "But . . ."

"But what?" Lil could hear the panic in her own voice.

"I'm scared to tell you anything else," Seven said. "I'm afraid of what will happen to the sisters." Instead of saying more, Seven slowly drew up the sleeve of her right arm to reveal three fresh burn marks. The skin was puckered and weeping. The wounds were in the shape of a sun.

"Oh my God. Seven." Lil's voice was full of tears, and the blood pounded in her ears. "Who did this to you? *Why?*"

"The Darkness must be burned out before we can enter the Brightness. I'm the Light's Gift, so I must be cleaner than all the others, for I will lead them into the Light."

"And my sister," Lil said, her voice shrill and terrified. "Are they going to do this to her?" Lil wanted to run out of the house, run to Mella, but she had no idea where to go. Her brain was doing somersaults, and all she could see were the burn marks on Seven's arms. If someone hurt Mella like that . . .

Kiran touched her hand, a tiny bit of her panic retreated, and she could breathe again.

Seven's eyes were enormous in her pale face. "I believe that your sister is safe."

"How do you know that?" Lil asked.

"Because of the laws of the Brightness." Seven drew in a breath. "I have to start at the beginning, so you will understand," she said hesitantly. "A prophecy surrounded my birth. I am the Light's Gift, the path to the Brightness. It is why I was made, why my mother bore me." She faltered and lifted her face to look at Lil. "What I am telling you is a secret known only to the sisters. Telling it will . . . May the Light forgive me. I don't know where the right path leads anymore." She drew herself up a little straighter; the candlelight caught in her eyes, making their brown shine gold. "I was supposed to lead my sisters into the Brightness. The place of Light for all sisters, for all eternity. Peace and happiness beyond this world of shadow."

"The Brightness. Is that like . . . like heaven?" Lil prompted.

"Heaven? I don't know what that is."

"Is the Brightness a place you go when you die?" Kiran asked, clearly trying to explain.

"No," Seven cried, horrified. "No! The Brightness is the place you go to *live*. But everything about the ceremony was wrong. The high priestess is the Light's guide on Earth, our spirit sister. It was her divine calling to instruct us in *The Book of the Light* in preparation for the coming Brightness. But she has strayed from the Light's path, into the Darkness."

"And Mella?" Lil asked impatiently. She didn't care about

Light and paths. She just wanted to know if her sister was okay. "How does Mella fit into this?"

"She is one of the sisters, and at tomorrow's Illumination, I was to lead her and the others into the Sun's fire, to be reborn in the Light."

"Fire?" Lil repeated, the hairs on the back of her neck standing up. Her eyes flicked to Seven's arms, where her long sleeves hid those horrific burns. She could see Kiran making the same connection in his head.

Seven spoke to the table, as if too afraid to make eye contact. "'At the Illumination the Light's Gift shall forge a burning path for her sisters. She shall be consumed by the flames, and her sacrifice will open the door to eternity.'" She looked at Lil. "I was cleansed with the fire, to ensure that I was free of the Darkness, but the pain from these burns was . . . I could not bear it. . . ." She began to cry. "I could not endure any more of the Sun's fire, not even for my sisters."

Lil's mind was whirring: *Burning path, consumed, flames, sacrifice.*

Oh my God.

"They were going to burn you alive." The words were out of Lil's mouth before she realized what she was going to say.

Oh my God.

This was where Mella was?

She only just made it to the kitchen bin before she threw up.

※

Kiran was looking at Lil, eyes wide with concern. He handed her a glass of water, and she held it tightly in both hands, taking small sips, to clear the rotten taste from her mouth.

When she was ten, Lil had accidentally put her hand on the hot iron, which had been left out on the kitchen table. She could still remember the hiss of her skin as it burned. The pain was immense, and she screamed so loudly she brought her mum and Taid running from the end of the yard. Her mum rushed her to the emergency room, and the whole way Lil had to breathe slowly, sucking in the air through her teeth around the pain. She could not imagine the agony of burning in a fire. Burned while you were still alive. *Consumed.* The terror—the horror . . . There were no words to describe it. Lil was dizzy with the enormity of it.

She looked at Kiran and saw her own feelings reflected back at her. His face was haunted, eyes dark pips, his lips drawn into a thin line. Lil knew that, like her, he'd never be the same again. Their safe, cozy world now blown apart by Seven's story and the knowledge that such hideousness could exist. Seven had escaped. She was safe. But Mella wasn't. That thought was almost too much.

"We have to get help right now," Lil said. She felt dizzy, like the world was spinning under her feet.

"I'll drive," Kiran said. "The roads'll be bad, but we'll make it somehow."

Lil hoped her eyes expressed how grateful she was.

"No!" Seven cried. "We cannot. The police will take the sisters away! They'll be forced into the Darkness."

"What?" Lil almost screamed. After everything that Seven had told them, how could she still be objecting to telling the police? What did this . . . this *Darkness* matter when Mella might be burned al—Lil couldn't bring herself to finish that thought.

Seven shook her head from left to right, left, right, left again. "You don't understand. The Illumination ceremony cannot happen without me. They're safe. I didn't abandon them. I left to *save them!*"

"What are you saying?" Lil asked. "That Mella won't be burned because you're not there?"

"Yes," Seven cried. "Yes! I'm the Light's Gift. Only I can find the path through to the Brightness. Without me, there's no path. The doorway won't open. Moon won't be able to start the ceremony. No one else will need to be cleansed. The sisters are safe."

Lil shook her head; it was so hard to understand what Seven meant. "But . . . but won't the high priestess . . . Moon . . . just choose another Light's Gift? Just find someone else to do what you were going to do. To find this path?"

Seven recoiled in horror. "No," she gasped. "*I'm* the Light's Gift. *I'm* the prophecy. There isn't . . ." She hesitated. "There can't be another one." Her tone was less sure. "I was born for this. I . . . I left to save them." Horror filled her eyes. "But . . . it has to be true. Moon told me. This was my purpose. *I left to save them!*"

"I think a lot of what you've been told might not be true," Kiran said softly. Seven's eyes filled with tears.

"I wanted to save them," she said. Then, full of panic, she added, "I should have told you everything earlier! If it's not true, then they're still in danger. . . ." She slumped forward, hands over her head, and face buried in the table. Her shoulders shook with the strength of her sobs.

"We have to go now!" Lil said. "We have to get to Porthpridd and find Sabrina." Her voice shook.

Mella. Oh God, Mella, please be all right. Hold on, we're coming for you. We're coming.

Everywhere there were huddled groups of sisters,
crying, angry, disbelieving, or all three.

"How could the Light's Gift leave like this?"

"Maybe something happened to her?"

"What will happen tonight at the ceremony?"

"How will we find the Brightness without her?"

"We can't."

"Moon will find a way."

Moon will find a way.

Brilliance couldn't get what had happened in the clearing out of her head. The look in Moon's eyes, the way
she'd spoken to Dazzle, and most of all, her words: "Find
my gift," she'd said. Not "the Light's." "*My.*"

Those words echoed around Brilliance's head, until
slowly she began to understand something. Moon was
the Light's representative on Earth. She was the reason
they were all here. She was kind and thoughtful and she
loved them. She was guiding them toward the Brightness,

tutoring them in the Light so they might achieve eternal Refulgence.

But only on her terms.

The thought came from nowhere, but like the mist rising on a bay, the truth of it became clearer and clearer to Brilliance. Everything here was done to Moon's specification, to her instructions. Because it was the way of the Light. But who knew that for sure, when Moon was the only one who could read from the Book?

The idea that Moon was less than perfect terrified Brilliance. Everything—*everything*—she believed was based on Moon's teachings, on her goodness, on her perfection. Because without Moon, what were they all doing here? What was Brilliance doing here?

Doubts niggled at Brilliance. Had she been stupid staying here? Was this going to be another failure?

Stop it, she told herself, and tried to capture some of her earlier happiness, but it was gone. Like sand, it had slipped through her fingers. *Damn it.*

Damn it.

She didn't want to be sad; she didn't want the Darkness back. She'd really believed this time would be different. That the Sisterhood, that Moon, might have something different to offer her. A path to a better her, a happier, calmer, more rational her. To someone with a purpose. Disappointment hit her hard. If not here, then where? She couldn't go home.

Anger rushed in too. How could Seven leave like this? She was their only chance at attaining the Brightness. How could she be so selfish? Without her, none of them would know the Light's eternal embrace, and Brilliance would never be free of the Darkness.

But . . . again the memory of Moon's reaction last night came back to her. Her words: *find my gift.* The way she'd spoken to Dazzle. How much did Brilliance, did any of them, really know about Moon? Perhaps Seven knew something no one else did. Maybe that was why none of them were allowed too near to her. Brilliance had spoken to her only once, early on. Moon had taken her to one side afterward and said that the Light's Gift was not to be bothered with the daily workings of the Sisterhood. "She is for a higher plane."

What a strange and lonely existence Seven must have had. Born here and never ever leaving. But not a part of life here either. Brilliance felt the girl's loneliness intensely. Brilliance knew what it was like to be in a crowd of people and still be alone. Maybe Brilliance could understand Seven's reasons for leaving.

But if Brilliance felt like that, then what was she still doing here?

The answer came fast: because she had nowhere else to go. A familiar despair caught hold of her. She tried to force it back. She needed some space to think, somewhere quiet, away from the other sisters. She could go up to the Sun's clearing, commune with the Light in private and ask for guidance.

She was about half a mile from the clearing when she saw Luster coming the other way. At the sight of Brilliance, fear crossed Luster's face. It was gone in an instant and she pulled her features straight, like she was settling a sheet, but Brilliance had seen it, and it brought up the hairs on the back of her neck. "Greetings, sister."

"May the Light be with you," Luster finished the saying, palm out, as custom dictated. She was clearly uncomfortable, though, and her gaze flicked back to the way she'd come. Brilliance followed it. She could hear voices in the distance. Moon's maybe?

"Where are you going, sister?" Luster asked.

"To the clearing," Brilliance said.

Luster hesitated; confusion, then doubt, flickered in her eyes.

Brilliance felt that tweak of fear again. "What's happening?" she asked.

"Perhaps you should come back to the house with me," was all Luster said.

It was innocent, but she wasn't fooling Brilliance. "Why?"

That hesitation again. Then Lustre seemed to decide something. "You are one of us now and . . . perhaps you can help her, sister. I know she looks up to you. Perhaps having you as witness will . . ." She looked about at the empty wood as though afraid of being overheard. "She's young and silly, but Moon can be unforgiving where she fears the Darkness lurks. With tenderness, kindness, Sister Dazzle will learn . . ." She let her sentence trail off.

"I don't . . . what are you talking about?"

Moon thinks the Darkness is upon Dazzle. She thinks she's the reason the Light's Gift left."

"What? But how could Dazzle . . . ? We aren't allowed to talk to Seven. What could we have done?"

Luster gave a small shrug. "The High Priestess of the Light knows best. She is our guide."

"Always," Brilliance finished, but it felt hollow. Did Moon always know best? Brilliance was beginning to have serious doubts.

"The high priestess believes Dazzle must be fully cleansed before the Illumination ceremony," Luster said. "We need the Light's forgiveness after losing Her Gift."

"'Fully cleansed'? What does that mean?"

Luster gave a sad smile. "I forget how new you are here. How pure." She rolled up her sleeve to reveal four burn scars, skin puckered and raw, each one in the crude shape of a sun.

Brilliance sucked in a breath. The agony . . . she couldn't even imagine. "Who did this?" But even as she asked, she knew. Moon had done this. Kind, generous, amazing Moon. Moon who had saved her, protected her. Moon who loved them all. *No, no, no, no, no.* What sort of place was this? *"Why?"*

"The Sun's Light cleanses and purifies. The Light is the only way to clear the Darkness out." Luster pulled her sleeve down again. "It isn't supposed to hurt, but sometimes the Dark is embedded so deep." She shook her head.

"I don't . . . how can she do this?"

"It's hard to understand at first, I know that," Luster said. "But we can't enter the Brightness unless we are pure. Dazzle most of all. The high priestess thinks there is so much Darkness inside her. I only hope the pain won't be more than Dazzle can bear." Luster hesitated, eyes dark with fear. "The high priestess doesn't believe the branding will be enough—"

"What?" Brilliance broke in, fear rising. "What do you mean? What's going to happen to Dazzle?"

CHAPTER TWELVE

The water in the driveway came up to Lil's ankles, and it was still raining. Gushing down like someone had slit the sky across the middle. It was insanity to drive in this weather at four in the morning, but what choice did Lil have? From what Seven had said, Mella and the others were in terrible danger. They had to do something to save them.

They headed to the car as quickly as possible, but all three were soaked through by the time they got there. Even Lil's bra was wet. Once inside, Kiran turned the key in the ignition. It spluttered for a second, and then the engine choked and roared. Kiran patted the dashboard. "Good girl, Astro," he said out of habit. Kiran's twin brothers had insisted on naming Kiran's car. Tan had suggested calling it 134340, in memory of Pluto.

After everything they'd just learned, the normal comment felt wrong. Everything felt wrong. Lil was sick with worry. "What if we're too late?" she asked Kiran.

Before he could answer, Seven spoke from the back of the car. "The Illumination ceremony cannot take place before sunset tonight. That's when the gateway between our world and the next is at its weakest. It's when we can pass through."

Lil cast a sideways glance at Kiran. Seven's words didn't offer much comfort. The rules of the Sisterhood might seem set to her, but who knew what this Moon would do, what "rules" she would change to fit her purpose?

"We'll get there in time," Kiran said.

Lil nodded. "Sabrina will know what to do." She said it again in her mind, and she held on to it tightly. It felt like a prayer. Besides, there was nothing else to be done right now. She hoped Seven was right about the timing of the ceremony and that Mella would be safe until then. Right now she concentrated on getting to her aunt.

She glanced around at Seven, who was staring out the window as if she expected something to emerge from the trees along the driveway. Lil remembered the flash of white she'd seen in the yard and shuddered. "Do you think the high priestess would have followed you here?" she asked.

"No. She would send Sister Evanescence, and she's far worse."

Lil glanced at Seven's arms, burns covered under the sleeves of Lil's sweatshirt, and wondered how this woman could be any worse.

No one spoke as they headed out onto the track that led to the main road. It was pockmarked with puddles. It was hard to see anything, even with the windscreen wipers slammed onto full, which Kiran always said were held on by "black tape and luck." Kiran sat forward in the driver's seat, driving at a snail's pace; it was too dangerous to go any faster. The road to Old Porthpridd twisted sharply down the mountain past the river. Below them, through the trees, Lil could see fields, or what used to be fields and were now mini lakes.

For the first mile or so, the road to Porthpridd was clear. Large puddles, but nothing more. *We're going to make it,* Lil thought. She let herself imagine arriving. They would park the car and tell Sabrina what had happened. She would know how to find Seven's home—she must investigate stuff like this all the time—and she would go there and bring Mella home. Lil would put her arms around her sister and say, *It's so good to see you.* And Mella would hug her back and everything would be okay; this endless missing and guilt would be over. If Lil knew that she was being blindly optimistic, she pushed the thought away.

They came to the turning lower down in the valley. A sign had been placed in front of it: ROAD CLOSED.

"I don't see any water," Lil said. "Maybe it's fine and they just haven't taken the sign down since yesterday."

"Maybe," Kiran said.

"We could always drive a bit of the way and see what happens?" she suggested.

Seven was leaning forward from the backseat. "Is there another way?"

Lil shook her head. "It's this or we turn around." She wasn't going back, not when Mella was in so much danger.

Seven weighed this up for a second. "We must try, then. Our sisters need us."

Kiran drove slowly forward. When they rounded the next corner, they realized why the sign was there. Water was running right across what had once been tarmac and into the field beyond. Kiran whistled.

"It might not be that deep," Seven said. "There is a ford near the compound. The water moves faster than that, and the sisters drive across it easily."

"Hmm," Lil said. "But you're meant to drive through fords. This is floodwater. . . ."

"What do you want to do?" Kiran asked, looking at Lil. "This is your call."

Lil stared at the water. It was madness to drive into a flood. It went against all her instincts, and yet . . .

"We risk it," she said. Mella was facing far worse. The only way Lil was keeping the fear for her sister at bay was feeling like she was moving forward, getting closer to rescuing her.

"Are you sure?" Kiran asked.

"Yes." There was no way Lil was going back to the house. Not for anything. She was going to make it to Sabrina. She was going to rescue Mella. No matter what.

"Okay," he said. His knuckles paled as he tightened his grip on the steering wheel. Lil knew he was readying himself. She was acting dangerously, recklessly, and she was doing it with Kiran and Seven, too. But she couldn't stop. Mella needed her and that was all that mattered right now.

The first few meters were all right. The car held steady and the water didn't come above the tire line. It wasn't until they were a good ten meters in and the water started flowing faster that she realized they'd made a massive mistake. The water was white on top now, with branches—some so big they looked more like trees—and other debris caught in it. As kayakers, they both should have known better.

"Kiran!" Lil screamed. "We're drifting!"

"I know!" Kiran said, frantically spinning the wheel. He slammed his foot on the brake, but it made no difference. The water, a swirling eddy, dragged them toward a clump of trees at what might once have been the side of the road. Then there was a jolt, and the front of the car dipped forward on Lil's side.

Lil gave another scream as water began gushing in around her feet. "Oh my God! Kiran. There's water!" Even as she spoke, the water was up to ankle level and rising. There was another jerk as the car shifted again, lurching even farther down on Lil's side, so that the water began trickling in through the window seal. "We're going to sink!" she said. This was her fault.

"We must ask the Light to bring salvation," Seven said from the backseat.

Lil bit her lip to stop herself from snapping at Seven. The Light? Seriously? How the hell was that going to help? She tried to open the door, and cursed under her breath when the water was too high. "Try the windows," she said. "Seven, press the button beside you. Will the window open?" Lil frantically jabbed at the button, but nothing happened.

"The water must have damaged the electronics," Kiran said.

"What are we going to do?" Lil yelled. The car tilted completely forward now, and the water was rising fast. With a lurching fear, she realized they could die in here. "We have to get out. Now!" she said.

Seven was chanting softly under her breath. Lil caught only the odd word: ". . . Light protect us."

"We'll have to smash the glass. Check the glove compartment," Kiran said. "There's an ice scraper in there. It's got a metal handle. It might be strong enough."

The car slid farther into the water as Lil jerked forward. Seven's chanting grew louder.

"Easy," Kiran said, "no sudden moves."

Lil tried to move steadily, but it was hard when the blood was thrumming in her ears. "I can't find it. I can't find it—oh, there." She tore the car manual out of the way and then snatched up the ice scraper. The car groaned as it tilted downward, straightened up a bit, and then dropped forward again. Water was gushing in at Kiran's feet now too.

"We have to get out of here," Lil said. "Can you climb into the backseat? It should give us a bit longer to escape if we crack the back window."

Seven's voice rose up: ". . . by the Light . . ." Her eyes were closed, and it took Lil saying her name a couple of times to get her attention. "We're going to break the window back there, okay? You need to move so me and Kiran can get in the back."

Seven nodded. Her mouth was still moving, the words silent.

Kiran and Lil climbed as carefully as they could between the front seats. Lil smashed the handle of the ice scraper into the back window. It reverberated fast, narrowly missing Lil's face. After several attempts a thin crack ran along the glass. It took eight more smashes before Lil managed to make a hole, and more than she could count to make it big enough for them to get through. Murky gray water gushed in; it was freezing cold.

"You go first," Kiran shouted. It was hard to hear him with the sound of the rain thrumming on the roof and the floodwater slamming into the car.

"Are you sure?"

"Yeah, I'll help Seven. We'll be right behind you. You're the better swimmer. I might need your help once we're out."

Water was trickling past the seats now. It smelled of sewage. "Go," Kiran said. "Seriously."

Lil went. She tried to avoid the ragged glass, but the car jerked and pain lanced through her arm as she ducked forward. She lost her balance, her calves banging against the trunk of the car as she slid headfirst into the murky water.

It snatched at her, wrapping itself around her and turning her over, dragging Lil down, so that she couldn't find her footing. She fought, legs kicking at the thrashing water as her lungs tightened. She clamped her jaw shut to prevent herself from gasping and taking in a mouthful of the dirty river. Once or twice Lil cleared the surface, only to be tugged back under again. Her body seemed to be ignoring signals from her brain, because her mouth suddenly opened, and with a huge gulp she took in a lungful of water. Her insides burned. She coughed automatically and took on more water. Panic boiled in her belly.

Then, through the muddy water, she saw Mella, hair in a French plait, the stripes on her wet suit luminescent despite the gloom. *Get a move on, Mouse*, she shouted. *Not the time for a paddle!*

And Lil swam toward her, legs that had been floppy and weak strengthening. Her feet found firm ground and she broke through the water, coughing and spluttering, to find herself knee deep. She was only a few meters from the dry road.

"Kiran!" she shouted, spinning around and wiping the water from her eyes. There was no answer, save the wind shrieking through the trees behind her. She couldn't see him. Dread rising up like bile, she turned around and around, shouting his name. She could just make out the top and rear end of the car. Had it sunk with Seven and Kiran inside? *Please, please, please, no.*

"KIRAN! SEVEN!" she screamed again, and there was an answering shout: quiet but steady.

She spun around, and there he was, farther along the flood and wading toward her, Seven beside him. Lil didn't stop to think. She ran to him, splashing the filthy water high and almost tripping several times in her haste, so that when she reached him, she barreled straight into him, nearly knocking him backward. Her arms were instantly around him and his were around her, and she was just breathing, breathing, breathing, because he was safe. They all were.

"I thought you'd . . . ," Kiran said, pulling back and brushing her hair off her face. "I'm okay, we're okay."

"We're okay," she said. She gave him a final squeeze before turning to Seven.

The younger girl stood to the side, looking small and scared, and Lil tucked her into the hug. She resisted for a second, body stiff as though she was unused to being touched, and then her arms slid around Lil as she hugged her back.

"I asked the Light to save us," Seven said. "And She did. May we forever be in the Light."

Kiran nodded over her shoulder at the car. "Do you think the Light can rescue that? Dad is going to go mental when he finds out."

"He'll just be pleased you're not dead," Lil said.

"Only so he can kill me himself."

"Come on." Lil tugged him. "We need to get out of here. Seven?"

The girl smiled weakly. Then, hands laced together, the three of them splashed through the water and back to the stretch of dry road.

"What do we do now?" Lil asked. The light was just beginning to surface, the dawn sun edging up on the horizon, and the rain was less. It was freezing, though. She was starting to shiver, and her arm was stinging from where she'd cut it getting out of the car. They'd been incredibly stupid to think they could cross that water.

Kiran sniffed. His arms crossed tight over his chest. "I guess we'll have to go back. We can't stay here."

"We can't go back!" Lil shouted. "What about Mella?"

"Lil, I'm so sorry, I don't know."

"What are we going to do?," Lil said, fighting against tears. This was such a mess. Her teeth were chattering now.

Seven stepped closer, putting an arm around Lil. She was so tiny she barely reached Lil's shoulder, but Lil appreciated the gesture. Kiran came closer too, and the three of them huddled together to keep warm. Lil didn't know how long they stood there like that. She had never been so cold. She knew they would eventually have to start walking home, but she couldn't bring herself to move. Doing so would be accepting defeat, accepting that they were unable to get to Mella.

Suddenly there was a shout behind them. She looked up to see a splodge of orange on the horizon. It was coming closer. "It's a boat!" Lil said. "One of those search-and-rescue things. Hey!" she shouted, jumping up and down and waving her arms. "Hey!" The occupants of the dinghy must have seen her, because the boat veered toward them. They waited for it to arrive on the side of the road.

A man and a woman clambered out. "You kids all right?" the man asked.

The woman's eyes narrowed. "That your car?"

Lil nodded.

"You saw the road closure sign?"

"Ye-e-e-es." Lil's whole body was shaking now, her teeth chattering like crazy.

"And you drove past it?"

"Yes," Lil said sheepishly. "We urgently need to get to Porthpridd. My aunt's a police officer. Sabrina Laverty."

"Wait," the man said, "you're Sabrina's niece? We were sent to come get you. You must be Kiran, eh? And you are . . . ?" He looked at Seven, who automatically shrank back farther behind Lil.

"A friend," Lil said, moving forward so Seven was better hidden from sight. "So you'll take us to Porthpridd?"

The woman spoke before the man. "That's what we came out for. You're lucky we found you when we did."

CHAPTER THIRTEEN

"Tell me again what she said about Mella," Sabrina said.

Lil and Sabrina were in the tatty kitchen of the village hall in Porthpridd. The journey here had been long, wet, and cold, although a much better trip with Kay and Don—the search-and-rescue team—than it would otherwise have been. The landscape around Porthpridd had transformed—what had been fields and road the previous day were now water. They'd gone in the dinghy for as long as they could, and then walked the rest of the way. By that point, Lil had been somewhere beyond cold, which she suspected was a dangerous place to be. Lil had nearly wept in relief at seeing the village hall. Kiran had walked head down most of the way, eyebrows so low they were practically on his chin. And Seven had been just as silent.

It was about six o'clock when they finally arrived at the hall. Sabrina rushed out to meet them. Lil let her aunt wrap her arms and then a blanket around her as she breathed in her aunt's smell of vanilla, the same perfume

Lil's grancha—Sabrina's mam—always wore. Sabrina looked very much like Lil's dad, with the same lively gray eyes and long, pointed nose. Sabrina had even inherited the same elfin ears. Mella had those too—the one thing she seemed to have taken from their dad. She hated them and always made sure her hair covered them.

As soon as she saw Sabrina, Lil blurted out what she'd found out about Mella. Her sentences were chaotic, her teeth chattering so hard, and Sabrina's face creased as she tried to understand. She frowned as realization sank in. "Lil," she said gently, "you mustn't get your hopes up, *cariad*." But rather than carry on, insisting that Lil put on the dry clothes the volunteers had collected at the hall, she grabbed another blanket and took her straight to the kitchen, where she put a cup of tea in front of her. Lil had tried to explain as best she could, but it was taking a while.

"She said that Mella has been staying with them," Lil said.

"And she's still there?"

"Yes, and she's in danger. This ceremony—"

"Why didn't you call me? Driving here like that was madness!" Sabrina's disapproval was clear in the thin line of her lips.

Lil stared down at the table. "The phones weren't working. I just wanted to get to you as quickly as possible."

Sabrina touched her hand. Her voice was gentler when she said, "I get that, I do, but tearing off like that—in this weather—it was very dangerous, *cariad*."

"Do you know about The Sisterhood of the Light?" Lil asked, changing the subject. She knew she'd acted dumb, reckless, but this was about saving Mella. "Have you heard of them?"

Sabrina hesitated and then said, "There was a story a few years back, about some sort of group farther up the valley. A cult, you might call it, but that's not . . . the proper term is 'new religious movement.' It's possible Seven came from there. A few of the locals made complaints about some strange practices." Her voice was calm, but Lil could tell she was agitated.

"What sort of strange practices?" Lil's stomach flipped.

Sabrina squeezed the top of her nose like she had a headache. "I don't know. I wasn't directly involved in the case. Witch stuff, rituals, dancing naked. That sort of thing. It was all very exaggerated, like something out of a movie. I think the locals just wanted them gone. You know what people can be like about anything different. They build up all sorts of prejudices, tell all sorts of stories. The complaints never came to anything. It was just a group of women living together and farming. Not a hint of satanic worship." She gave Lil a grim smile. "But now after what you've told me about Seven . . . This is serious, Lil. She didn't give you any more details about the ceremony?"

Consumed.

Lil shivered. "I didn't ask too much."

"Maybe we can get more out of her."

"She's terrified of the police."

"I'll go easy. Officer Burnley is talking to her now. We

have to be careful, though. Gentle. It sounds as if she's been through a lot, and no doubt she's traumatized. If it weren't for this bloody storm, we could have taken her into the women's center, gotten her some proper support." Sabrina looked worried. "I don't have access to any systems. I've only got Officer Willoughby because he lives in the village, same as me. Officer Burnley's only here because she popped into the village last night to check on her mum and got stuck here. It's a bloody mess. Still, we'll work it with what we've got. Seven's a pretty distinctive name, if it's her real one. No surname, though, or none that she shared, anyway. I tried calling the HQ at Caerwen to have them put what info we have into the database. They're flooded too. Place is chaos. The constable I spoke to managed to run a quick check. Nothing. It's like she doesn't even exist. You say you found her on the road?"

"Yes, I told you that already." Lil knew she sounded rude, but she didn't want to answer any more questions. She wanted Sabrina to focus on her sister. "What are you going to do about Mella?"

"I'm going to send a team up to Seven's home as soon as I know where it is. I know this is frustrating, going over the same thing, but the more information we have, the more chance we have of finding this group, and without a location, I can't do much."

"But what about the group from a few years back?"

"I asked Caerwen about them, but by all accounts, they've moved on. We'll obviously follow up, see if we can find out where they went, but . . . I don't know. It would be hard enough without this storm. They might not even be part of the same group."

Lil nodded, although she was frustrated, more with herself than anyone else. She had been naive to think that Sabrina would be able to find this place with so little information. She'd just hoped the police would have a database or something, but what? A database required data, and they didn't exactly have much to go on.

"Did she give you any idea about which direction she came from?"

"I didn't ask." Lil mentally kicked herself for not pressing Seven for more details.

"Where was she coming from when you found her in the road?"

"The Sisterhood, I guess, but she didn't say anymore." Lil felt like she'd asked Seven all the wrong questions, but as soon as she'd heard about the ceremony, everything else had left her head. "I just wanted to get to you as quickly as I could."

"Of course, darling. You think a car hit her?"

"No. She fell down the bank, I reckon. You know it's steep there and probably slippery when it's wet. There were a load of broken branches."

"Why didn't you call anyone? An ambulance?"

"I tried. I mean, I would have, definitely, but my phone got smashed when I fell off my bike."

"You know it's incredibly dangerous to move someone after an accident?" Sabrina said. "This is very serious, Lil. You could have done real damage!"

"I know." Lil plucked at the sleeve of her sweater. "I've been so stupid. I should have told you last night when you called, but she threatened to run if I told anyone." Lil dropped her eyes to the table. She had a terrible thought. If she'd spoken up sooner, could they have saved Mella by now? If only Seven had told her more last night . . . Lil shook herself. It was pointless to think like that, but she couldn't help it.

"And Kiran, was he with you when this happened?"

"No," Lil said quickly. "He came around after. He wanted me to tell you. It was my decision not to. He doesn't have anything to do with this. I don't want to get him in trouble." Lil shivered again. She was still so cold.

"Do you want another blanket?" Sabrina asked gently. "Are you all right? You must be worn out."

Lil shook her head. She was tired, but she wanted to finish this. "Will Seven be okay? The cut on her head? It didn't look so serious once I'd cleaned it, and she seemed fine. No obvious signs of concussion, but I would feel awful if something happened because I . . . I did the wrong thing."

"We think she'll be fine," Sabrina said. "Nothing's broken, and she doesn't seem to have done any permanent damage to her head, but she has got a nasty bump. You should definitely have called in the emergency services or me, but you looked after her pretty well on your own. You kept her safe." Sabrina smiled gently but distractedly. She was in police officer mode. She tapped her nail against her teeth, something she always did when she was thinking.

"You said Seven mentioned maybe being followed, by this high priestess?"

Lil shook her head. "Not her. Seven said she'd send someone else, someone worse. I can't remember the name she gave. It was long." Lil thought for a second. "Evanescence," she said. "I think."

"And did you see anyone? Either on the road when you found Seven or later at the house?"

"No. But . . ." How to explain her feelings? "It felt like we weren't alone. I didn't actually see anything, not properly, but I just sensed there was someone else there." Lil paused. She wasn't clarifying this well. "And when I was in the yard last night, I thought maybe I saw . . . I don't know . . . someone. But it was dark. And . . . I don't know. It's hard to explain."

Sabrina frowned. "Our brains can play all sorts of tricks when we're—"

Lil cut her off, irritated. "I didn't imagine it. I can't tell you what I saw, but I know it was real. I'm sure there was someone in the yard, watching us, watching the house. And Seven said Moon would send someone after her." Lil shuddered at the memory of that flash of white in the yard. What had that been? A trick of the light? No, definitely not. Someone had been there; she knew it.

"Well," Sabrina said, "you'll be safe here; there are lots of people around. No one will be able to get in here without someone noticing." It was clear she disregarded Lil's concerns as fancy. Sabrina didn't go in for sensing things; she liked cold, hard facts: witness statements that included height, weight, eye and skin color, clothing, and preferably an exact time and location.

"I can't give you more details, but it was real," Lil said with passion. Sabrina pressed her lips into a line, and Lil sighed and changed the subject. It was pointless to argue with her aunt about this. There were other, more important things to discuss. "What are you going to do to find this place?"

"Honestly? I don't know. There's not a lot to go on, but I'll do whatever it takes." Sabrina rubbed her eyes. There were dark circles under them. She'd clearly been up most of the night. "You should go and have a rest after you've eaten something." The remains of Lil's sandwich sat on the table between them, along with the cooling cup of tea. Lil couldn't eat them, her stomach replaced by a stone.

Sabrina touched her cheek. "Oh, *cariad*, this is hard on you."

Lil drew back. She was close to tears, and Sabrina's kindness was making it worse. "Have you heard from Mum? Is she okay?"

"Yes, she called very early this morning, about five."

"Really? How? I thought the phone lines were down."

"We've got the emergency ones working and, thank God, the backup generator in this place."

"And she's all right?" Lil asked. "Mum?"

"Yes, pet, don't worry. She stayed over in Chester. Roads were a mess. She's going to try to get back today. I reassured her that all was fine."

"She must have been worried when she couldn't get me on my mobile or the landline."

Sabrina smiled gently. "We kept in touch. She's okay. Honest."

"I should call her. Can I borrow your phone?"

"Of course. But it might be best not to mention anything about Mella for the moment, okay? We don't want to get her hopes up. You know how hard she finds these false leads."

Lil went outside to make the call because the signal was stronger. It was still raining, and the low-slung clouds turned everything a murky gray. The trees around the parking lot threw long shadows, concealing anything that stood among them. Remembering that pale, ghostly figure in the yard, Lil shivered and stayed close to the door of the hall. But surely, no one could have followed them here. If there had even been someone at the house.

She dialed her mum's number, thinking about what Sabrina had said about not mentioning Mella. That would be hard, but Lil knew it was right. She didn't want her mum to worry.

Her mum answered after one ring. "Sabrina! Have you found her? Is she okay?"

"She's okay," Lil said.

"Oh, Lili! I've been so worried. I couldn't get through to you—"

"I know, Mum. My phone got smashed." She had no intention of telling her mum anything else that had happened. Sabrina was right; it would only send her into a panic.

"When? How? Were you in an accident? Are you all right?" Her mum's voice rose several octaves. In her mind Lil saw her mum's hand tightening around the handset.

"I fell off my bike, but no permanent damage. How are you?"

"Better now I've spoken to you. I didn't sleep last night."

"But Sabrina told you I was okay?"

"I was still worried. I wanted to drive right back, but Sandi and Sabrina said I should wait. That the roads weren't safe."

"You did the right thing staying there."

"Are you sure? I think I should head back now, but I'm so tired."

"Then stay. Get some sleep. Drive later. The roads might be clearer then."

"Do you think so? I guess you're probably right. You're so clever and sensible, Lils. Sandi suggested that too, but I feel better hearing it from you. You always know best. I don't know what I'd do without you. If anything happened to you . . ." Her voice broke.

"Nothing is going to happen to me, Mum. All's good here. Now rest up a bit. That's an order!"

Her mum laughed. "Okay, Mouse."

The sound of Mella's nickname made Lil's throat dry.

"You'll stay with Sabrina?" her mum asked.

"Like a shadow." Lil paused and then asked, "Has Dad

called?" She tried for lightness, but the question rang heavy anyway.

There was a pause. "I doubt news of the storms has hit Australia yet. They are, what, seven hours ahead in Sydney?"

"Nine." You shouldn't have to wait for the international news to inform you about your daughter.

Their dad had done very little when Mella ran away. Lil had stood on the landing and overheard her mum talking to him the week after Mella went missing, when they'd finally managed to pin him down. He'd been rehearsing with the orchestra in some remote backwater in Australia, or that's what Lil gathered from her mum's side of the conversation.

"I'm not being hysterical. Gareth, please . . ." Her mum's voice broke. "I don't know what to do. I'm so worried about her. She could be anywhere. . . . I don't know. They're trying. But they . . . she took some belongings with her, clothes and that. Some money. They think she's run away, because she's done it before. But Mella always came back. She's never been away this long. She would call. I know she would. . . . I just . . . I thought maybe she might come to you. Or that maybe you would know what to do. . . . Please, don't shout. Gareth, please, I didn't know what else to do."

Their police liaison officer said that Lil's father might have trouble seeing Mella's disappearance as "real." "Because he's so far away. It might be easier for him to just pretend it hasn't happened. Put it out of his mind. He doesn't know how to handle it."

Because of course Mum and I know exactly how to handle it, Lil thought sarcastically.

Secretly she hoped her dad would swoop in and make everything better, like when she was five and he immediately picked her up after she fell. Because she really didn't know how to handle this either. She desperately wanted someone else to pick her mother up off the floor, take her into the kitchen, and make her a cup of tea (that she wouldn't drink) and some toast (that she wouldn't eat). And hold them both while they cried.

But there wasn't anyone else. So it didn't matter what Lil wanted.

Lil walked down the stairs to her mother and took the receiver out of her hand. "Call us if she gets in touch," she said to her father. Then she hung up. She hadn't spoken to him since.

Because not knowing what to do was not an excuse to do nothing.

We do not seek knowledge, lest we
stumble blindly into Darkness.

—THE BOOK

M ella tore through the trees, panic-horror-terror fuel-
ing the adrenaline gushing through her veins. She
was no longer Brilliance; she'd cast that name aside when
Luster had told her what was going to happen to Dazzle.

The forest floor was uneven, strewn with undergrowth
and bracken that seemed to be deliberately twisting around
Mella's ankles. She tripped countless times—her legs were
scratched, one knee bleeding—but she didn't let it slow her
down. She hurtled across the ground. As she broke through
a patch of densely packed trees, she saw it, flickering in
between the branches, silhouetting their slender arms: an
orange glow. The Sun's fire. They'd already lit it.

Mella put on an extra burst of speed, which two seconds ago she would have said was impossible. *Don't let me
be too late, please, please.* The fear lent wings to Mella's feet,
and she flew over the last couple of hundred meters, with
no stumbling on the rutted ground, no clutching of her
ankles by weeds or bracken.

She pulled up to a stop at the edge of the Sun's clearing, breathing heavily, assessing. Relief was a cool balm to her tight chest and aching limbs: There was Dazzle. Moon stood on one side and Evanescence on the other. Mella had no idea when Evanescence had come back. She wished she hadn't.

The three of them stood with their backs to Mella. Some of the other sisters were in a semicircle on the opposite side of the fire; all were dressed in brightly colored tunics, the painted suns on their cheeks. Luster had said that they would be there as witnesses of the Light. It made Mella sick to think that they were just going to stand and watch Dazzle be tortured.

She had to catch them off guard, grab Dazzle somehow, and run. Then what? She didn't know exactly. Keep running, she supposed, until they could get to safety. Since she arrived, she'd left the compound only twice. They just had to keep going, head for a main road, and hope they came across a car that would give them a lift.

As Mella stood watching, Moon raised her hands. "Sing, my sisters," she cried. "Sing the Light into being."

The Sisterhood began to dance and sing, their colored gowns swinging out wide around them.

"I dance with the fire in my heart."

For a moment Mella was caught up in the dance, eyes catching on the flames, the way they moved like liquid. The peace came over her, a oneness with everything. Her eyelids were heavy. It was hard to focus. She breathed deeply, the familiar heavy air. . . .

Her eyes flew open again. The incense in the seven stakes around the fire . . . it smelled so sweet, too sweet. It got in your head, right in there, and it made your senses dull, sluggish. Like the time Mella tried a joint at Cai's. It made her feel heavy, out of her own body. She hated it. This was the same feeling. How had she not realized it before? Moon was drugging them! *That* was the communion with the Light, *that* was the feeling of otherworldliness.

Mella dragged her sleeve over her hand and covered her mouth, trying to breathe shallowly and as little as possible. Her head cleared a little, but it still felt like she was moving through a woolen blanket.

A bird cried and then Moon's voice cut across the clearing: "We must help our sister Dazzle out of the Dark and into the Light, so she is pure enough for the Light's eternity."

As one, the sisters began to move, circling around the fire toward Dazzle. Moon gripped one arm, Evanescence the other, and Mella's fear became a fire. It rose up from her belly, burning as it went, until a scream shot from her mouth: "Stop!"

Everyone turned to Mella as she strode out from the shade of the trees. The sisters' eyes were wide, Moon had one eyebrow raised, as cool as ever, Dazzle's mouth had opened in a little O, and Evanescence looked furious. "How dare you interrupt your sister's cleansing!" she shouted savagely, baring her teeth. "Do you want her to perish in the Darkness?"

"It's all right, sister." Moon was as cold and distant as the stars, and all of Mella's hope about her disappeared. How could she have been so blind? But there was no time to consider that now. "Sister Brilliance," Moon said, "please join your sisters. You can be witness too."

"My name is Mella."

The Sisterhood gasped as one. It was forbidden to reveal your Dark name. To do so in the presence of the Light was sacrilege.

"I'm not going to let you hurt Dazzle," Mella said.

"Hurt her?" Moon laughed like it was the funniest joke ever. "I'm going to save her."

"You're going to kill her," Mella said. "She'll never be able to stand it." To Dazzle she said, "I don't know what you've been told, but"—Mella drew a deep breath and forced the words out—"you're going to die, Dazzle. She's going to . . . to burn you in there." She pointed at the bonfire.

Another collective intake from the sisters, whether from the idea of Dazzle being burned or from Mella's interruption of the ceremony and blasphemy against the Light, she couldn't tell.

Dazzle merely bowed her head. "It is the Light's way. I'm full of Darkness. I must be cleansed."

Mella was overwhelmed with sadness and sympathy for Dazzle. "You are not full of Darkness, Dazzle. Don't listen to them. Please. This isn't right!" Mella was surprised how sure she felt about that. Usually she was so uncertain about everything, but she knew with crystal clarity that this was wrong. Then the full horror hit her; Moon had not lied to Dazzle. She had not told her she would survive this. She'd convinced her that this was the only way: to die in agony so that she might achieve eternal Light. Somehow the brutality, the cunning, of that, the years of abuse and manipulation that must have been involved, were so much worse.

Mella moved. She had no plan other than to get Dazzle away from this woman who had brought her up to die, to *willingly* die as though her life meant nothing. Mella didn't know what she was going to do as she flung herself at Moon. It didn't matter, because Evanescence was there, snarling, teeth bared, arms like a wall defending her high priestess.

Mella landed in a scrunched heap on the ground.

"Take her away, sister," Moon said with a casual flick of her hand. She turned her back on Mella as if she was irrelevant. "Sisters," she said, "shall we continue?"

Most shifted back to her immediately, but some looked confused; they exchanged glances. A soft murmuring rose up from them.

"Quiet!" Moon said. She did not raise her voice, but it was an earthquake rolling out from its epicenter. The force of it made the sisters take a step back. No one else moved; no one else dared to speak.

Mella's mouth was covered so she couldn't scream, but she fought. Muscles screaming in pain, back aching from her rough landing, she fought with everything she had. It made no difference. Evanescence held her fast, face pressed into the ground. She had no idea what Evanescence would do to her, but it couldn't be good. Mella didn't care; she was more worried about what they were going to do to Dazzle.

Mella couldn't move or see anything but the muddy grass in front of her, but she heard Moon speak: "And unto the Light we give our sister, so that she may be cleansed in Her fire."

Dazzle screamed. It was barely human. A vacuum in time that, like a black hole, dragged everything toward it.

CHAPTER FOURTEEN

After calling her mum, Lil tried googling "Sisterhood of the Light" and "Wales," but she couldn't get an Internet connection. After the third message saying "Server timed out," she gave up and went back inside. Sabrina sat hunched over the table, scribbling in her notebook. She was sucking on a strand of her hair, something she did when she was concentrating.

Lil handed Sabrina her phone, noticing that there was a sheen on Sabrina's cheek from her wet hair, like a snail's trail. "Mum's going to take a nap and drive back later. She was a bit panicky but generally okay."

Sabrina nodded. "Good. Oh, I meant to say. The Colchesters are all right."

Lil felt herself color at the mention of Rhiannon's surname and the fact that her aunt had thought to let her know that Rhia was safe. She didn't realize that Lil hadn't spoken to her for weeks.

"That's great," Lil said guiltily.

Sabrina smiled gently. "Why don't you go and get some rest? You look all done in, sweet pea."

Lil started to protest but stopped to stifle a yawn. God, she was exhausted. It had been a long night without much sleep, on top of a lot of worry and anxiety. Neither of which was over. "What about Mella?" she asked, and then yawned again. It seemed as though she'd finally given her body permission to be tired and now she couldn't control it.

"We're doing everything we can, *cariad*," Sabrina said. "The best thing you can do now is get some rest. Whatever happens, I promise you'll be the first to know. Sleep now while nothing's happening, then you'll be ready when it does."

It was logical, but Lil still struggled to accept it. How could she rest when Mella might be in danger? That thought was one she'd grappled with for over four months.

"Go," Sabrina said, gently pushing her to the door. "That's a direct police order and you can't disobey those."

"You promise you'll let me know—"

"Cross my heart," Sabrina said.

As Lil walked across the hall, she wondered what life would have been like if Sabrina had been her mum. If it was Sabrina who had taken charge in the days and hours after Mella left.

When the police finally came around on the morning after Mella's disappearance, pushed in no small way by Sabrina, they asked loads of questions, although they knew the answers to most of them already. They'd asked them all before. "How old is Mella? What was she wearing when you last saw her? Does she have any health issues? Who are her friends? Boyfriends? Have there been any arguments recently? Your husband is not around, right, Mrs. Laverty? Any chance Mella could have gone to see him?"

Lil answered them all. Her mum was crying too hard.

The village hall was full. There had to be about two hundred people in there; most of them were huddled in blankets on makeshift cot beds. There was no electricity in any of the houses in the village, so a lot of people had come up here, where it was safer and, thanks to the backup generator, warmer. Also, they'd gotten an old gas stove going for food.

Lil stopped in the bathroom to change out of her wet clothes. When she came out, she saw Kiran, his dad, and his twin brothers. She lifted her hand to wave but then saw that Kiran and his dad were deep in conversation. Lil didn't like to interrupt. She hoped Kiran's dad wasn't too mad. Insurance would cover flood damage, right? Or car-lost-in-flood damage? Lil knew that Kiran's dad couldn't afford a new car. Money was even tighter for them than it was for Lil and her mum. Lil's mum wasn't working much now, but at least her dad sent the alimony payments regularly.

Lil recognized a few kids from school, but none of them were in her year. Porthpridd didn't have a secondary school, so, at thirteen, everyone went to the one in town. Lil smiled at a girl in year nine whom she saw on the bus sometimes.

There were some volunteers taking bedding and cups of hot tea to people. Some were in search-and-rescue uniforms, but most seemed to be just regular villagers. Lil saw the vicar and his wife, Gwen. They'd helped a lot when Mella first went missing, bringing up meals to the farmhouse and organizing a couple of the searches. Lil's *nain* had been a big member of the church. Gwen hugged Lil when she saw her. "What's up, love?" she asked in Welsh. "You look wiped out." Gwen motioned to a couple of spare beds over toward the back of the hall. "You get yourself some rest. Your aunt go up to get you, did she? It flooded around you, too?" She didn't wait for an answer, which was good, as Lil didn't know how to explain the reason they'd left home. "That young girl is over there too," she added, pointing to a corner of the room, where Seven was sitting on a cot.

Lil thanked her and headed in that direction.

There was a man reading a newspaper on a bed nearby, a battery-operated radio lying next to him. As Lil passed, she heard the newscaster mention the floods and stopped to listen.

"It's seven forty-five a.m., and much of North Wales remains under water this morning after heavy rain caused flash floods overnight. The Gwynedd area was among the worst affected, with water waist-deep in some places. The Environment Agency issued a flood alert for the tributaries of the river late yesterday. It is expected to stay in place until at least tomorrow. The agency says water levels remain high but are gradually dropping. Makeshift accommodation for those affected has been set up . . ."

Lil walked on to join Seven. There was a spare cot next to her, and Lil sat down on it. "All right?" she asked Seven.

Seven looked at her fiercely. "They asked me many questions." She said it like it was Lil's fault.

"They're trying to help," Lil replied, wrapping one of the blankets around her shoulders. It smelled of mold, but at least she was warmer. She was about to wrap another blanket around her knees when she saw that Seven didn't have one, so Lil held it out to her. When she didn't take it, Lil put it around Seven's shoulders and then sat back down on her own bunk.

"I do not trust the police. Only your aunt." Seven's fists were curled tightly in her lap. Lil recognized the posture from Mella. Seven was trying to seem angry when really she was scared. Her eyes kept darting around the room.

"Sabrina's in charge. The officers have to do what she says. And she's going to talk to you later. Everyone just wants to help."

"When will they go to the compound? I need to know that the sisters are safe."

Lil understood Seven's impatience. She felt exactly the same way. It was agony to sit here waiting while Mella was still in so much danger. But if they didn't know where the Sisterhood was, how could they rescue them? Seven was the only one who knew anything. Surely, she must remember something about the route she took yesterday. "Did the officer who talked to you ask you where the Sisterhood is?"

"Yes," Seven said, "but I don't know. I have never left the compound before now. I know only what I can see from behind its walls."

"And what's that?" Lil asked, desperate for any piece of information that might help.

"There is the sea on one side and three high walls on the other."

"You can't tell us anything else?" Lil tried and failed to keep the frustration out of her voice.

"I would watch boats pass from the cliff top, and in a nearby bay children would play sometimes."

Boats. A beach. That could be literally anywhere on the Welsh coastline. Lil tried not to feel irritated. It wasn't Seven's fault. "What about when you left? What did you see then?"

Seven's brow furrowed. "It was dark. I did not see much and I was very scared. I ran very fast, but . . ." A pause. "The gates of the compound open onto a narrow road, overhung with many trees. But it was too dark for me to see anything. I ran for a long time, until the sun started to come up.

Great, Lil thought. She held in a sigh.

"I'm sorry I can't remember more."

"Maybe something else will come back to you."

"Perhaps." She didn't sound convincing.

"Did you tell the police all of that, about the sea and the beach and that?"

Seven nodded.

It was pointless to keep asking questions when Seven

didn't know the answers. Yawning, Lil lay down on the bed, then said, "The police have no record of you." Seven's lack of official documentation seemed sinister, like someone was trying to hide her or deny her existence. Given what Moon had planned for her, both were probably likely reasons.

"Record?" Seven repeated.

"You know, like a passport or a birth certificate—a piece of paper that says you've been born."

"Do I not prove I've been born?"

Lil smiled. She couldn't argue with the logic. "It helps you get a job and that. And a bank account." Lil was unable to imagine Seven getting a job or going into a bank. "It's different where you come from, right?" she said.

"I was special," Seven said quietly after a pause. "That's why I was never registered. The other children at the compound had birth certificates, but I didn't."

"Tell me more about the Light," Lil said, rubbing her eyes. She was exhausted, but she couldn't sleep yet, not when she was so worried about Mella. Talking to Seven made her feel like she was doing something active to find her sister. "I want to understand." She needed to know what it was about this group that had appealed to Mella. "When you talk about the Light, you don't mean this"—Lil waved her arm around vaguely—"do you? It's something else."

"In some ways it is the same. The Light is everywhere. That is what makes it so special. It's what gives us life, what creates us."

"Yes, but what is it?" Lil pressed. "How does it create us? It's like a god?"

"The Sisterhood has no god. We do not worship the Light, but we venerate it. We believe it is a life source that comes from the sun in its purest form. It travels through all of us, and it guides us toward the right path to live. It is beauty and truth and hope. It is love. It is what makes the plants grow and so gives us the food we need to sustain us."

"And Mella believed this. . . ." Lil bit off her words. She sounded skeptical. Rude, even.

Seven just smiled. "Many are like you when they first encounter the Light. Your sister was different. She *wanted* to believe. She was looking for the true path her whole life. It took her time, though, to come to see the Light as the *way* and not an escape from herself."

An escape from herself. That's what Mella had been look-ing for her entire life. Had she really found her way at the Sisterhood? Lil suspected not, the Light most likely being another escape route, like the countless other things Mella had believed in for a while: tarot cards, the Magic 8 Ball, Christianity. Running away.

"How long was she with you?" Lil asked.

"It's been fourth months since you sister joined us."

"Four months?" What had she done in the weeks she was alone? Lil shivered as she imagined what Mella had gone through. Why hadn't she just come home? Lil wished more than anything that she could go back to the morning Mella left and change everything.

"What do you mean by 'the Dark'?" she asked, trying to push those thoughts out, to focus on what she could control: asking Seven questions. "You mentioned it last night. Something about opposites?"

"Yes, it's all about balance, about opposing forces of nature. Light and Dark coexist; one cannot be without the other. We respect the Dark because it gives us the Light, and we fear it because it has the power to take that Light away."

Lil nodded. She could see a sort of logic in that. She could definitely see how it would appeal to Mella. It must have done. Four months was a long time for Mella to stick with something. "Where did you find her? Did she say?"

"A sister does not force that knowledge which is not given willingly."

So Mella had refused to talk about it.

There were so many questions Lil wanted answered. They jostled in her mind, each one fighting to be the first one out of her mouth. There was something that had really been bothering Lil, though, since Seven told them about knowing Mella. "Did Mella tell you to come to me?" she asked. "When you left the Sisterhood?"

"No, not specifically, but when she talked about you, she said you were full of Light, and I knew that although you were not a sister, you would help me." She smiled sadly. "She was right. You are one of the Light's chosen daughters."

Lil smiled inwardly. After everything that had happened between them, it really meant something that Mella still trusted her, still believed in her. "But how did you know where to go? You were so close to the house when I found you."

Seven hesitated. "Your sister wrote a letter, to your

mother. It is forbidden at the compound to communicate with the outside world, so she left it on the cliff top. She said she would let the Light carry it to you. I was afraid that the high priestess or Evanescence would find it, so I took it. Your address was on the front." She paused, then added, "I memorized it. I don't know why. The Light was perhaps guiding me without me knowing it. Your sister was kind to me. She told me about *Alice's Adventures in Wonderland.*"

"Did she?" Lil smiled. "Is that why you called yourself Alice?"

Seven nodded. "We only spoke once, but I have never forgotten. Many of the sisters would not speak to me at all. It was forbidden. A couple of them were kind to me, though, in secret. Your sister and one of the Alphas, Luster."

Lil felt intense sympathy for Seven then. To live in a place where no one spoke to you? It was horrible. Lonely. "But an address wouldn't have led you to me," she said. "Had you heard of Porthpridd, this village?"

Seven shook her head. "The Light in all Her bountiful goodness led me to you."

"And Mella didn't . . . she didn't come with you?"

Seven shifted position, the color rising to her cheeks. "I left in secret. I believed my departure would be their salvation too. Now I realize that was an untruth, and I was naive to believe it so easily."

"I just want to find them," Lil said. "I want to know she's safe."

"So do I!" Seven said with passion. "I have been asking the Light to help the high priestess fight back the Darkness and let the goodness shine in her once more."

Lil appreciated how concerned Seven must be. Whatever had happened at the Sisterhood, these women were her family, all she'd ever known, but Lil didn't find her prayers (was that the right word?) to the Light that reassuring. Moon was obviously dangerous, incredibly so, and possibly insane. She'd branded Seven and would have burned her alive if she hadn't escaped. Who knew what she might do to the rest of the Sisterhood? *Oh, Mella, please be okay.*

"I'm glad you found me," Lil said with feeling. At least now, with Sabrina's help, she had a chance of saving Mella. But more than that, she was genuinely pleased that she could be there for Seven. She'd been through so much, and Lil wanted to make sure she got the support, help, and love she needed. "But what if you hadn't, what would you have done? Could you have gone to your mum? You said she left? Isn't she somewhere outside the compound?"

"I do not know where. I've never heard from her."

"Never?" Lil asked.

"No. She and Moon had a disagreement," Seven explained, fiddling with the blanket. "I was not yet in my fifth sun, so I remember very little of it. We lived in a different house. A great distance from here. There was another high priestess. Moon had a dream in which the Light said that she was to be the new high priestess because the old one had been cast into Darkness. A lot of sisters mistrusted this prophecy, not least because it came to Moon during the darkest part of the night. My birth mother was one of them. There was a split in the Sisterhood between those who followed Moon as the true high priestess and those who continued to trust the false one. Moon led the true sisters away from that place of Darkness and we found a new sanctuary. Moon brought me with them. I am the Light's Gift. She could not have left me behind. She could not have risked the coming Illumination ceremony and the sisters' ascension to the Brightness. She gave my mother a choice: Stay with the false prophet or come with your daughter. My mother chose to stay."

"And *abandon* you?" The words were out of Lil's mouth before she knew what she was doing. "Sorry, that was . . . sorry. But your mum left you with Moon? She didn't try to keep you with her?"

"You do not understand. The Darkness is as powerful as the Light. It is blinding. My mother's faith was strong. She did not know that it was the Dark that guided her. Moon *protected* me! She safeguarded my gift. If I had remained with my mother, I would have resided in the Darkness."

"Is that . . . is that what you really believe? I mean . . . Moon would have burned you al—"

Seven cut her off. "Moon *saved* me." Her bottom lip jutted out stubbornly, and Lil could see how hard it was for her to accept that so much of her life was a lie.

"Perhaps . . . ," Lil began gently, "perhaps Moon was not telling the truth about your mum. Perhaps she wanted you and . . ." She trailed off.

Seven's eyes filled with tears. "I am a boat caught in a tide. How can I find shore again if everything I have ever believed is a falsehood?"

When Mella first left, people would tell Lil, "It's all right. There, there. It's okay." But sometimes things weren't okay. It was a lie to say that they would be. So Lil didn't tell Seven it would be all right. Instead she sat down beside her and took her hand.

Seven smiled, eyes shining with tears. "I can see the Light inside you. The high priestess said recreants were cruel and selfish and full of Darkness, but you're not like that at all."

"Thank you," Lil said, a touch of humor in her voice. Seven's world sounded so dramatic. Everything in stark contrast, with no shades of gray. But wasn't that exactly what life was? The spaces in between. No one was just one thing.

"Kiran isn't like they said they were either," Seven said.

Her turn of phrase pulled Lil up short. "Like they said who were?"

"*Men,*" Seven said in a hushed whisper, as though it were a dirty word.

"What?" Lil cried.

"I have never conversed with one before."

"You've never spoken to a *guy*? How? How is that possible?"

"There aren't any men at the compound."

"None? At all?" Lil could hear the incredulity in her voice.

"No. Little boys, yes, once, though not now. They must leave the compound before their twelfth sun. I used to think that male children became female when their sun turned twelve, until Sister Luster told me the truth. It is strange to me that the Light would cast someone out because of the way they were born. The Light is for *everyone*. She *shines* on *everyone*—so how can only certain people be allowed to enjoy Her glory and Her Brightness?"

Seven spoke with such conviction. Lil wondered how it felt to believe so utterly, so unfailingly, in something, even after everything Seven had been through. "I can't imagine growing up with no boys. No men. That's . . . so . . ." *Unnatural.* "But," Lil added, a thought occurring to her, "you said there were babies at the compound. How did . . . ?"

"The women arrived pregnant. But, oh." Seven ducked her head, cheeks coloring. "Sister Luster explained that to me also . . . how they . . . they became that way." She looked up suddenly, cheeks aflame. "You know, don't you? I don't have to explain?"

Lil held in a laugh. "I know. It's okay. I don't need the birds-and-the-bees talk."

"The birds and the bees? Luster didn't mention them." Seven's forehead creased.

"It doesn't matter," Lil said quickly. "A turn of phrase. So, huh, no men. I can't . . . wow . . ."

Seven rolled onto her back and was staring up at the ceiling, eyes closed, a gesture that said, *I don't want to talk anymore.* Lil turned to watch the goings-on in the hall. She would never be able to sleep now with everything that Seven had told her spinning around and around in her brain.

People moved about the hall, eating, sleeping, and, in one couple's case, arguing. "I told you to buy sandbags," the woman said. "But, oh no, you wouldn't listen."

A couple of little girls were playing a clapping game next to them. The younger of the girls, who was maybe seven or eight, kept glancing over at the couple. Her parents, maybe, Lil wondered. Every time she did so, the older girl started clapping and singing louder, to bring her back to the game. Seeing them reminded Lil of her and Mella. They'd played the same game when they were little, and Mella had always been doing things to distract her from their parents' fighting. At night, when the raised voices could be heard through the thin walls of their London flat, Mella would climb into Lil's bed and sing loudly, right in her ear, so Mella's voice was all she could hear. The memory brought up a lump in Lil's throat. *I miss you, Mella,* she told her sister in her head.

"What are they doing?" Seven asked, nodding at the two little girls.

"It's a clapping game."

"Why?" Seven asked, so confused that Lil laughed despite everything.

"For fun? For a competition. I used to play it with my sister."

Seven nodded, watching the girls a moment longer before saying, "She missed you. She talked of you. Not to me. To the other sisters, sometimes. A sister called Dazzle especially. It was forbidden to talk of the outside, but I heard them whispering to each other, at night."

"And Mella talked about me?" Tears rose to Lil's eyes. "Did she say why she left? Did she say it was my fault?"

"I never heard her say anything that was unkind or angry about you," Seven said, and then added, "I do not believe your sister ever blamed you. She loves you. She said you are *brilliant*." She put Mella's emphasis on the word, making Lil smile widely. "You are her best friend."

"But she still left me." Lil's voice was fragile, like something easily broken.

"Yes, but the Light gave your sister something she was missing. Hope."

The tears cascaded down Lil's cheeks. Her sister had lived for seventeen years without *hope*. "I never knew," she said. "I had no idea she was so unhappy."

You did know, said a tiny voice in her head. It sounded so much like Mella. *You just didn't want to see it.*

Oh God, Lil thought. *Oh God, Mella. I'm so sorry.*

"The Light can seem cruel sometimes," Seven said, "but She has Her plan."

Anger mixed with Lil's grief and it burned brightly. "This is her *plan*? My sister leaves me? You nearly get burned alive. That's a *plan*? And you're okay with that?"

Seven's tone was calm and gentle. "We can't know the Light's thoughts. If Mella hadn't left, she wouldn't have found the Light. I wouldn't have found you. And I can't . . . I can't regret that, no matter what happened to make it come about."

Lil's rage subsided a little.

"If Mella hadn't come to the compound, I would not have had anywhere to run to that night."

Lil didn't know what to say. She would have done anything to stop her sister leaving, but Seven was right. Perhaps some things were meant to be. But a guiding Light? . . . Lil shook her head. It was so implausible.

There was a giggle from the girls on the other side of the room.

"So," Seven said, "how does this game work?"

"It's silly," Lil said.

"I'd like some silly, please," Seven said. "I think up until now I've had far too much seriousness."

Lil smiled back at her. "Okay," she said, holding out her hands, "but I warn you, I'm very good at this. . . ."

As they played, she thought about Mella. The same refrain on repeat in her head. *Please let her be safe. Please. Please. Please.* She paused and then added, *By the Light, please let her be safe.*

CHAPTER FIFTEEN

Lil took in another lungful of air. It wasn't exactly fresh, surrounded as she was by water that seemed to have come from the local sewage plant, but it was fresher than the village hall. With so many people in there, it was beginning to stink.

Lil had come out here when she woke; she and Seven had been sleeping close together, limbs entangled like conjoined twins. She'd detached herself from Seven slowly, so as not to wake her. Seven had been dead to the world, though, barely stirring even when Lil accidentally knocked her head getting off the bed.

Lil hadn't remembered falling asleep. The clock in the hall had stopped, she didn't know what time it was, but she couldn't believe she had slept at all with everything going on with Mella. She felt guilty.

It was cold out here, but the rain had finally stopped, and the sky was red and orange as the sun tried to break through, pale, though, murky, like the color bleeding on one of those watercolors Mella used to paint. She didn't have the patience to wait for the layers to dry, so all the colors ended up leaking into one another and turning gray.

Lil's back ached and she knew it was from sitting so stiffly, every part of her tense against the wind whipping about her. It wasn't just the cold. She was on edge about Mella. No more news yet, just that the police were continuing to investigate possible locations and leads, which was proving even more difficult, thanks to the weather. It was all taking too much time. Sabrina reassured her that they were doing everything they could, but it didn't feel that way.

Lil stared angrily out at the valley, a river now. It glistened below her, uncaring and unheeding that it was stopping her from reaching her sister. Lil longed for a plane, or a helicopter, or a boat that would carry her across that foul water to Mella. But even if she had the transport, she didn't know where to go. As infuriating as it was, Lil's only choice was to wait for the police to pinpoint the location of the Sisterhood. All she could do was hope that they did it quickly.

She wished this were all over, that Mella were at home, safe, and the three of them were eating one of the croissants Mella always made on birthdays. It was ironic because Mella burned toast and possessed zero interest in cooking, and yet fiddly, fancy, buttery French patisserie—she was a genius at it.

Course you wish you were eating one, Mella piped up. *They're amazing! So good you want to die!*

Which you would if you ate too many.

Yeah, but what a way to go! Mella paused and then said, *Are we all right?*

You're in my head, Mella. Of course we're not all right.

You know the first stage of madness?

Hearing voices in your head?

Nope. Hairs on the back of your hand.

Lil laughed. *And the second stage is looking for them.* Lil drew a deep breath. Tensing up was not keeping her any warmer. *I know things were bad at the end. You and me . . .* Lil trailed off.

Mella wasn't listening. She'd stuck her fingers in her ears and was singing at the top of her voice.

You have to be serious sometime, Lil said.

Yeah, right, that coming from the girl hearing voices.

One voice. Yours. I miss you. So much.

Miss you, too.

There was a long pause. Then Mella said, *I didn't want to leave. If you hadn't . . .*

It was Lil's turn to metaphorically jab her fingers in her ears, trying to force her sister's voice out of her mind. She didn't want Mella to finish that sentence.

The memory of Sabrina's birthday, the last one before Mella left them a few months later, filled her head. Sabrina was working a late shift, so she came over in the morning. Mella had been in a funny mood all week; she'd come back late the night before and hadn't made croissants. The atmosphere at breakfast was tense.

"Would it hurt you to smile?" Mum said. "Honestly, Mella."

Mella didn't answer or look up from where she was picking her toast apart but not actually eating any. Sabrina and Lil exchanged a glance. Lil wished her mum wouldn't try to get a rise out of Mella.

Mella looked tired and thin. Lil could see the sadness in her, beneath her aggression; like tentacles, it wrapped itself around everything, sucking the joy from all of them. Lil wondered why Mum couldn't see it. Maybe she could, and shouting at Mella was easier than addressing it.

Lil nudged Mella gently under the table to get her attention. She wanted to smile at her, to say, *It's okay, I know.*

"Stop kicking me," Mella said angrily.

Lil colored. "I didn't . . . I . . ."

Mella stood up so fast her chair clattered to the floor. "I've got to go," she said. "I'll be late for college."

"Mella! Get back here right now." The words died on Mum's lips as the front door slammed. Mum sighed. Her face settled into a series of hard lines. "Honestly, that girl. Doesn't know how lucky she is."

"She seems a bit down," Sabrina ventured. "I've thought for a while that—"

Mum cut her off. "She's moody. She's a teenager." She snatched up her plate and dumped it in the sink. "You finished eating, Lil? Let's get this done, so that Sabrina can be on her way."

Lil flinched at her mum's words and tone. Lil mouthed a sorry at Sabrina, who smiled, but her eyes were distant and Lil knew she was thinking of Mella.

Mella always took up more space than anyone else.

Birthdays, holidays, were full of Mella: either running off, or fighting with their mum, or sulking. Sometimes it felt like even when she was gone, Mella sucked up all the space, so that there was nothing left for anyone else. But Lil didn't care. She'd give up all her oxygen, all her *everything*, to have Mella back safe.

Come home, Mels. Please.

Leaning forward and pushing her fists into her eyes, Lil swallowed the rising ball of panic and dropped her head into her hands. She didn't know how long she had been sitting like that, but when she sat back, Mella was on the bench next to her, so close Lil could smell the bubble gum of her lip gloss. She was dressed in her sunshine-yellow T-shirt with the cute panda on the sleeve, her ripped jeans, and Lil's DMs. *Don't be angry, Mouse. Please.*

I'm not mad, M. She got no further. She blinked and Mella was gone. Never really there.

There was a movement at the corner of Lil's eye and, startled, she turned quickly to see Kiran coming toward her. "It's freezing! What you doing out here?" he asked as he drew close.

Lil forced a smile, pushing her grief for her sister back inside. "Enjoying the sweet, sweet smell of raw sewage." Her voice was flat and Kiran hesitated.

"Are you okay? I mean, if you want to be alone, I can . . ."

"What? No. Seriously. Sit with me. Take in the view."

"Nice weather," he said, sitting beside her and tugging his sleeves down over his hands.

"Hey, this *is* nice for Wales."

"Are you sure you're okay?" he asked. "You look kind of . . . and finding out about Mella and stuff . . ."

Unfinished sentences must be catching.

"I'm fine. Just a lot on my mind, you know." Lil smiled gently at him and felt that pull, like she and Kiran were joined by string, and no matter what happened, they kept getting tugged back together.

He wore a dark-green beanie hat with luminous orange trim on his head, and he'd changed his T-shirt. The new one was long sleeved, with a fake bloodstain on it, shaped to look as though something with huge teeth had taken a massive bite out of him. The caption said, "Bite me!" His dad must have grabbed it from home for him. Kiran owned a vast collection of "humorous" T-shirts. At least his clothes were clean, although he must be cold out here without a sweater.

Lil suddenly felt self-conscious in the sweater Sabrina had found for her. It smelled a bit moldy. She tucked her hair behind her ears. It was greasy, and she wished she had a hair band. Why was she thinking like this? She saw Kiran every day. Why would he care what she looked like?

Lil looked deep into Kiran's dark-brown eyes and saw a kaleidoscope of memories, despite having known him only a few months: the time he'd brought her soup when she had the flu, and when he'd left the first bluebell of the season on her desk at school because she'd said they were her favorites, the crease he got between his eyebrows when he was concentrating, the way he sucked the end of his pencil, and the way she sometimes caught him looking at her. A sliver of feeling blossomed in Lil. She closed an imaginary fist around it and squeezed. She couldn't afford distractions. She didn't deserve them, not when Mella was missing. Lil pinched her arm, to give herself some focus.

There was concern in Kiran's eyes now, but it was chased by wariness, like a twist of iron in a rope to make it stronger. "Any news?"

"No. Sabrina's working on it."

He whistled. "I don't know what to say . . . They'll probably—"

"What time is it?" she asked, cutting him off. Some things were too hard to talk about. She turned his wrist so that she could see his watch. It was a chunky thing with a bright-orange strap and had so many different dials on it that it took Lil a little while to work out which number gave the time. One measured his heart rate, the depth of the river, the distance from the sun, the number of days left before the world ended. Then she found her eyes wandering. She'd never noticed the inside of Kiran's wrist before. The skin was paler, like something hidden. She felt shy suddenly and let go of him, without registering the time properly. Tenish? Elevenish?

Kiran had that clear, concerned look in his eyes again. The one that made her feel exposed. Undone.

"You tell your dad about the car?" she asked.

Kiran didn't answer immediately. "Here," he said, handing her a Twix, her favorite. He opened a packet of potato chips and ate a couple of handfuls before saying, "If Sabrina hadn't been around, I reckon I would be decomposing slowly in a shallow grave right about now."

"I'm sorry, K. He was probably just worried." It was something Lil recognized from her mum's reaction to Mella.

"Yeah. Wish his worrying involved less shouting." He ran his hand through his hair, making it stick up and getting chip crumbs in it.

"You have . . ." She gestured at his head.

"Mad professor, eh?" Kiran said with a grin, flattening his hair down.

Lil smiled back. "Just a bit. And there's chips . . ."

"Oh, right." He ruffled his hair, dislodging the chips but making the strands stick up again.

Lil opened her mouth to say something, then closed it. He looked cute.

Cute, eh? Mella said in her head. *Ooh, Mouse!*

You shut up, Lil told her gently.

Mella began to sing: *Lil and Kiran K-I-S-S-I-N-G.*

"I keep thinking about it," Kiran said, interrupting her thoughts. "Being trapped in that car. I played it down to Dad, but we could have died, Lil."

"I know." Lil shivered. "I guess I'm trying not to think about it either. I hope Sabrina doesn't tell my mum. That's the last thing I need now. Do you think your dad will tell her?"

"Maybe. I don't know. He won't be about for a bit anyway. He's going out with one of the search-and-rescue guys to assess the damage. At least it won't take him long. Water, check. No car, check. Listen, though, that wasn't why I came out here. I wanted to warn you: Cai is coming here."

Lil's stomach turned over. After trying and failing to get Cai to admit he'd seen Mella shortly before her disappearance, Lil had concentrated on avoiding him. It wasn't easy. It was a small town, and besides, he was always at the kayaking club. Lil couldn't stay away from there; it was Mella's favorite place—Lil's closest connection to her.

"He was lucky," Kiran said. "He stayed on to help Gavan and Jon close up the kayaking club. They put on the shutters and that to try to stop the water getting in. He'd have been caught in the flash flood otherwise." Cai lived in the trailer park near Porthpridd. It was low in the valley, so it would definitely be flooded.

"How do you know all this?" Lil asked.

"Gavan told Dad. The search-and-rescue went out for Gavan and Jon about a half hour ago. They're all coming here."

"Great," Lil said.

"You don't have to talk to him. Just stay out of his way."

"I wish he'd drowned instead of your dad's car."

"Bit harsh, Lils."

"Is it?"

"I know you and Cai have history."

"History?" Lil hated how mean her voice sounded. "Cai made my sister leave. If it hadn't been for him, she would be with us. Safe."

Liar, liar, pants on fire, Mella whispered in her ear.

Lil colored. Luckily, Kiran took it for anger about Cai.

"I know Cai's an idiot, but . . ."

"But nothing," Lil said, letting her rage swallow up the guilt, which was much harder to live with. "Why are you defending him?"

"I'm not."

"Sounds that way."

"Seriously, I hate Cai. He should be left on the beach and have crows feast on his liver."

"You're just saying that to placate me."

"Is it working?"

"No!" Lil said, but she was smiling. "He just makes me so mad."

Kiran looked uncomfortable and Lil felt embarrassed. "Sorry," she said automatically.

"Why are you apologizing?"

"I don't know. You looked . . . I don't know. Automatic response."

There was a moment's awkwardness, and then Kiran asked, "How's Seven? I was going to check on her, but then I got caught up with Dad . . . and I didn't know what to say, to be honest."

"Shaken. She's sleeping now." Lil filled Kiran in on what she'd said about the Sisterhood's beliefs.

"It's a shame we can't get the Internet to work. I tried on Tan's phone earlier, but there's no signal."

"I tried too," Lil said. "I can't believe all this stuff was going on so close to home. How come we've never heard about it?"

"How often do you read the local news?" Kiran asked.

Lil smiled. "Never." She didn't watch TV much either or, if she was being completely honest, look up national news. She felt bad suddenly. Her citizenship teacher was always saying to take an interest in the world—"read one news article a day"—and she'd never taken any notice, and now this *massive* thing was going on so close to her home and she didn't have a clue.

"What are you thinking, Lil?" Kiran asked. "You look miles away."

"I don't know. That a girl I found on the road in the middle of a storm turned out to be from some crazy cult. The same cult where my sister has apparently been living."

"Oh, that. Yeah. I can see how that would get into your head."

"And other stuff."

"Other stuff?"

"More Mella stuff," Lil said very quietly. "I keep thinking that if the police don't hurry, she won't be there anymore. Or something bad'll happen to her. I know Seven said this ceremony can't happen until sunset, but how likely is it that Moon will wait? And now Cai's coming here. I don't care what anyone says. I don't care that they checked his trailer. He knows something! He does. He was her *boy-friend*. She went to his house every single other time she ran away, why not then?" She realized she was shouting and drew in a deep breath. "Sorry. It just makes me crazy. The thought that he knows something and isn't saying!"

"You don't have to say sorry," Kiran said. "I'd be mad

too, and . . . you can talk to me anytime you want. About anything," he added in a softer tone that raked up the hairs on the back of Lil's neck. "I'll always be here for you."

Lil loved the sound of that, and she smiled. "Why do you bother with me?" she asked. The words were out of her mouth before she thought about it. If she had, she definitely wouldn't have said them.

"Because you're worth it." Kiran groaned. "Did I really just say that?"

"Uh-huh. Yes, you did."

"Corporate branding. Seeping into my brain. It's the subliminal messaging. We should be wearing tinfoil on our heads."

"You joke, but I know you totally would, if you thought you could get away with it."

"How do you know I haven't got foil on already?" Kiran raised an eyebrow. "Why do you think I'm wearing this hat?"

Lil laughed, and it felt so good, like opening a window in her chest and letting in the fresh air.

After a pause he added, "This is nice."

"What? The rain? The lack of electricity? The enforced camping? The subliminal messaging? The dangerous cult?"

"No, this. Us. The two of us."

"We're often us." A warning beep was beginning to sound in Lil's head.

"Not like this."

"We're probably both just high on sewage fumes," Lil said, trying to ignore the fact that all her internal organs seemed to have grown wings and were flapping about inside her. Seeing Kiran's lips move to form the word "us" made her think about kissing them. "It really stinks out here, doesn't it?"

"Oh, you mean, that's . . . that's not,"—his voice dropped to a whisper—"you?"

Lil hit out at him playfully. He caught her arm, his fingers sliding down her wrist. Their gazes snagged, and her chest tightened. The beep in her head grew louder, became one long note, started to flash red. She couldn't do this. She tugged her arm out of his grasp, snapping her eyes from his to the smears of chewing gum on the ground.

Lil could feel some of the tension disappearing and realized with a gasp that she hadn't thought about Mella for five minutes. That never happened. Sitting here on this bench with Kiran, she actually felt happy. As happy as she did before Mella left. Guilt swam through her like a dark cloud, eating up her joy as it went. Her sister was out there somewhere, alone, frightened, possibly injured— how could Lil have forgotten her for a second? For half a second? For a heartbeat?

"Lil," Kiran said slowly. "There's something I have to tell you."

The warning light in Lil's head was going crazy. "You don't," she said. "I'm kind of tired. Can it—"

"Please, I need to tell you this. I feel bad I haven't before. I guess I was worried what it meant. What I wanted it to mean. I'm putting this badly. I'm just going to say it. I like . . . well . . . I mean, there's someone I like—really, really like."

The response to this was so obviously *Who?* But Lil couldn't ask that because the way Kiran was looking at her meant that Lil already knew the answer, and she couldn't go there. They were friends. *Friends.* So what if sometimes she noticed the way his stick-out ears were kind of cute, or the fact that he could make her laugh more than anyone else? So what if her heart was beating faster and her brain was screaming at her to lean forward and kiss him? Those things could not happen. That release, that happiness, was not hers to take.

Lil jumped up off the bench. "I'm sure whoever she is is very lucky," she said awkwardly. "I mean, you're really . . ." *Wonderful, amazing, funny.* "Erm . . . you know . . . nice." It sounded so lame. Nice? Of all the words, Lil's brain had given her "nice." "And it's great being your . . . I mean, I like that we're friends, you know. 'Cause you're really nice and *friends* is good."

Mouse! Mella said. *Seriously, why not just go right ahead and kick the boy in the balls?*

Shut up, Lil said.

Aloud she said, "I . . . I've got to go. Sorry, Kiran. I'm . . . sorry." She said "sorry" a couple more times; in fact, she was unable to stop saying it. Then she looked at Kiran's face. It was a study of the term "face falling." The sight of it hurt Lil somewhere right in her chest. *Oh, in my heart,* she thought with a sudden clarity, and then felt stupid because you didn't love someone in your heart. Not actually.

Love, Lil thought. *No. I can't. I don't.*

And so she said sorry again. She was worried she was

about to say it again, when a voice called out Kiran's name. It was Tanuj. He was the older of Kiran's twin brothers by two minutes.

"Hey, Tan," Lil said enthusiastically. She wanted to hug him for arriving at just the perfect moment. Then Tan did what he usually did when joining conversations, which was to stand and stare at you. Tan stared at her for what felt like a long time without blinking.

Lil shifted from foot to foot, wondering how a nine-year-old could be so intimidating. "Well, I . . . ," she murmured. She could sense Kiran staring at her. She'd hurt him, she realized.

"Did you know that neutron stars can spin at a rate of seven hundred rotations per second?" Tan said.

"I did not know that," Lil said. She almost flicked a glance over at Kiran but stopped herself just in time. Tan was sensitive as well as smart. He and Kamal were starting to get picked on at school. "They make googly eyes at each other when we talk," Kam said.

"They think we don't notice," Tan added.

"But we do," Kam finished.

Lil didn't want Tan to think she was making googly eyes at Kiran, so she smiled and said, "Thanks, Tanuj."

He nodded. "You're welcome." Then he turned to Kiran. "Daddy says you're to come back now."

"Tan, that's rude. I'm talking to Lil."

"S'okay," Lil said. "I'll catch you later. I need to . . . you know." She darted across the parking lot. She was relieved. Kiran wasn't good for her. He made her forget;

he made her happy and she had no right to be that, not when Mella was who knew where. She needed to focus on getting Mella home. That was all that mattered.

Lil walked head down, deep in thought, so that she didn't see the wall of person blocking her path until she had smacked right into him and rebounded onto the ground.

Lil looked up to find Cai Jones standing in front of her.

Cai Jones. His hair was perfectly tousled—the word seemed invented for his *What, this? I fell out of bed looking this good. Maybe tomorrow it'll be your bed* hair. The worst thing about Cai was that Lil could see why Mella fancied him. Lil would never admit it—not even under torture—but she'd thought him cute the first time she saw him.

Now he was the last person Lil wanted to see. Ever.

She scrambled up, wincing as she realized how hard she had landed. "Get out of the way, Cai."

"Nice to see you too."

"Well, it isn't nice to see you." Lil sounded like a sulky child. Cai always made her feel like an awkward twelve-year-old.

"You still blame me, huh?"

"Yes, because it was your fault."

"Still think I've got Mella's body buried under the decking of my trailer. Or curled up in the septic tank."

"Don't joke about that! What's the matter with you?" These were the images Lil fought against every day. She didn't need someone *joking* about them. Cai was such an idiot.

He grinned. "You think you know your sister so well. Perfect Mella. You and her were so close. No way she would ever leave without telling you. *Never. Not my bestest friend Mella.*"

"Piss off, Cai. I don't have to talk to you."

"No, you don't. You don't have to do anything that might change your worldview. Just keep on believing your big sister was bloody brilliant."

Lil stormed back into the hall, her heart beating frantically in her chest. She hated Cai. *Hated* him. But most of all she hated how he got in her head and made her thoughts all twisty and dark. How could he joke about Mella being dead? How could he even bear to *think* it? Suddenly Lil wanted her mum. Her hand went automatically to her pocket for her phone so she could text her. But it wasn't there, of course. She channeled a message instead and willed it out across the waterlogged Welsh valleys. *Hope you're okay. Love you.*

She looked about for Sabrina. She'd be busy, but maybe she'd have a couple of minutes for a cup of tea, and surely there must be some news about Mella by now. Her aunt was nowhere, but Officer Burnley was there. Lil knew her vaguely. She thought her first name was Angharad maybe. She was nice, but Lil still felt shy going over to her. "Is my aunt around?" she asked, after saying hi.

Officer Burnley recognized her immediately and gave Lil a full-beam smile. "No, love, she's gone up to check on some of the houses by the river. Report of a break-in. Honestly, can you imagine? Now? Just kids, I suspect, but still . . ."

Lil didn't want to get into the specifics of the break-in

right then, so she turned the conversation. "Did she say when she'd be back?" she asked.

Officer Burnley smiled kindly, eyes infused with a sympathy that made Lil squirm. "You'll be worrying about your sister, no doubt. Wondering what's going on? Sabrina is chasing it up with the Caerwen police station. They'll be doing everything they can, love. It'll be a challenge in this weather, mind."

"No news, though?" Lil pressed.

"Not yet." The woman's smile was sadder. "Have you eaten?"

Lil shrugged. Some volunteers had set up a makeshift kitchen, using the gas stoves to heat things up in vats. She couldn't eat anything, though. There was a lump the size of Wales in her throat. No news on Mella. And now no Sabrina. She tried not to feel annoyed that Sabrina had left to investigate those houses. Did she think that was more important than Mella? Lil cut off that thought. Of course she didn't. She was doing everything she could, and those people needed help too.

Lil thanked Officer Burnley and turned away. She was about to walk back toward her bed when there was a shout from behind her. She turned to see Sabrina hurtling across the hall.

"Oh, Lili," she cried as she drew close, "they've found her." She gripped Lil's hand. "'They've found your sister.'"

The Light will protect, as is Her will.

—THE BOOK

The sound of Dazzle's scream went on for a long time. It felt like eternity to Mella as she lay, face pressed into the ground, feeling the weight of Evanescence on her back. She couldn't get enough air, and what she could breathe was mostly grass and dust and mud. She felt dizzy and sick. There was blood on her face, and her head throbbed. It was bad, she could tell. Her vision shrank to a gray squiggle and then disappeared completely.

When she came around, the clearing was empty apart from her, Moon, and Evanescence. "Let them go," Moon was saying. "If they refuse to follow the Light, then the Darkness is welcome to them." She sounded tired.

"The Darkness is close now, High Priestess," Evanescence replied. "We should stay inside the walls of our Sisterhood, where it is safe from prying eyes."

Mella tried to lie still, to hear more, but there was dust in her throat, and a cough built until she could no longer contain it. As she moved, Evanescence lunged forward to stand right over her again, her face ferocious; her expression said, *Don't even think about running.*

Mella shrank back from her, coughed again, and then sat up. Her back hurt. "Where is she? Where's Dazzle?" she asked.

Moon smiled sadly. "The Brightness is not for us all."

"What does that mean?" Mella heard Dazzle's scream again inside her head, and she knew. *She'll never be able to stand it.* She was dead. Oh God, she was dead. Tears sprang to Mella's eyes. It was too late. She hadn't saved her.

Moon crouched before her, taking her chin gently in her hand and wiping away her tears. "Don't cry for her. Think of yourself. I can still save you, if only you'll let me."

Mella yanked her head back. "You killed her."

"No," Moon said softly. Her voice was as quiet as a whisper; it was the exact same tone she'd used when they first met. The sound of it made Mella want to throw up. "She chose the Darkness. There was nothing I could do." She stroked Mella's cheek. "Don't you know that everything I do is for you, for my sisters?" She smiled. It was like a maggot crawling out of the apple you'd just taken a huge bite out of. "Let me help you. Let me take you into the Light. Let Her burn the Darkness from you."

Burn.

Dazzle's screams rang in Mella's head again, only this time they were her own. Mella's heart seemed to stop in her chest as panic crashed like a tidal wave over her. She didn't think, only moved as though the fire were already devouring her. Kicking out as Evanescence made to grab her, Mella was up and fleeing for the trees.

Chapter Sixteen

They've found your sister.

"Mella," Lil said. "Mella. They found Mella." It was idiotic because she had only one sister, but her brain couldn't take on the words. "They found her!" Lil said. It was like she'd been underwater for four and a half months and was suddenly bursting through into the sunshine. Somehow she was holding Sabrina, and Sabrina was holding her, and they were both crying and laughing and shrieking and saying the same words over and over again.

"They found her." Lil.

"Yes." Sabrina.

"But they *found* her."

"Yes. Yes. Yes. Yes!"

Lil's legs gave way. Sabrina caught her and eased her to the floor as the world whitened out at the edges. There was too much happiness flying around Lil's body and not enough oxygen. She just needed a moment. She rested her arms on her legs and dropped her head forward, taking in deep, long breaths. Somewhere far away Sabrina was rubbing her back and saying, "I know it's a shock."

A shock. A shock was getting an A on a maths exam or coming downstairs and finding you'd been burgled. This was a miracle. It was waking up one morning and discovering you could fly, or walking out of your house to find it was raining chocolate bars. It was celebrating Christmas every day. It was everything you'd ever wished for and then some.

Because Mella was coming home.

"Can I see her?"

"Yes," Sabrina said, "yes, *cariad*, of course you can. I'll take you to the hospital now."

"Mum!" Lil shouted suddenly, making a couple of people look up. "Does Mum know?"

"Yes, she's going to meet us at the hospital."

"What did Mum say when you told her?" Lil asked, and then because there seemed to be some kind of delay between the world and her brain, she said, "Hospital. Is Mella hurt?" Lil's stomach did a somersault. *Please don't give her back to me only to take her away again.*

"We'll know more when we get to the hospital," Sabrina said.

"Sabrina!" Lil cried, exasperated.

Sabrina held up her hands. "Darling, I know this is hard, but I really don't have anything more to share. They mentioned a head injury and that's all I know. Let's get to the hospital and find out. Okay?"

Lil nodded. "How did they find her?"

"As far as I can gather, a car picked up a young woman

who had been walking on the main road to Caerwen earlier today. She was very distressed, and they took her to the local hospital. The medical team called the police. One of my team went up there and confirmed that it was Mella."

"And did she say she came from the same place as Seven?" A flicker of something crossed Sabrina's face. Lil couldn't read what it meant, but it scared her. "There's something you're not telling me."

"Please, Lil," Sabrina begged. "The main thing is Mella has been found and is receiving the care she needs."

Lil could see it was pointless to keep questioning Sabrina. She either didn't know or wouldn't say more right now. That was Sabrina's way. She only spoke truth, and if she didn't know something for sure, she wouldn't say it, no matter how much you pestered her. "Did she ask about us?" Lil inquired instead.

"I don't know any more than I've said. I'm sorry. I'll get a full report later."

"Will we make it to the hospital in the rain?"

"If we have to learn to fly, we'll make it," Sabrina replied.

It took Lil and Sabrina ages to get to the hospital. At one point it looked like they might not manage it. But Sabrina found a back way where the river water was lower. Lil could barely keep still, and she was unable to stop asking questions long enough for Sabrina to answer them.

The first one she asked was, "It's really her?" Or rather,

her mouth asked. Lil felt entirely disconnected from the rest of her body. There had been sightings and "findings" before. Not for a long time. At the beginning they'd gone hurtling off to Cardiff, Manchester, and even London because someone was absolutely and completely positive they'd seen Mella. Not a young woman matching Mella's description, but actually Mella. The journeys there had been like this one: long but full of excitement. The journeys home had been long and quiet. No one had spoken; there had been nothing to say.

"It's her," Sabrina said. "The officers checked."

The road was very wet with puddles all along it. Lil knew driving must be difficult. She should let her aunt concentrate, but she couldn't. She'd waited over four months and she couldn't wait a second longer. "Sabrina," she said. "Is . . . is it bad? Did they hurt her?" All the terrible things that could have stopped Mella from coming home filled her head.

Sabrina reached across and patted her knee. "She's safe now, that's the important thing."

"But I want to know what happened to her. She'll . . . if it was bad . . ." She'd been gone for months; of course it was bad. "She'll need help. I want to be able to support her, and I can't if I don't know what she went through."

Sabrina glanced across at Lil briefly, her eyes shining. "You're such a good sister, Lil."

Lil had to look away. *Don't be angry, Mouse.* Lil had let Mella down once before. She was never doing it again.

Lil's mum wasn't there when Lil and Sabrina arrived at the hospital. Sabrina talked to the nurses while they waited, and Lil got a hot chocolate that tasted more like coffee from one of the vending machines, then sat in the small waiting room.

After a while Lil picked up a magazine, turning the pages without registering what was on them. In the end she let it lie, unread, on her lap. Her stomach was in knots. She couldn't eat the dry sandwich Sabrina had insisted on buying her from the café on the ground floor of the hospital.

Lil was relieved when her aunt came back. Anything to escape her thoughts. She stood up. "Is Mum here?" she asked, and then she saw her mother standing in the doorway.

"Lil!" Her mum stepped forward, and then they were holding each other and crying. "Oh, Lils, can you believe it?" The hope in her mother's voice scared her.

Fear had begun to creep in alongside Lil's happiness now. What would Mella be like? She'd been through so much and she'd been fragile before. Something told Lil that getting Mella home might only be the beginning. Would her mum be able to cope with it? *Please be strong,* Lil begged silently. *For Mella. For me.*

"Can we see her?" Mum asked Sabrina, her voice full of happy tears. "Can we see my daughter?"

"Yes," Sabrina said, but she made no move toward the door. "But I want you to prepare yourselves. I didn't get the full information before, but . . . Mella is in a bad way."

Her mum gripped her hand, and Lil tried to hold steady for both of them, Sabrina's words echoing around her head. She hung back as they went out into the corridor, leaving Sabrina to take her mum's hand. Lil needed more time to think. What would she say? What would Mella say? Over four months was a long time. How would Mella look? Would she look different? How bad was bad?

By the time they reached her sister's room, Lil couldn't breathe. Her lungs were replaced with a plastic bag. Lil hovered outside the room. She wanted to rush forward and throw her arms around her sister's neck, but her body wouldn't cooperate. She shut her eyes briefly, imagining the scene. Mella in her mum's arms. Both of them crying. Laughing. Happy. Finally her mum would draw back. She'd dab at her eyes with one hand, while holding Mella tightly with the other. Then Mella would look over at Lil for the first time. "Mouse!" She'd smile, and the memory of the last agonizing months would be wiped away—

A scream broke into Lil's thoughts. It was followed by a shout.

Lil's eyes flew open and she darted into the room.

Her mum was backing away from the bed, one hand over her mouth. She was the color of icing. Sabrina held her as she was shouting for help, and she looked pale too but also angry, two spots of red rising up on her cheeks. Lil didn't understand what was going on. Why were they shouting? Mella had only just come back. Shouldn't everyone be so happy they could burst?

Then she looked at the girl in the bed.

She was dark haired, curls escaping from the loose plait that hung over one shoulder. There was a bandage covering half of her face and another around her arm.

Lil's legs turned to water.

The girl in the bed wasn't Mella.

"Trust in me," saith the Light, "and I
shall never fail you."

—THE BOOK

Mella's head hurt; in fact, the whole left side of her body was one giant bruise. She was lying down, somewhere dark and warm. She struggled to sit up, eyelids sticking. The room she was in wasn't as dark as she'd first thought. A fire burned in a large glass orb on the long wooden table. It cast orange shapes on the wooden floor. A low voice whispered in the gloom: Moon. Head ducked over the orb, she muttered to herself. There were other shapes. Sisters. Mella counted ten women. Where were the others? Had some escaped? Or were they dead too?

Mella felt sick. She'd been an idiot not to see what was going on sooner. But how? Moon had always seemed so kind, so loving. Mella was angry with herself. This place was just another of her mistakes.

She shifted position, easing herself up to sit, using the wall to help her. She didn't think she'd be able to stand. Her left ankle was all puffy and purple. Not a good look. But how had this happened? Who'd brought her here? The last thing she remembered was running from Moon and Evanescence . . . oh, and the tree root. She'd tripped and landed headfirst on something solid. She must have knocked herself out and twisted her ankle, and Evanescence found her and carried her here. To the Great Hall, with the other sisters, and Moon babbling like a lunatic to the Sun's flame.

"You're awake."

Mella jumped and, turning, saw Luster leaning heavily against the wall beside her. The congealed blood on her face and neck gleamed against her dark skin like rubies in the firelight. The sight of those injuries hurt Mella. She didn't deserve to be treated like that. None of them did.

"Are you okay?" she asked.

Luster raised an eyebrow. It said, *Do I look okay?*

"Where are the others? I know Dazzle is. . . ." *Dead.*

The older woman shook her head. "I don't know. Dazzle hasn't come back. I'm hoping by the Light that means she got away."

"Got away? How?"

"When they realized what Moon was going to do, some of the sisters intervened. They pulled Dazzle to safety and then they ran. I followed you up to the clearing. I tried to help as best I could . . . but some of the sisters fought back. . . ." She gestured to her face.

Mella glanced around at the women in the room, wondering who it had been.

"Don't blame them. Many of them have been here nearly all their lives. . . . Without the Light, they have nothing."

"But Dazzle's okay? She's alive?"

"She was when I saw her. Hurt, badly, but alive, yes."

Hope blossomed inside Mella. "And if the others got away, if they can get to the police, tell them what's happened..." She broke off as Luster shook her head. "What?"

"We rarely leave the compound. Moon has filled their heads with tales about the people outside. Dark-filled recreants. Even if they do make it out, even if Dazzle survives, I don't know that they'll trust anyone enough to—"

"But one of them will, surely?"

"Maybe." There was no hope in her voice.

"So we're on our own, then."

Luster didn't answer. She didn't need to. Fear clutched at Mella's chest. Moon had told them: "Let me take you into the Light. Let Her burn the Darkness from you."

"We have to do something! We can't just sit here, waiting." But even as she thought it, she knew it was hopeless. They were in the Great Hall; its windows had bars, and its iron-studded door was shut and locked. Even if it wasn't, Mella wasn't sure she could walk, let alone run. Then there was Evanescence.

Mella could see her now, prowling across the doorway like a caged tiger. Maybe if enough of them ran at her. But which of the sisters would stand against Moon? These were the ones who'd stayed, who had hurt Luster to do so.

She looked at them now, silent and hunched, sitting in small groups. Mella barely knew them. How could she convince them to turn against everything they'd been taught? They knew about the cleansing. They'd seen what had happened to Dazzle. It had probably happened to them in the past, and still they'd stayed, still they'd obeyed Moon and done nothing. Why would they go against their high priestess now, when the Brightness was so close?

Mella looked at the barred windows. "How will we escape?"

As if in response, the fire surged upward, cackling like a maniac.

CHAPTER SEVENTEEN

On the night of Lil's sixteenth birthday, her mum and Mella had an argument, the biggest yet. It was their third that week. None of them had seen Mella since Tuesday. Rhia was over for dinner. They waited as long as they could to eat, until everything that wasn't burned was cold. The meal sat in Lil's stomach like cement.

Rhia and Lil were in the kitchen washing up when Mella came in. It was past ten. Lil was trying not to be angry at Mella, but she could feel the rage burning up inside. It was her birthday. Why couldn't Mella just be nice for one night? Just not make everything unpleasant for one night.

"Where the hell have you been?" Mum shouted from the hallway. "I've called everyone we know. Mrs. Forster said that it's a shame I can't keep track of my own children."

Mella laughed. "Yeah, well, Mrs. Forster has always been a bitch." She came into the kitchen, tugging off her boots. "Sorry I'm late, Mouse."

"Is this some kind of joke to you, Melanie?" Their

mum stood, arms folded, face thunderous, in the door-way, while Mella went through the fridge. "Do you think it's funny to make us worried sick about you? To call the police and almost hear them sigh. 'Gone missing again, eh? What do you do to her, Mrs. Laverty?'"

Mella took out a piece of cheese and began to eat it. Lil could tell she was drunk. The anger inside her rose higher. She hated her sister when she was drunk.

"This has got to stop," Mum said.

"Or what?" Mella shouted suddenly and the noise exploded around the room until Lil wanted to put her hands over her ears.

"Stop it," Lil said. "Stop shouting. Mum, Mella's here now. It's fine. It doesn't matter. Just stop shouting, please." What she wanted to say was, *Mella, just sit down, can't you? Just be my big sister. The fun, kind one who draws silly pictures of goats for my birthday.* Lil had been looking forward to tonight for ages. Mella had promised to be home early. She had promised not to argue with Mum. Yet here she was. Late. Drunk. Argumentative.

Rhia blushed scarlet and looked as though she wished the floor would open up and swallow her. *You and me both,* thought Lil. Rhia gave Lil a reassuring smile and then said, "I'll just . . . ," before slipping from the room.

"Stop shouting at each other," Lil said again. She was angry, but no one noticed because no one was listening to her. As usual. Lil was surprised at how bitter that thought was.

"Where have you been?" Mum asked Mella.

"Fairyland."

"Have you been drinking?"

Mella just smiled stupidly.

"I know where you haven't been recently—college."

Mella whitened. She glared at Lil. Lil opened her mouth to say, "It wasn't me," but she was too late, and who cared? Mum was shouting again and didn't need an excuse. Besides, Mella hadn't been at college. She was always out with Cai. All the time.

"So where have you been going? Hanging out with that boy? Don't tell me it's true love. I can tell you now, Melanie, you do not end up staying with the guy you met when you were seventeen. Unless you get pregnant. Then what? You'll get stuck in this valley, watching all your dreams disappear, just like . . ." She trailed off, but they both knew what she had been going to say. *Just like me,* stuck in the middle of nowhere, no husband, two children, having given up the career she loved before it really began.

"Yeah, 'cause we've made your life so difficult." Mella put her hand on Lil's shoulder. It was trembling. Lil wanted to hold her. She wanted to hold her mum and sister both so tightly that they couldn't get any more words out and then they would have to stop shouting at each other. Lil was no expert, but she knew that some things once said couldn't be taken back.

"Mum," she said, voice overly cheerful. "Didn't you say there was cake? Let's have that."

"Lilian, I am talking to your sister. Please don't interrupt."

You are not talking, you are shouting, and it's my birthday! But Lil didn't say anything. She just went out of the room and into the hallway. She needed to breathe. This was like her sixth birthday and her seventh and her twelfth all over again. For once could Mella just be . . . ? Be what? Less selfish. God, her sister was so selfish. Everything was always about her. Lil was sick of it. Her anger was a red-hot coal in her stomach, and Lil fanned it with bitterness until it began to burn.

Rhia was sitting on the stairs. She held her hand out for Lil to pull her up just as Mella shouted from the kitchen. "God, you're such a ——!" And she called Mum a name that was so awful it seemed to reverberate around the house. "No wonder Dad left."

Lil flinched.

"Come on," Rhia said, putting her arm around Lil and leading her into the living room. She pushed her down onto the sofa and then went to turn on the stereo.

Lil shook her head. "I want to hear." She knew it was a bad idea, but she could feel her irritation with her sister burning up inside her, and she wanted to add oxygen to that fire. She was tired of always being okay with everything, of always being the one to act as peacekeeper, apologizing again and again for both of them.

Rhia hesitated and then nodded. "Probably sensible to check they don't kill each other."

There was the sound of a glass smashing and any humor was lost.

"You think it's true love, you and Cai, do you? Wake up, Mella!" Mum shouted.

Lil closed her eyes, breathing deeply, so she felt rather than saw Rhia sit on the sofa next to her and drag the blanket over them both. Nain had knitted it, and if you held it close, you could sometimes imagine it still smelled of her jasmine perfume. Tonight it did nothing to calm Lil.

There was another shout from the kitchen but quieter.

"Maybe they're calming down," Rhia said.

"Maybe."

Rhia pulled her hand out from under the blanket. "Thumb war?"

Lil smiled. "You hate thumb war."

"It's your birthday. I'm feeling magnanimous."

Lil took her friend's hand. It was warm. They both wore the same nail varnish. Bright orange. The color Rhia had bought Lil for her birthday. Lil felt a bit better. "One, two, three," she said.

From the kitchen she heard, "You don't think about anyone except yourself."

"Four," Rhia said.

"You don't know anything about me and Cai."

"I declare a thumb war," Lil said.

The kitchen door opened. Mella's voice was loud and clear. ". . . end up like you!"

Before Lil registered that her body was moving, she was out in the hallway. Her hands were in fists, and she was shaking so hard she could barely get the words out. The sight of her sister just enraged her further. "It's . . . it's my birthday!" she spit, anger rising as she realized she sounded like a small, stupid child.

"It's my birthday," Mella said in a horrible singsong voice.

In that moment Lil hated her. "You ruin everything, Melanie," she snapped. "You're so selfish. You know that? Why don't . . . why don't you just piss off and leave us alone. Go to Cai's. Stay there. I don't care if I never see you again."

Out of the corner of her eye, Lil could see Rhia's pinched face. She heard her sharp intake of breath. Lil folded her arms across her chest, keeping the anger inside, not yet ready for it to burn out.

"Fine!" Mella retorted, opening the door and then slamming it so hard behind her that the sound echoed around the whole house.

Rhia moved closer, slowly, like she was approaching a wild animal. "She'll know you didn't mean it," she whispered, squeezing Lil's hand.

Lil snatched her fingers away. "I meant it," she snapped. Her words came out even more irritable and mean because the anger was seeping away and regret was seeping in, and she didn't want Rhia to see it. She stormed up the stairs to her room, closing her eyes as she leaned against the doorframe. When she opened them, she was surprised to find that the house was still standing around her.

Lil collapsed into one of the chairs in the hospital waiting room and dropped her head into her hands. She'd run from that room and the girl who wasn't her sister as fast as she could. She hadn't waited for an explanation about the mistaken identity. At that moment her disappointment was too great, the sound of her mother's cries too much to bear. She needed some time on her own to regroup, to settle her thoughts. Just because this girl wasn't Mella, it didn't mean Mella wasn't at the Sisterhood. Seven knew her, had said she'd been there on Friday night. This was a mix-up. They would still find Mella. They would still bring her home. That was the rational train of thought, but Lil's brain refused to stay rational. She felt hot and dizzy, and each breath was painful, like it was ripping itself from her lungs.

Sweat was gathering at her neck and under her arms. She tugged her sweater off. Everything felt too close in here, like something was pushing in. Lil was afraid that when she looked up, there would be no space left.

She felt despair creeping up inside her. She was exhausted from hoping and wishing and getting excited every time there was a lead. And this time she'd thought they had finally found her. But they hadn't. Yet another false hope. How could hope feel so hopeless?

Where was Mella? Was she still with the Sisterhood? What was happening to her? Lil remembered the burn on Seven's arm, the haunted look in her eyes, and she was more scared than she'd ever been in her whole life.

CHAPTER EIGHTEEN

Lil went to bed angry on the night of her birthday, her heart racing like she'd run a marathon. She did not go back downstairs, and her mum drove Rhia home. Lil was ashamed of how she'd behaved, but that just made her angrier. Why did Mella have to be like this? Ruining everything and making Lil act like a jerk. She nursed her anger all night, tossing and turning, as she thought of everything that she wanted to say to her sister. *Why are you so selfish? Why can't you just think about someone else for once? It was my birthday and you are so thoughtless. I bet you didn't even get me a card.* On and on the arguments went, right through Lil's dreams, so she barely knew if she was awake or asleep. She woke up properly when she heard someone come into her room. Her sister said her name. Lil didn't move. Her anger was a rock pinning her to the bed.

"Don't be angry, Mouse. Please," Mella said. "I know I keep messing up. I just . . ." She drew a deep breath. "I don't blame you for not wanting to talk to me. But don't be mad, Lil, please. I love you. I'm sorry. I'm so sorry."

Lil bunched her hands into fists to stop herself from flinging the duvet back and saying it didn't matter. It did matter. Because Mella kept saying sorry and then she kept doing the exact same thing again. Lil didn't want her to be sorry; she just wanted her to stop—to stop what? Being Mella?

"You know what? You probably are better without me." Mella gave a small, humorless laugh. Then Lil felt the weight ease as Mella stood up, followed by a soft click as the bedroom door closed behind her.

Lil fell into a grumpy sleep after that. When she opened her eyes next, it was morning. The sunshine was peeking through her striped curtains and the room was empty. Mella was gone, but Lil could still taste her vanilla perfume in the air. There was an envelope on the floor by her bed. She opened it to find a card with a picture of a baby goat wearing red Wellington boots on the front. Goats were Lil's favorite animals. Mella always drew her goat-related cards for her birthday. Inside Mella had written:

> Doctor, doctor, I feel like a goat. How long
> have you felt like this? Since I was a kid.
> Happy birthday!
> Love,
> Mella x

When Lil went downstairs a little while later, she found her mum at the kitchen table. She was on the phone with Cai. It was clearly his answering machine, because she was saying, "If my daughter's with you, can you please ask her to text me so that I know she's alive? Thank you." There was no concern in her voice then, only irritation. She smiled at Lil and rolled her eyes. "Your sister's done a runner again. Call Erin, will you? Check if she's seen her." She got up to refill her coffee cup.

That moment was frozen in Lil's memory. It was always bright and full of light, and all the memories that came after were grayer, like the world had turned to black and white. Because that was the last moment their lives had been normal.

Two hours later they would be calling everyone Mella knew, again and again, and the permanent fear on her mother's face would have begun to settle into the lines around her eyes.

Because Mella wasn't at Cai's.

She wasn't at Erin's.

She wasn't at the random girl's house she'd met at life drawing last week.

She wasn't on the riverbank drawing the sycamore trees because their branches were just so divine, like women dancing.

She wasn't at the kayaking club.

She wasn't replying to the seventy messages that Lil had sent.

She wasn't in any of the local hospitals.

She wasn't at Caerwen train station.

She wasn't anywhere.

She had completely disappeared.

And the never-ending, mind-numbing panic, fear,

desperation, misery, guilt, despair, took up residence in the space she'd left, taking the light, the life, out of everything because—

Where was Mella?

Where was she? Where was she? Where *was she*?

How could someone just completely vanish?

Vanish like she'd never existed in the first place.

And how was Lil supposed to live with that? How was she supposed to begin each day with a hole torn right through everything?

Chapter Nineteen

"Lil?"

Sabrina walked toward her. Lil wanted to run into her arms and stay there until their closeness filled up all the empty spaces inside each of them. But Lil couldn't move.

"Are you okay?" Sabrina asked.

Lil nodded, then shook her head.

Sabrina crouched in front of her and brushed Lil's hair back from her face.

"Where's Mum?" Lil asked.

"She was very upset. She's having a rest now. One of the nurses is with her."

"Is she okay?"

"She will be. What about you?"

"I feel sick."

"Like you might be sick or just . . ."

"Just sick. In here." Lil pointed at her heart. "It wasn't her," Lil said. "I can't believe it wasn't . . ." She didn't bother to finish her sentence. She dropped her head into her hands. Sabrina sat down next to her and drew Lil close, wrapping her arms around Lil so tight it felt like they were the only thing holding her together.

As Sabrina led Lil to the car park, Lil felt the shock and grief retreating inside her, to form a knot in her throat. Sabrina opened the passenger door of her car and helped Lil inside. She strapped her in like she was a child. Lil didn't fight it. Memories flew through her head. Nothing really stuck. The argument on her sixteenth birthday, her telling Mella not to come back. *Don't be angry, Mouse. Please.*

It was only after Sabrina reappeared, getting into her side of the car, that Lil registered she wasn't initially next to her. Her mouth felt dry, her throat sore. She needed to cough before the words would come out. "What's happening?" she asked. "Is Mum coming?"

Sabrina handed Lil a packet of chips. "Thought you might be hungry." Then she said, "They're going to keep your mum in for a bit. She's exhausted. She needs some rest. We'll go back to Porthpridd. Come back for her later."

Lil held the chips in her lap. She wasn't hungry.

Sabrina's phone rang. "Yes," she said. "What's going on? . . . Did you run a trace? . . . Nothing? What about the path reports? . . . I want to know how this happened. Hmm. Yeah. . . . Okay. . . . And what about the girl? . . . Well, just keep an eye on her. I'm on my way back now. . . . Yeah, bye." She clicked the phone off. "Right, let's go."

"I should stay with Mum," Lil said. "She worries if I'm not around."

Sabrina gave her a watery smile. "I think you need a break too, Lils. Your mum puts too much on you." She drew a deep breath. "I should have done more. I didn't realize how shattered your mum was."

"She doesn't sleep."

"And you?"

Lil shrugged and looked out across the car park. "Sometimes."

"I should have been there more, Lil. I'm sorry. Not just now but . . . before. I knew your mum was struggling. . . . After my brother left and you came back here, I wanted to do more. I tried to be there, but work was always so busy. I told myself you were okay. But I knew you weren't. I knew Mella needed help. I just . . ."

Lil squeezed her hand. "You've always been there for us." Lil's heart felt too big for her chest. "Will Mum be all right on her own?"

"I think Sandi's going to come up. She'll be all right." Sabrina glanced in the rearview mirror. "I look a state." She puffed up her hair and wiped away the mascara from under her eyes. Then she turned on the engine. As she indicated and took the turn for the road back to Porthpridd, she said: "I'm so sorry we didn't find your sister today. What a mess. I can't believe we put you through that."

Lil looked out at the water glistening on the fields as they drove by. "Who is she? The girl, I mean."

"Her name, well, the one she eventually gave is Dazzle. I don't think it's her real one, but that's all she'd give us."

"Why did they think she was Mella?" Lil asked.

"I'm still getting to the bottom of it. Dazzle was in a very bad way when she was brought into hospital. Her burns are incredibly serious, and she has a nasty gash on her head. She was so terrified she wouldn't talk at all at first. The officer in charge knew we were looking for Mella, so there seems to have been some misinformation. I honestly don't know what happened. But trust me. I am going to get to the bottom of it. Dazzle is distraught that she caused you such pain."

"So where is Mella?" Lil asked.

"Well, that's the one good thing that's come out of all this. Unlike Seven, Dazzle wasn't born in the commune, so she was able to give us more details about where it is."

"Where is it? Near here?"

"It's up by Caerwen. We're not sure exactly, but we're hoping to get more information soon. We also got another lead. A call came in while we were in the hospital. Did Seven tell you how she got to you?"

"Not really. I didn't ask. I assumed she ran?" Lil said, remembering Seven's dirty pumps.

"She must have for part of the way, but she got a lift, too. From a woman. Picked her up on the side of the road and drove her toward Porthpridd. She was suspicious, though, and when Seven fell asleep, she called the police. Seven must have woken up. The woman said when she got back to her car, Seven was gone. The police up at Caerwen only put two and two together this afternoon."

"And this woman knows where the Sisterhood is?"

"What she said helped us to narrow down the search to near Cragen Beach."

"Cragen?" Lil repeated. They'd gone there every summer as kids. How many times had Lil and Mella stared up at those cliffs without realizing what was there? Lil shivered and glanced up to where the sun was peeking through the trees. There were so many weird coincidences—like this was predestined somehow, as though there really was some kind of divine guidance involved. No, that was just silly.

"And Mella's there? Is she all right?" she asked.

Sabrina's eyes were dark as shadows, huge in her pale face. "I don't know. This high priestess burned Dazzle. . . . She tried to push her into a fire, but some of the other women stopped her. They ran away too, but they got split up somehow. Dazzle doesn't know if Mella made it out or not. If she didn't . . ." Sabrina didn't finish her sentence.

Lil knew what she had been going to say. *If she didn't, then Mella is in grave danger.*

Lil thought she might be sick.

Sabrina gripped her hand. "I'm putting the best that the Caerwen police force has on this. We are going to get Mella out of there. I promise."

CHAPTER TWENTY

Lil followed Sabrina into the village hall. Images from a movie about a cult flicked through her mind, mixing with memories of reports of a headless body found in the river Thames and linked to "religious sacrifice." She and Sabrina had been quiet for the rest of the journey. Lil hadn't known what to ask, and she'd been afraid of the answers anyway. As they entered the hall, she said to Sabrina, "How soon can we go up there?"

"We?" Sabrina looked confused. Her eyes were glassy. Lil wondered how much sleep she'd had the night before.

"To the Sisterhood. To get Mella? How soon do we leave?"

"As soon as the warrant is in place. But . . ." She hesitated. "You're not coming, darling. You can't think . . ."

Lil knew, of course, that it was ridiculous. That Sabrina would never take her. "I could wait in a car. I have to see her!"

Sabrina hugged her. She didn't need to say anything. It was still a no. Lil opened her mouth to protest, when she was cut off by some sort of commotion near the entrance to the hall, just past the door to the kitchen. She glanced up to see Cai and Officer Burnley. Cai was up close, in the woman's face, shouting and waving his arms. "I just want a chance to tell my side. Just a chance; that's all I'm asking for. Jesus, you coppers."

Sabrina moved quickly. "What's going on?" she asked.

Officer Burnley looked relieved. "Mr. Jones wanted a word with you, ma'am. I said you were still out, but . . ."

"It's okay, Angharad. What's going on, Cai? What do you want? I'm busy right now, so make it quick."

Lil could hear the strain in Sabrina's voice. Lil knew she wanted to get on with rescuing Mella, not waste time talking to Cai.

Cai, though, puffed out his chest. "I just want to get my side of the story across."

"Your side?" Sabrina asked. "What are you talking about?"

Cai cut right across her. "Well, you've heard what she's got to say, so you ought to hear me out before you start jumpin' to all sorts of conclusions. I know what you cops are like."

"Sorry, Cai, I don't—" Sabrina began.

"Mella. You found her, right? Well, I don't care what she told you about that morning. It didn't go down the way she tells it, right. It was an accident."

Lil realized that Cai was talking about the last morning that any of them saw Mella. *An accident.* What did he mean by "an accident"? Had he done something to Mella?

All these months Lil had believed she was the last person to speak to Mella. It hadn't mattered how many times people said it wasn't her fault; how could she have known that what seemed like a regular argument would be the last one anyone ever had with Mella? In the weeks and months after Mella left, more and more kept coming out about how much trouble she was in. She hadn't been going to college. She'd missed almost a whole term of work. The week before Lil's birthday, they'd kicked her out.

Sabrina always said it wasn't just one thing that made someone run away. But that mattered so little to Lil. If she'd shouted less at Mella that night, if she hadn't ignored her the next morning, then maybe . . . just maybe . . . she wouldn't have left, and she wouldn't have ended up with the Sisterhood. . . .

Now it turned out that someone else had spoken to Mella that morning.

Cai. By the sound of it, he'd done more than that. He'd hurt her!

Lil wasn't a violent person. She'd never hit anyone in her life, but now she darted across the hallway and pounded Cai in the chest. Hard. She was actually a couple of inches taller than him, although she always forgot that because he made her feel so small. All of her fear about what was happening to Mella at the Sisterhood, her terror that they wouldn't find her in time, fueled her fists. She was shouting, too, but not words. Just incoherent noises.

Cai didn't fight back. He just put his hands up to protect himself as Lil bashed him again and again. She wanted to hit him so hard he would fly out of the atmosphere and land on the moon. No, she wanted to punch him right back in time so she could stop him before he got to Mella, so she could change that morning. *I'm awake, Mella. What do you want? Let's talk! Tell me what's wrong.*

Her aunt was saying her name over and over. Finally she grabbed Lil by the shoulders and pulled her gently but firmly back. "Let him speak, Lili," she said gently.

Lil was still angry, but she could see that what her aunt had said made sense, and besides, her hands hurt. No one ever told you how solid the human body was and how much it hurt to punch it. She was gasping and sweaty. Her fists shook at her sides and adrenaline lit up her body like a power station.

"What's this about, Cai?" Sabrina asked, voice icy. "We don't have time for you to mess about right now. When you say 'that morning,' do you mean the morning Mella went missing?"

Cai nodded. He rubbed his neck. "Does she have to be here?" He jerked a finger in Lil's direction. "Ain't a confession supposed to be private?"

"Is that what this is?" Sabrina asked. Her voice was calm, but Lil knew her aunt well enough to recognize the anger and fear in the twitch of her mouth.

"No!" Cai said. He rubbed his neck. "You know it's not. You found her now, so you know anything I say here—"

"Who told you we'd found her?" Sabrina asked.

Cai looked sheepish. "Overheard it, didn't I? Two police were talking and I just . . ."

Sabrina's lips had narrowed into two thin lines. "So this is why you've decided to talk to us now, because you think we found her, so whatever you say, whatever you did to her, doesn't matter?"

Cai shook his head as color rose to his cheeks. "It's not like that. I would have told you before, but . . . you guys were always on me. And she never liked me." He nodded at Lil. "She always wanted to blame me."

"Why do you think that is?" Lil said, the words exploding from her mouth. "You were horrible to Mella. You made her miserable!" *Horrible, miserable.* Lil sounded like a child. Cai had almost *destroyed* Mella.

"She was that way long before I came along," Cai said. "It's like my ma used to say: Some people are born happy. Some are born sad. You can make the sad ones happy for a while, but not forever. You can't change what they are."

"That isn't true!" Lil began. "Mella was fine before she met you." But she wasn't. They blamed Dad leaving; they blamed the fights before he left; they blamed the move to Wales. Mella had always been emotionally vulnerable, prone to ups and downs.

"I loved her!" he shouted. "You don't know anything about it. Always bitching about me. Turning her against me. It was you and the rest of the village sticking their nose in. 'He's a bad un, Melanie. Watch him, Melanie.' You're the ones that turned her. Caused rows and that."

Lil was so angry. She couldn't believe that Cai might have known something all this time and was only saying something now, and only because he thought they'd found her. "We didn't . . . at the hospital, it wasn't—"

"Right, Cai, you'd better start talking," Sabrina said, cutting her off. Lil read in her eyes that she didn't want Cai to know they hadn't found Mella.

"We don't have time for this," Lil said. Sabrina needed to get on with rescuing Mella from the Sisterhood.

"It's in hand, *cariad*," Sabrina said, pouring meaning into her words. "The wheels are in motion." She turned back to Cai. "Let's focus here," she said. "You say you spoke to her, Cai. When? Can you tell me exactly what time?"

"Is *she* going to stay?" He nodded in Lil's direction again.

The twitch by Sabrina's mouth got stronger. "We can continue this conversation in private down at the station, if you'd prefer. No? Then I suggest you start talking. Shall we go in here? Bit quieter." After she led them into the kitchen off the hall and shut the door, she said. "I know you and Mella had a turbulent relationship, but right now I only want to know about things if they are relevant to her disappearance. So, I say again, what time and where did you last see my niece?"

Cai sat down at the table and looked sheepish. "It were about seven a.m. or thereabouts, I reckon. Listen, what sort of trouble am I in for this?"

"That depends on what information you held back."

"I didn't do nothing to her, right. Not deliberate, anyway. She told you that, right? When you spoke to her today?"

Sabrina ignored his last question. "But you did lie when the police came to question you. You said you had not spoken to her since the previous afternoon. Are you now saying that isn't true?"

"Yeah, but I was scared. The way you lot get on to me, you can't hardly blame me."

"Cai, I'm happy to discuss any grievances you have with my team at a later point. But right now can you give me a full account of the last time you saw Melanie Laverty?"

Cai's eyes darted round the room, like he was looking for an exit. After a minute, as though he realized there wasn't one, he began to talk. "It was a mistake. I didn't mean it. It—it just got out of hand. Mella and me, we had our problems, but I loved her. You got to believe me."

Lil's heart was no longer bouncing around. It had curled up small and tight in the center of her chest. Sabrina's words came from far away. "Did you hurt her? Is that what you're saying?"

Mella. Lil gave a wail, and Sabrina put her arms around her and held her tight. "What happened, Cai?" Sabrina asked, voice shaking.

Cai began to talk. His sentences were jerky and hard to understand, but after a while it began to make sense. Mella had called Cai on the night of Lil's sixteenth birthday at around midnight, after the row with Lil's mum where she stormed out of the house. *After I told her to go*, Lil added in her head. She'd asked if she could stay with him. He'd been at the Castle Pub, drinking. He and Mella argued when he said he wouldn't go straight home. "I'd just bought a round." Then, come closing time, the barmaid there, a girl called Susie, told him he was too drunk to drive home and drove him herself. She then went into his trailer for a coffee, "because it was late and dark and I didn't want her crashing or something when she drove back to hers."

Mella called him again, he thought, around two o'clock. There was another fight. He didn't want her coming over because "Susie was there, weren't she, and Mella might get the wrong idea." *Or the right one*, Lil thought. He couldn't remember exactly what they'd said, but it was ugly. Mella had hung up on him.

When Sabrina asked what time Susie left, Cai shifted uncomfortably. "After . . . after the argument with Mella, I was kind of wound up and . . . well, Susie was sweet. She listened to me and said all the right things. I don't know . . . it was stupid, really stupid, one of the dumbest things I ever did."

Lil was so angry she was shaking, and a vein pulsed in Sabrina's neck.

"Then there's this banging on the door," Cai said. "It was the next morning—early—before seven. I don't know exactly what time, and it's Mella. And she's saying sorry and she's trying to kiss me . . . and Susie . . . well, Susie's right inside the trailer in my bed. . . . I know that I've made a massive mistake, and I just want to forget the whole thing ever happened. I tell Mella: 'Let's go for a walk. Stay out there. I'll get my shoes.' She's suspicious, 'cause why do I want to go for a walk at half past six or whatever in the morning?

"Then she gets this look in her eye, like she knows, and she tries to get into the trailer . . . and I . . . I don't want her to, because Susie is inside, and I just think if she doesn't know, it'll be all right. I'll never do anything so stupid again." Cai broke off then. His eyes were distant, like he was back four months ago. When Sabrina asked what happened next, to prompt him, he jumped, like he'd forgotten they were there. Lil was wound tight: both desperate to hear the rest of the story and afraid to.

"So Mella tries to get inside, like she knows Sue's there, and so I put my hands out, just to stop her, like, but I'm too strong or something, because she falls back and she knocks her head on the patio table and then there's all this blood. I've never seen so much blood. She's shouting that I . . . punched her. But I never! She just walked into my fist, you know. Then Susie comes out and she's standing there in one of my T-shirts. Nothing else. She puts a hand on my arm. I shake it off quick, but Mella sees it and she knows. She's shouting so much. I think that maybe if I let her go, she'll calm down and then we can talk and she'll forgive me."

He looked up, his eyes red rimmed. "I swear that was the last time I saw her. I swear it." And he broke down, his face collapsing like melting wax. "I know I messed up. I should have told you ages ago. I just needed a few days to get my head around it. I thought she'd calm down. If I gave her time. Then I heard that no one had seen her, and you guys were checking my trailer, asking all these questions. I knew if I told you I spoke to her, you wouldn't believe that it was an accident. You'd think I was lying. That I did something to her. I wouldn't. I loved her." He dropped his face into his hands. "I loved her so much."

When the Light is upon you, it burns in
your fingers, in your toes, in your veins,
in your soul, in your heart.

—The Book

✷

M ella had lost count of the hours they'd been in the
Great Hall. It was impossible to guess the time
with the thick curtains pulled across the windows. The
Sun's fire burned on endlessly, and Moon continued her
whispering. She made no attempt to talk to Mella or the
other sisters. Mella's ankle throbbed and her tongue was
a sponge in her mouth. She'd never been so thirsty.

Aside from Moon's whispering, the room was largely
silent. Mella could feel the sisters' eyes on her from time
to time, but no one spoke to her. She didn't know what
they were thinking. Were they terrified as well and all
wishing they'd never come here? Or were they desperate
for sunset and the Brightness? Mella couldn't stop thinking about Dazzle and the others. Had they made it out?
They must have done, surely, otherwise they'd be here
too. Or had something happened to them?

"I just don't get it," Mella said. "You knew what would
happen to Dazzle, but you did nothing to stop it."

"We all have our duty in the Light," Luster added quietly.

"That's rubbish," Mella said, amazed at the force of her anger.

Luster flinched. "You're a new sister. It's hard to understand."

But Mella did understand. She was just sick of people here blaming the Light for their actions and expecting some other force to come along and take control of their lives. Then it hit her: That's what she'd been doing her whole life. How many times had she said, *There has to be more than this? There has to be a purpose. We can't just be on our own, responsible for our own screwups.* Because that was terrifying. Not to believe in a grand plan, to believe you utterly controlled your own destiny, was what Mella had been most afraid of. She wanted a safety net. No, she wanted someone else, *something* else, to blame when things went wrong. *It's not my fault, it's written in the stars, it's my horoscope, or my tarot, or God, or Cai, or my mum, or even Lil.* And finally, it was the Light.

"We control our fates," she thought now with absolute certainty. "We make our own choices; God or whatever doesn't do that for us."

Cai had been a jerk that morning. All the mornings, in fact, and the afternoons. He was just a jerk. She still remembered how he'd knocked her out of the way, so keen to hide that bloody Susie from her. Mella had been angry with Lil for not listening to her when she needed to talk. But it had been Mella's choice to go and to stay gone, to avoid humiliation, to avoid saying sorry, and most of all to avoid having to face up to what a mess her life had become. It hit her hard to realize suddenly how her actions must have hurt her mum and Lil. *Oh, Mouse,* she thought. *I'm so, so sorry. I put too much on you.* She'd always expected her sister to cheer her up, to make it better. She'd never given a thought to how difficult that must have been for Lil. What a toxic sister she must have been sometimes.

"*We* make our own choices and then we have to stick by them," she repeated more firmly.

Luster cupped Mella's cheek. "Maybe you're right. Or maybe there is some greater force involved than you realize. You once said you didn't feel anything you did made a difference. You wanted to know what your purpose was. I hope you found it tonight."

Mella was surprised. Was it true? Had she done that? Her desperate search for answers, for meaning, for purpose, had led her here. But was here exactly where she'd needed to be? She smiled at Luster. She felt something unfurl inside her, blossoming like a flower, beautiful and fragile. It was a sense of belonging she'd never had before. Not to a place but to herself.

Chapter Twenty-One

After what Cai had told them, Sabrina insisted Lil let her talk to him alone. "It's important that I get all the details down, Lils. Because of the conflict of interest, I'll need to get Officer Burnley as a witness." She stroked her niece's cheek. "I promise to tell you everything I can, all right?"

Lil nodded. She was numb, like someone could set fire to her and she wouldn't even notice. She winced. That was a bad analogy. She'd found out so much today and didn't know how to process it all. Lil sat down on the floor of the little entranceway to the village hall, unable to make the decision of whether to go inside or outside. She was exhausted, mentally and physically. Knees up, she let her head drop against them.

Cai had seen Mella after she left home, and he hadn't said anything. In over four months. He'd only spoken up now because he thought they'd found her. He thought he was safe, free from blame.

Mella hadn't intended to leave like she did. She only

planned to stay at Cai's for a bit until everything calmed down, like always. But Cai hurt her, humiliated her, and rather than admit the truth—that Cai was a waste of space and their mum had been right—Mella stayed away. That was why she hadn't come back. Right? Because of Cai, not because of what Lil had said. Lil rolled the idea around in her head, trying to make it fit. It didn't. Cai was a crappy boyfriend. He was always going to let Mella down, but Lil was her sister; she should have been there for her.

Whatever Cai said, it wasn't love that he'd felt for Mella. You didn't treat someone you loved like that. You didn't make her feel guilty for seeing her friends or talking to other boys. Nor cheat on her and finally hit her. But— and the thought brought Lil up short—maybe it had been love, from Cai's point of view, because he didn't know any better. How much love had he been given? Not a lot, probably. From what Lil knew of his background, he'd experienced a pretty rubbish childhood and now wasn't in touch with either of his parents. To be only nineteen and living alone in a trailer must be pretty bad, although before it had just made him seem grown up. "He has his own place," Mella would say. None of that was any excuse, though.

And—this was hard to admit—Mella had been unhappy before Cai. "We're concerned about Mella," a letter from school would say. "We'd like to discuss the possibility of weekly meetings with the school guidance counselor. We think Mella might benefit from some one-on-one support on how to manage her anxiety and emotions." The head of school requested a meeting with Lil's mum. "Such a drama queen," Mum said of Mella, and she blamed their dad for leaving, and then the move to Wales, and finally Cai. But those were all surface things. They affected Mella, sure, but it was more than that. "I hate being inside my head," Mella would say. "I just want . . . I want out of it. To be quiet, you know. It's never just quiet in here." And she jabbed her forehead. Lil didn't know what to do, because how did you help someone whose own head was a dangerous and frightening place? So she ignored it, pretended everything was okay. Mella was just a bit sad. Mella did love the drama. She'd be fine. In a little while, she'd be happy again. But she never was.

Lil was consumed with guilt, she was drowning in it, and it was hard to breathe. They could have stopped this. Her and Mum and Sabrina. If only they'd listened, if only they'd *seen* how much Mella was suffering. If only they'd stopped blaming everything else and really, *really* asked Mella what she wanted, what she needed.

Oh God, Mella. I'm so, so sorry. If she ever got Mella back, she would never ignore her pain again. Lil would help her in whatever way she could, because no one deserved to hate being in her own head. Lil would find a way to make it better for Mella.

If she ever got Mella back.

If.

Only two letters, but their meaning was devastating.

Lil gripped her knees, remembering the conversation she had with Sabrina a few months ago. It was three weeks after Mella left. "She'll be back for Mum's birthday," Lil said. "I know she will."

Sabrina turned her face away from her, trying to hide the tears in her eyes.

Lil touched her aunt's shoulder. "She'll be back. She *will*."

Sabrina gave a half nod, then rubbed her eyes. She took Lil's hand, holding it tight in her own. After a long while she said, "Lili, hope is good. It's important to believe in Mella, but . . . at some point you might have to face up to the fact . . . Mella was very unhappy before she left. . . ."

"No," Lil said. *"No." Not that. Never that. Please.*

"Cariad, we couldn't find any leads on where she might have gone. There's no evidence that anyone is holding your sister against her will. You know this. We searched the woods around your home, the mountains, everywhere. Nothing. It was like . . . like she just vanished."

"But she's coming back!" Lil almost screamed the words. "The fact that you couldn't find anything doesn't mean . . . it doesn't mean . . . She *is* coming back. She is. She *is*."

"Of course, sweet pea, of course." There was no conviction in Sabrina's voice, and Lil felt despair creeping up inside her. They'd been dancing around this conversation since Mella left, but still Lil hadn't been able to accept it. Her sister was not dead. She had not killed herself. She hadn't been that unhappy. They would have known—but would they, really? And would they have taken enough notice? The idea terrified Lil and she buried it deep inside her, never to think about again. She couldn't bear it.

Sabrina kept talking, softly, about preparing for the future, moving on, just in case. Her voice was soft but her words were too sharp, like a knife slipping under Lil's rib cage.

Chapter Twenty-Two

Someone nudged Lil's leg, and she looked up.

Kiran.

Lil stood up and threw her arms around him with such force that she flung them both back against the wall.

"Oof," Kiran said. "Wow. Do I have a terminal disease that only you know about?"

Lil didn't answer. She squirmed closer, breathing in his Kiran scent of Lynx deodorant, lemons, and Tri-Flow, the stuff he used to keep his kayak rust-free. He hugged her back, and they stood like that for a long time. After a while Kiran whispered, "So what am I dying of? Is it something cool? Like I was in a fight with a shark?"

Lil laughed and pulled away. "I needed to see you. I just didn't realize until I saw you."

He touched her hand, sliding his fingers through hers. The weight of them felt good, warm. She held on, heart pounding. What was she doing? After what Kiran said earlier, it was clear how he felt about her, and this wasn't fair. She didn't know what she wanted. She gently let her fingers drop away from Kiran's. The movement was awkward and unsubtle and Kiran felt it.

"Oh," he said, an involuntary sound, and he took his hand back.

Lil cringed. "Sorry, I . . . I just . . ." She just what? "I don't want to hurt you," she finished finally.

"So don't."

"It isn't that . . . simple. I . . . I . . . you know what I said before about you and me and about you being . . . nice?" *I meant incredible, amazing.*

"You're going to say I'm not nice?" Kiran asked. His tone was light, but Lil could hear the hurt underneath it, the embarrassment.

"No! Of course not. You are nice, *so nice*. It's just with Mella and . . . everything . . ."

"It's okay, Lil." He ran his hand through his hair nervously, avoiding her gaze. "I get it. I didn't mean to . . . to push you or make you feel awkward. I care about you."

I care about you, too, Lil said, but only in her head. A voice was screaming at her. It sounded a bit like Mella. *Tell him! Tell him, you idiot!* Lil didn't know how, and she didn't want to risk hurting Kiran or making a mess of stuff. She just needed to find Mella, and then everything would be clear.

"I'm sorry," Lil said finally, again, because that seemed to be her default response to everything.

Kiran smiled his crooked smile, and the sight of it sent her brain into a spin. "It's okay." There was a pause, and then with a monumental effort that made Lil's heart swell so much it almost exploded out of her chest, because she knew he was doing it for her, to make her feel okay, he said, feigning lightness, "So, Lilster, why you hanging out in the corridor?"

Lil drew a deep breath and then it all tumbled out in a gush: Cai, the girl at the hospital not being Mella.

Kiran was silent for a moment, and Lil had to remind herself that even at times like this, Kiran's responses were always considered. Finally he swore. Loudly. Maybe "considered" was too strong.

"Yeah," Lil said. She slid down the wall to sit on the floor again.

Kiran sat next to her. "I mean . . ." He swore again. "I just . . ." He ran his hand through his hair, making it stand on end. "Lil. I'm sorry . . . I can't . . ."

"It's okay." It wasn't, but Lil felt she needed to say something.

"I can't imagine how you felt seeing that girl . . . and it not being Mella."

Lil drew her knees up to her chest and wrapped her arms tightly around them. Kiran put his hand over hers, very lightly, just for a second, but the warmth of his skin fizzed through her. That touch said more than any words.

They sat side by side for a while in silence, and then finally Kiran said, "I can't believe Cai. Seriously, what a . . ." He cut himself off. "Well, you know." He gave another crooked smile, which made Lil smile. Swearing three times in one conversation was clearly too much for Kiran. He was such a dork, a gorgeous, lovable dork.

"Why didn't Susie tell anyone?" he asked.

"They agreed it was better to keep quiet, apparently. Avoid trouble. I get the impression Susie would do anything for Cai. The idiot." Lil sounded so bitter. She didn't really hate Cai and she certainly didn't hate Susie. Cai was what he'd always been, and he'd done to Mella what he was always going to do.

Why didn't you tell me, Mells, how much you were hurting? Why did you have to be so proud and stubborn? she asked in her mind. *Why didn't you make me see that you needed help?*

I am who I am, sugar. A duck can't change its spots.

Leopard, Mells. Ducks don't have spots.

Huh. Not even teenage ones? Mella laughed loudly.

Humor. Another thing Mella hid behind, and Lil had let her, because it had been easier than facing the truth.

"So Mella isn't at the Sisterhood?" Kiran asked, interrupting Lil's train of thought.

"No, she is. At least we think so." Lil brought him up to speed with what Dazzle had said. "I'm so scared, K. What if something already happened? What if—"

"Don't think it; it's going to be fine. Sabrina'll go marching in there, and she'll sort it."

Lil nodded. "I hope so," she said quietly. There was a muddy stain on the jeans Sabrina had lent her, and she scratched at it with her nail. "I hear her sometimes," she said quickly before she changed her mind. "Mella. I mean, in my head." She didn't look up. She was too afraid to see Kiran's expression.

"I used to talk to my mum too," Kiran said gently.

"After she died. I just couldn't get my head around the fact that she was gone—I'd never see her again—so I imagined that she was still with me. I'd tell her stuff, about my day and that. I still do it sometimes."

"This is more than that," Lil said. "This is, like, whole conversations. I actually *hear* her. I'm worried I'm going crazy."

"Hey," Kiran said, "hey, look at me. You're not crazy. Seriously, Lil, look at me." Lil raised her head. Kiran's eyes were shining with understanding, full of kindness and love. "Whatever makes it easier is fine. It doesn't mean you're crazy."

Lil wanted to tell him how guilty she felt for being angry with Mella that night. But she didn't have the words, and she was too scared that Kiran would hate her for it.

"Come on," Kiran said, "let's get some fresh air."

"We should find Seven. She'll want to know what's happened, and maybe she can help. She knows the compound better than anyone. The more the police know about the place, the easier it'll be to find Mella and get everyone out safely."

As they stood up, Kiran pulling Lil to her feet, Sabrina reappeared. She looked harassed.

"Everything okay with Cai?" Lil asked. "You get his story down?"

Sabrina nodded but was clearly distracted; she barely seemed to register Lil's question.

"Are you okay?" Lil asked. "Has something happened?" She was fearful suddenly. "Is it Mella?"

Sabrina hesitated and then said, "I don't want you to panic, but . . . it looks like we're going to have to wait a bit longer before we go up to the Sisterhood."

It was a punch in the stomach. "What? No. No! You've got to go. Now!"

Sabrina shook her head. "We're really short on officers, and this sort of operation requires top-level people. We're severely understaffed, and some of the phone lines are still down, which is making it even harder."

"Don't they realize how serious this is?" Kiran asked. "Lil told me everything. . . ."

Lil was grateful to him for speaking up. "Yes," she added. "They've got to know how important this is! What Moon is planning! Sabrina!"

"This is the highest priority. I've got everyone working on it. It won't be long. Trust me." Her phone rang, and Sabrina made an apologetic gesture as she walked back into the kitchen. "Hello? . . . Yes. . . . Right. . . . Can you say that again? You're breaking up. . . ." Her voice was lost as she closed the door.

"I can't believe this," Lil said. "How can the police not get the seriousness of it?" Kiran touched her shoulder and she turned into him, tears burning her throat. "I can't lose her, Kiran. I can't, not again, not again."

Kiran held her, and Lil wanted him to carry on doing it forever. A series of images ran through her mind: Cai knocking Mella to the ground; Mella, bloodied and tearful, at a train station; Moon picking her up, promising her a safe place. Mella screaming as the flames rose up . . .

There was a movement behind them. Lil turned to see Seven standing in the doorway.

"The police won't go up there," Seven said. There was no question in her voice.

"You know? About Dazzle and what she said?" Lil asked.

"Officer Burnley told me. I should never have left them. What have I done? Oh, by the Light."

An idea began to form in Lil's mind. It was crazy, more than crazy: dangerous, stupid, reckless, and Sabrina would be absolutely furious. Yet once it was there, the thought grew, taking root in her brain.

"Let's go. The three of us," she said quietly. "To the compound. Just to check on them. I think I know the way. If it's right by Cragen Beach. I've been there loads, and we might even be able to get into the compound. We can scope it out. Call the police. Hey, we could even sneak in! Rescue Mella and whoever else ourselves."

There was a second's silence as Kiran and Seven took in what she'd said.

"Please," Lil said. "I have to do this. I . . . wasn't there for Mella before. I can't let that happen again. Seven, I know—"

Seven cut her off. "I will help you. Perhaps I can even save them. If I am truly the Light's Gift, She will guide me."

"You still believe . . . even after . . . everything?" Kiran asked.

"Yes," Seven said solemnly. "It is the Darkness that has

led the high priestess astray. The Light is good and pure and true, and it is everywhere out here, in this world that I was never meant to see. Recreants are not dangerous." She grinned. "They are you, Lil, and you, Kiran. The Light loves you, too. She led me to you." As if in response to her words, although Lil knew that was impossible, sunlight flooded the hallway. A star of pure white light, it turned the linoleum floor from gray to gold.

They all gasped, and Seven smiled. "See?" she said.

"It's just the sun," Lil said. "The rain's stopped, so it was bound to come out eventually." In her head, though, she was thinking how beautiful even this dank hallway looked in the sunshine. She remembered how the light had shone when she and Seven first met. It was stupid, impossible, and yet something in her wanted to believe just a little bit.

Kiran reluctantly agreed to drive them to the compound but almost changed his mind when Lil told him how they were going to get there. They were going to take her aunt's car, which was parked up against the fence. Her little Peugeot, thankfully. Kiran would definitely have refused to drive an actual police patrol car. It would be easy. Sabrina never locked it—no one did in Porthpridd—and she kept a spare set of car keys taped to the inside of the glove compartment.

"Your aunt the police officer's car?" Kiran said, his voice going very high pitched.

"Yup."

"Your aunt the police officer, who has given you full

permission to drive her car and head up to a potential hostage situation?"

"Sure, yes," Lil said. "If that makes you feel better."

Kiran groaned.

"Look at it this way," Lil said. "It'll put the whole you-drove-your-dad's-car-into-a-river thing into perspective."

Chapter Twenty-Three

Lil, Kiran, and Seven drove for a long time, partly because they needed nonflooded routes and partly because none of them could read the printed map in Sabrina's car. "There's no arrow thing to tell you where you are," Kiran said.

"It's a book!" Lil replied. "It doesn't have GPS!"

"Well, it should," Kiran muttered, turning the map around for the hundredth time.

Lil was just glad they'd managed to sneak out of the village hall and drive away without anyone noticing. As they crossed the parking lot, Lil kept expecting someone to stop them. No one did. The vicar's wife even waved at them as she passed, arms full of blankets. "Your aunt inside?" she asked.

Lil nodded without looking back, hoping that Sabrina's telephone call was a long one.

"What happens when we get to this beach?" Kiran asked now. "Are we going to be able to find the compound?"

"I'm hoping Seven will remember the way," Lil said quietly. She was in the front passenger seat beside Kiran,

Seven was in the back. She was quiet most of the journey, staring out the window, but Lil was certain she wasn't taking in the scenery. What was she thinking? The last time she'd come along these roads, she'd been running for her life. "Do you recognize anything?" Lil asked her.

Seven took a moment to answer, turning to Lil slowly, as if coming from very far away. "No," she said. "I'm sorry. It was completely dark when I ran, and I was very scared." She gazed up at the sky. "I am asking the Light for guidance."

Great, Lil thought, and exchanged a glance with Kiran.

"We'll just keep driving," Kiran said as they passed a sign for Cragen Beach. "Up every road and lane there is around here until we find it."

How did she get so lucky to have a Kiran in her life? "Thank you," she whispered, grateful he was here.

Kiran only nodded, but his eyes were full of meaning: *Anything for you*, they said.

Lil colored and turned away. There was no point denying how she felt about him.

Finally! Mella said in her head. *Kiss him already!*

Lil blushed deeper. *Not yet. Not until you're safe.* Everything would wait until then.

Oh, Mouse. What if I'm . . . ?

Then everything will be over, and the certainty of that struck Lil with the force of a gale.

Seven gave a shout and Lil turned around. "What?" she asked, frightened.

"There!" Seven cried. "There! That road. I remember. *I remember!*"

They'd just passed an overgrown lane, and Kiran did a U-turn to drive back to it.

"Are you sure?" Lil asked. The path was nearly identical to about seventy million other ones they'd passed in the last hour or so.

"Yes," Seven said. "Look. The Light!" The clouds had broken overhead, and Lil didn't know how it was possible, but a shaft of light was spiking the trees over them. Like a finger, it pointed down that road. She exchanged another glance with Kiran. His eyebrows were so far up his head it was a wonder they hadn't disappeared. But he took the turning without saying anything; Seven sounded so sincere, and what else did they have to go on but her memory? *And her faith*, Lil added silently.

The fading evening sunlight caught Lil full in the face, warming her. She drew a breath. The tension in her neck eased, and she felt hope for the first time since the journey to the hospital. It felt good to finally do something. She was going to find Mella. She was going to bring her home. She thought about what Seven had said back at the village hall, about the power of the Light. *Help me find my sister*, she said in her head. *Please. Please.*

After driving only a short way down the road, they came to a pair of gates.

Kiran drew the car to a stop. "This it?" he asked.

"Yes," Seven said.

There was a handwritten sign on one of the gates. It was covered in a plastic envelope to protect it from the weather, but the ink had still run: WELCOME TO THE LIGHT. Beyond the gates the road carried on, deep in shadow, even though it wouldn't be dark for another four hours or so. Lil was glad of the daylight. There was something creepy about this place, which Lil would have expected, given everything that had happened here. But it was more than that somehow: an energy seeped into the trees, into the ground, even into the air. Seven made the Light sound good, but how could something like that come from this place? Evil seemed etched in the very gravel of the overgrown driveway.

"So what's the plan now?" Kiran asked, and his voice, jovial and aiming for brightness, sounded too loud in the small car. "Storm the castle? Save the princess. Princesses?"

"I don't know. I hadn't really gotten past 'Get here,'" said Lil. Her eyes flickered over the gateway again. Was someone watching them? Was someone standing in the shadow of that road waiting for them? Goose bumps broke out on her arms.

"You want to drive up to the house?" Kiran asked, his tone lower now, almost a whisper, as though he was scared of drawing unwanted attention.

"We should walk," Seven said. "We will be quieter. It is better if Moon does not anticipate our arrival."

Her words hung heavy. It was reckless coming here like this. Who knew what they would find? But Mella needed her, and so Lil was going to help her, come what may.

The three of them agreed to park up on the road and walk the rest of the way. Lil was on edge, torn between not wanting to leave the safety of the car and her urge to get to the Sisterhood, to find Mella as quickly as possible.

After leaving the car on a nearby bank, they headed back

to the gates. Seven walked a little ahead. There was a determination in her now: A strength Lil hadn't imagined existed in her tiny frame. "The Light wants me to save our sisters," she said.

"You all right?" Kiran asked Lil.

She wasn't. Who could be? But she nodded anyway and gave a small smile. She touched him fleetingly on the shoulder. "I'm glad you're here."

He nodded and said softly, "Always."

Seven called, and the two of them hurried to catch up.

The uneven path was overshadowed with trees. It was hard to keep a firm footing, and one or another of them kept stumbling. Lil tripped over a pothole and landed heavily, scraping both her knees. The other two helped her up and she gave a hiss of pain. Both her knees hurt, and she was sure she could feel blood dripping down her leg. "I'm all right. Let's keep going." She was eager to get to the house, to find Mella, and to get off this path. The wind picked up and was blowing through the trees and making the branches hum. Every now and then there was a rustle in the undergrowth nearby: an animal, obviously, but Lil couldn't get rid of the sense that someone was following them, edging closer and closer.

There was another noise, right behind them now, and Lil increased her pace, wincing at the pain in her knees. They kept going for what felt like a long time, barely talking, and anything they did say was so quiet it wasn't even a whisper, just a breath. After a while they turned a corner on the drive and the way ahead was brighter. The trees were less dense, and through them Lil could see a lighter patch in the dark. The moon, she thought at first, although that made no sense because it was too early.

Then they took a final twist in the road and came out into the open. The house stood before them. It was enormous and old, and beautiful. Ivy ran like veins over its Welsh stone walls and around its many paned windows. It had three arched gables, each one topped with some sort of stone sculpture. The building looked like something out of a Jane Austen novel. No, from *Jane Eyre*. They'd studied that in school, and Lil could imagine Bertha Mason peering out from a small attic window.

"How did you get this place?" Lil breathed. She'd imagined a run-down old farmhouse, or just outbuildings. Nothing as grand as this.

"It was gifted to the Light by one of the sisters. It had been in her family for generations."

"It's immense," Kiran said, and whistled.

"And very cold in winter," Seven said. "Come. We must hurry—"

A scream shredded the early-evening sky. Shrill and sharp and terrified. For a second Lil thought her imagination was now a reality. This was Rochester's house, on the night of the fire. Then with a horror that turned her insides to water, she realized this was much worse than that. This was real. The sky turned a livid red. There was another cry.

"Fire!" Seven shouted.

Lil broke into a run, with Kiran and Seven tearing after her.

"If you follow me," saith the Light,
"I must consume all that you are."

—THE BOOK

At last Moon stood and turned to face the women gathered silently in front of her. A smile slithered across her face, malevolent as a snake; her teeth glittered unnaturally in the firelight. "I have made my peace with the Light. She is ready to accept our sacrifice. Come, my sisters! The flames await us."

As she spoke, one of the sisters began to sing: "I dance with the fire in my heart, in my soul, in my veins. I dance until it rises up for me. I dance into the Brightness. Into the Light." Evanescence and some of the others joined in, their voices mingling to become a wail.

"Please," Mella said, hating herself for begging but not able to help it. Her mind was whirring with ways to stop this. "Please don't do this!"

"You're afraid, sister," Moon said. "I understand. You have doubts and so you fear the fire. If you are a true sister, the flames will embrace you tenderly, lulling you to sleep. Otherwise, I cannot vouch for the Light's gentleness. As you saw with our sister Dazzle, the Light only cleanses those pure of soul; in others the Darkness must be burned out." Her voice rose to a shriek, like that of an owl before it swoops on its prey.

"High Priestess," cried one of the other women, "please! We don't want to die."

Another woman—Mella thought she was called Luminescence—nodded. "The Light loves us. Surely, there's another way."

"No other way," Moon screamed. "I will bring my sisters from Darkness into Light for eternity. We *will* enter the Brightness." With that, she picked up the Light's orb and flung it against the wall. The glass smashed in a shriek of fire. There was a second's pause and then the flames shot up the curtains and ate up the wooden floorboards. Stretching, stretching, stretching until all was fire and heat.

Chapter Twenty-Four

Lil moved more quickly than ever before. She was close enough to the house now to see the fire. Flames peeped over the crescent of the roof, and smoke rose like tarred feathers. She ran on, faster and faster, until the other two fell back behind her. Her stomach was solid with fear. She was dimly aware that running headlong toward a burning building was idiotic, but she didn't care.

She could feel the heat now, a slow, steady burn that was getting stronger, as was the smoke. It caught in her throat, making her cough. She tried to quell her panic. Where was her sister? Had she escaped? Was this fire an accident?

No!

This was no accident.

"Moon," Seven said breathlessly, drawing up alongside Lil, as if reading her mind. "Moon did this!"

They were at the back of the house and could see the fire pulsing inside like a red heart. It was mainly concentrated on the ground floor, in what looked like one long room that ran most of the length of the back of the house. Behind the tall, narrow windows the fire burned in shades of orange, flickering and dancing with its own heat.

"Do you think anyone is trapped in there?" Lil asked.

Seven's silence said it all.

Mella? Lil screamed in her mind. *Mella! Are you there?*

Silence.

I'm coming for you. Hold on. Hold on. Lil sent the thought out into the burning house, and in her mind it flew through the smoke-filled corridors, a flash of white, like the wings of a bird.

She stared at the building, trying to work out how to get in. Perhaps if they could break a window . . . Then: "Oh my God," she said. "There are bars on the windows! How will they get out?"

"They'll try to come out the other way," Kiran said. "Through the house, to the front." He was standing a little farther back, his dark eyes glittering and scared, caught in the firelight. "The rest of the house isn't on fire yet."

"They won't be able to," Seven said. "Moon will have locked them in. It's the Illumination ceremony. Everyone must pass through the Sun's fire. She must have found another path, a way to reach the Brightness without me."

"We have to do something!" Lil said.

"We can't go any closer," Kiran said. "It's too dangerous."

"So we just stand here and *watch*?" Lil screamed. They had been so stupid coming here like this, with no plan as to how they were actually going to help, just a vague notion to check it out. No one even knew where they were. *Idiot, idiot, idiot.* "What are we going to do?" she asked desperately.

Seven shook her head, the flames reflected in her wide, unblinking eyes.

"I'll get help," Kiran said.

"How?" Lil asked. "We've got no phones!"

"I'll run back to the car, drive to the nearest village."

"There's no time!"

"We have to try, Lil," Kiran said calmly.

He was right. Panicking wasn't helping anyone. They may have been foolish coming here, but they were here now and they were the only hope for those women trapped inside that building. They were Mella's only hope. "Yes," she said, reluctant to see him leave but knowing it was their best chance at getting help. "Go. Go."

"I'll be as quick as I can. Don't do anything brave when I'm gone. Okay?" His eyes held Lil's for less than a second, but it was enough. *I love you.*

Lil met his stare. *I love you, too.*

Then he was gone, hurtling over the grass.

Lil turned back to the house. The fire was vast. Even in the time they'd been standing there, it had spread across much of the ground floor in this part of the house. Perhaps by going around the building, they might find a window without bars, a place the fire hadn't hit yet. Maybe they could get inside. Then they could try to find something to break down the door of the room at the back, and start trying to get people out.

Lil shouted to Seven, telling her what she was going to do. Seven nodded, and the two of them edged around the house, looking for a way in. The smoke was thicker now, dropping over everything like a veil and making it hard to see and harder still to breathe. It scorched Lil's eyes and coated her throat, making her hack, and each time she did, she dragged more of it down into her lungs. She pulled her sleeve over her hand and put it to her mouth.

The flames were hotter too; they were a good ten meters away, and it was like standing in front of an open oven. It seemed impossible that they were going to get close enough to break a window.

Everyone inside will be dead before Kiran even makes it to the car.

The thought made Lil want to drop to the ground and cry, but she couldn't. She had to find a way in. She had to do *something.* As she passed around the side of the building, miraculously the smoke cleared a bit. Up ahead, near the front, she could see a part of the house that the fire didn't seem to have reached. She ran for it, and when she got there, she realized that it was an annex, with a tall, narrow window in it. Peering in, she could see what looked like a storeroom, with sacks, boxes, and bags on the floor. There was no fire.

Getting through the window would be a squeeze, but Lil reckoned she could just about manage it. She ignored the part of her brain that was screaming at her not to go into a building that was on fire, and she tried to open the window. It was a sash one and the wood was rotting.

After a couple of attempts she was able to shove the lower part up, the lock splintering and then giving way. Seven stood behind her, watching silently. "Is it safe?" she asked.

"Probably not. But I don't know what else to do."

"I will fit better."

"No," Lil said. "I'll do it." This was her stupid idea; no one else should put themselves in danger.

She was scared, though. It could be an hour before Kiran managed to raise the alarm, and what if Lil got trapped in there? The thought of the fire made her legs weak, but Mella was already in there, and Lil couldn't just leave her.

"What will you do when you get inside?" Seven asked.

"I don't know. Maybe I can get the door to that room open. Get them out . . ." Lil trailed off. If she thought about this too rationally, she wouldn't do anything at all.

She pulled herself up onto the window ledge and then eased herself through sideways, before dropping down onto the other side. The room beyond was hot, small, and smoky, but nothing like the density of smoke at the other side of the house. She moved toward the wooden door.

She should have known what was waiting for her when she touched the handle. It was burning hot. Still, her brain didn't register and she pushed the door open, saying to Seven over her shoulder, "I'll check if it's safe and then you can fo—"

She got no further. As she opened the door, the heat was immense, taking her breath away and blasting her skin. She fell back as the fire that had been raging down the corridor beyond gave a giant roar and ducked into the room, licking the paint off the walls and surging up to the ceiling.

Lil screamed and scrambled back toward the window. Feet scrabbling up the wall, she tried to get out, but the window seemed to have shrunk in size, and she couldn't work out how she'd ever made it through. Seven was shouting her name, and Lil turned to watch the flames rush toward her: the red, the purple, the blue. A kaleidoscope of color. It was almost beautiful if you didn't think about what was burning. If you didn't think what it meant.

I'm going to die here.

Above the sound of crackling flames came voices, and running feet, and sirens. Seven was crying out, yelling for someone to come and help. Suddenly hands grabbed Lil, tearing her through the window, ripping her sweater on the rotten wood, but dragging her out of the pall of smoke and into the clear evening air. Lil gulped down mouthful after mouthful like she was drowning.

"Can you hear me? Are you hurt?" a voice said.

Lil looked up. A female firefighter was standing over her. Lil had no idea how Kiran had raised the alarm so quickly, but she didn't care. "You're here!" she said.

The woman gave a serious smile. "Just in time, by the looks of it. Can you tell me what's happened here? Are there more people trapped inside?"

"Yes! At the back of the house. In that long room. It was started on purpose—the fire. You have to help them. My sister's in there!"

"Okay," the woman said. "Okay. I'm Stacey Curby, the watch manager here. Can you tell me your name?"

"Lil." Her voice shook with adrenaline and fear. She could hear the fire roaring at her back.

"Okay, Lil." Stacey gestured for one of the other firefighters to join them. There were four of them on this side of the building, working to rig up a hose from the fire engine. "There are people inside," she told him when he came over. "You okay to get on sorting the breathing apparatus? Look for a route in. The front, probably. Ask Rob to get on the radio to the station. We're going to need all the reserves we can get, and tell him to see what he can do about the water supply. We've only got what's in the engine at the moment."

The man nodded. "There's a lot of floodwater down the valley. Might be able to set up a pump. I'm on it." He ran off, shouting for two men to follow him as he headed back to the fire engine.

Stacey turned back to Lil. "I need as much detail as you can give me. Anything, however small, could save lives. What was the situation inside? Were you able to determine the source and location of the fire? How many people are in there? Where are they?"

"I don't know much. I was trying to get in, not out."

"You were trying to get in?" Stacey sounded incredulous. "In there?"

"I was scared no one was coming. I couldn't leave my sister."

Stacey's eyes darkened with compassion. "I understand

how worried you must be, but going into a building without proper equipment is very dangerous. Where is your sister located? How many people are with her?"

Lil explained as quickly as she could about the Sisterhood, how Moon had started the fire. "She locked them in that room at the back," she said. "The one with the bars. Seven will know more."

Seven was standing quietly beside Lil, but she stepped forward at her name and answered Stacey's questions about layout with more detail than Lil would have believed possible. She was obviously scared and worried for her sisters, but a calmness, a sense of purpose, seemed to have taken her over. As Stacey's questions came more rapidly, Seven's answers grew more fluid and even more direct.

As they were talking, there was the sound of an engine behind them and a police car drew up. A moment or two later Sabrina got out. *"Diolch i Dduw . . . ,"* she said, clutching Lil to her.

Stacey and Sabrina exchanged introductions. "We reckon there's up to fifteen women trapped inside," Sabrina said. "One definitely escaped. Some others might have too, but we can't say for sure."

Stacey nodded. "We're getting ready to go in." Her radio crackled, and she held up a hand to say *Excuse me* as she turned away to answer it.

Lil held Sabrina tightly. "Mella," she breathed. "Mella's in there."

Sabrina said nothing but held her closely. She put her

arm out to pull Seven into her other side. Now that Stacey was no longer quizzing her, the full horror of the situation seemed to crash over her again. Seven was pale as a cloud and shaking. Lil took her hand.

"I shouldn't have left them. By the Light, what have I done?" Seven said.

Lil squeezed her hand. "They'll get them. The firefighters, won't they, Sabrina, they'll rescue them all?"

Sabrina didn't answer. She was staring at the flames lashing at the building. Lil turned to look too, and she felt sick.

The fire was a monster. It looked absolutely unstoppable. The hoses of water were barely penetrating it, despite the pressure, which was so great that it was rising up like steam. But the flames devoured it thirstily in moments and then leaped on, dancing across more and more of the building. If anything, the heat was even stronger. How much longer could someone survive in there? Seven, clearly asking herself the same, let out a little wail, like a cornered animal. Sabrina's arms tightened around Lil's shoulders.

Mella, Lil whispered. *Mella*.

She lost all track of time. It could have been minutes or hours. Another police car arrived, with three officers inside. Eventually Stacey came back over. "We're going in," she said. "Two ambulances are on their way, and hopefully another fire engine." She didn't add, *I hope it'll be enough*. She didn't need to. Her uniform was streaked with soot, her face pale and sweaty.

Lil's insides turned to water.

Sabrina gave Lil a squeeze and the three of them stumbled after Stacey, half blind with the smoke, to the front of the building.

"You'll need to stand far back," Sabrina said. "The fire's not out."

"But they're going in!" Lil was incredulous.

Sabrina avoided her gaze. "They can't risk waiting any longer. They're sending a team in with breathing apparatus and infrared cameras. It'll be too smoky in there to see much. And hot."

Can't risk waiting. Lil's insides twisted. *Mella. God, Mella.*

Lil, Seven, and Sabrina arrived at the front of the house just in time to see the first of the firefighters going in, masks on their faces and oxygen on their backs. They battered down the front door. Lil was astounded by their bravery. The fire was still raging. This part of the house was relatively untouched as of yet but the fire rose in gusts against the darkening summer sky.

The wait for them to emerge was agonizing. Seconds became a minute became five. *Oh my God, they're all dead. Oh God.* The thought sent a shock wave through Lil. She grasped Sabrina's hand. Beneath the soot, her aunt's face was pale as a ghost's, her teeth clenched as though in pain. Seven was muttering under her breath. Lil knew she was talking to the Light. She was filthy too, hair and face covered in ash. Lil was sure she looked the same. Her hands and arms were black.

Lil moved closer, putting her arm around Seven, who leaned into her, clearly welcoming the support.

Then the first firefighter finally came out from the house, supporting someone in his arms. He carried her clear of the thickest part of the smoke and let her stand alone. She staggered as though her legs were too weak to hold her, but then stood tall.

Seven gave a gasp and then a cry. "Sister Luster!"

The woman turned. Her eyes lit on Seven and she smiled, arms open wide. Seven ran into them. They hugged for a long time. Lil turned away to watch another member of the Sisterhood brought out. Younger, and she was being carried by a firefighter, who laid her gently on the ground, clear of the smoke. The next woman came walking. Then another, and another. A few were walking, supported by firefighters, but a lot were carried. A couple were screaming. Lil wasn't close enough to see their injuries, but she knew they must be bad. Her insides turned over at the thought of how monstrous some of their burns must be. Mella still hadn't been brought out. Where was she? Lil felt sick. Not everyone would have survived that fire. *Oh God. Please don't let us be too late. Please please please please please.*

A woman came through the door next. She was tall, nearly as tall as Lil. She reminded Lil of a silver birch tree in autumn; red hair, like leaves, and her bright-white dress and pale skin glowed through the murky gloom. She seemed untouched by the fire, to the point that her dress didn't even have ash on it.

As she appeared, a hush fell on the group, and a chill crept up Lil's spine as she realized who this was. The high priestess, Moon. Lil couldn't stop staring at her. There was something mesmerizing about her.

She was held between two huge firefighters, but she shrugged them both off as if they were flies. "My sisters!" she cried. Her voice was husky and smoke-laced but still melodious and sweet. Like honey, it spread all over you, and held you fast. Something about her manner made you want to do the right thing, to not disappoint her. "Today the Darkness came to our door and we let it in."

There were two police officers with her now. They were clearly trying to silence her, but even as they held her, she kept talking. "Will you let the Darkness take you? Will you succumb?"

A spark of energy jumped from sister to sister as she spoke: a tenseness in their spines, almost a readiness to obey, no matter what.

"My sisters, didn't I shelter you when no one else would? Didn't I bring you in from the cold and the Dark? Didn't I show you the Light?"

The less-injured sisters shuffled uncomfortably, looking at the grass, at their feet, anywhere but at her. A couple stood up and began to move toward her, eyes dazed, their movements jerky, as though something beyond their own will controlled them.

"Come with me now. It's not too late. We can still be saved." Moon's voice reverberated off the walls, off the trees, off the gravel, as loud as anything Lil had ever heard yet as quiet as a whisper right in her ear. It brought up the hairs on her neck. "Come with me into the Brightness!"

Moon twisted, suddenly and sharply yanking herself free of the police officers—and before anyone could stop her, she ran back into the building. As she reached the doorway, where there had been no fire, there was a spark and a flash of white light. Then flames spiraled out from where she stood. They spun like a pinwheel in orange, and blue, and purple. For a second, with her arms outstretched and lit up from behind, she looked like an angel. Then the fire gushed upward—even at this distance Lil could feel its intensity—and Moon screamed, her body twisting with pain, and then as suddenly as they'd appeared, the flames died down and disappeared. The darkness from inside the house seemed to reach forward, and Moon was swallowed up in it.

There was a long silence. Lil didn't know how to process what she'd just seen. Where had the fire come from? How had it vanished again so quickly?

A murmuring began among the sisters, and it grew louder. "The Darkness," they whispered. "The Darkness got her."

Even Lil had to admit it looked like that, although of course that was impossible. The dark wasn't a living thing. It was just the absence of light.

The first ambulance arrived and two paramedics came forward with a stretcher. Lil could see them working in the doorway of the house, covering the body—Moon—with a sheet and then carrying her away. Lil turned. She didn't want to see. She didn't want to think about it . . .

The firefighters who'd gone into the house were standing in a huddle talking to Stacey now.

"What's happening?" Lil asked Sabrina. "Why aren't they going back in?"

"I don't know."

"They need to go back in!" Lil said, voice rising. "They haven't got everyone." *They haven't got Mella.*

"I know, *cariad.* I'm sure they're just regrouping. Working out their next move." Sabrina's eyes were on the group of exhausted-looking men and women. Some of them were taking off their helmets, unhooking their oxygen tanks.

Stacey walked toward Lil and Sabrina. "Detective Laverty," she said, "can I have a word?"

Behind her, more of the firefighters began taking their gear off.

"What's going on?" Lil asked. "Why aren't they going back inside?"

Stacey glanced at Sabrina and then shook her head gently.

Sabrina ducked her head, tears squeezing out of her eyes. "My God," she said.

"No," Lil said. "No! Mella's in there." The two women stared at her, her aunt tearful, Stacey compassionate.

"Mella's still in there!" Lil shouted.

"Lil," her aunt whispered, and Seven clutched at her.

Lil stepped back sharply, throwing up her arms, shaking off both Seven's hand and Sabrina's words.

"No," Lil said. "No, no, no."

"It's just too dangerous," Stacey said. "The team . . ." She turned away, tears clouding her own eyes.

Sabrina said something softly to her and tried to reach for Lil, but she backed away.

"No," Lil said again and again, until it was no longer a word but a wail that rose on the wind, a sound that was not a scream or a cry or a shriek, but a combination of the three. She could feel something breaking inside her, something small and precious that she hadn't known existed until that moment, but she knew with absolute certainty that she could not live without it.

Her aunt said her name again, but Lil couldn't bear it. She turned and ran. She had no plan other than movement, escape, something to keep that terrible ripping inside her at bay, but she found herself at the back of the house again, staring into the mouth of the flames. Staring at the bars on the windows.

She was numb, hollowed out. Empty.

She stumbled about, watching the fire crews work. There were more of them now; another engine must have come while they were at the front. They set up a line of freestanding hoses, closer to the building, where it was hottest. Some sort of aerial platform was rigged up too, and water was pouring down onto the second floor of the building as well. But still the fire burned, as strongly as ever, stronger in some places, and Lil could see it was hopeless. The building was gone. Whoever was left inside . . . She couldn't finish that thought.

A team of firefighters had peeled off from the main group, taking some heavy-looking equipment around the side of the building. Seven was still with Luster, and

Sabrina was with Stacey. Lil felt close to despair. It was all over. Mella was . . .

Then she heard something. Someone was crying. Very small at first. It sounded like Mella. "Mella?" Lil said, moving closer to the house. "Mella?"

"Mouse?"

It was so faint, less than a whisper. Lil moved closer again, skirting around the building to avoid the firefighters. She said her sister's name again. Nothing. Had she imagined it? Was it Mella or just Mella's voice in her head?

She took another step forward, so that she was right up close to the building now; the walls were black, and chunks of them had fallen away. "Can you hear me?" she said aloud. "Mella? Are you okay? Answer me, please. We're coming for you. Just hold on."

There was a shout behind her.

"Lilian!" Her aunt's voice tore through the air.

Lil turned to see her aunt gesticulating wildly above Lil's head. She looked up in time to see the rotten carcass of a window frame plummeting toward her. It fell heavy and it fell fast, and Lil was too close.

Lil threw her hands up to protect herself, stumbling backward at the same time, legs tripping over each other. She fell, head connecting with something solid. The words she'd been saying for the last four months, thirteen days, and so many, many hours rose up in her throat.

"Mella. Find her. Find Mella."

And then there was nothing but darkness.

CHAPTER TWENTY-FIVE

Lil was trapped in the flooded river again, but this time she could not break the glass and escape. Instead of water filling the car, it was fire. Lil was close to drowning, but every time she thought her lungs would explode from lack of oxygen, the fire would fling her up to the surface again, to a tiny portion of the car not consumed by flames, and she would tug down a mouthful of scalding air. Then the flames would surge, and the whole dance would begin again. She wasn't sure how long this went on for, but suddenly she was aware of something beyond the fear and the panic and the searing heat in her lungs. A voice, shouting. Then something that wasn't boiling touched her. It was soft and it wrapped itself around her. It tugged her up toward the surface and held her there while she drew lungful after lungful of air.

"You're all right," someone said. "You're all right."

Lil woke with a sob. For a second she didn't know where she was and then she came to full conciousness. She was on a blanket on the grass. Her head ached. Sabrina was there, brushing Lil's hair off her face. "You're all right," she said again.

Lil whimpered like a kitten.

"Shh," her aunt said. "I'm here. Shh. I'm not going anywhere."

Lil rolled into her aunt's arms, allowing herself to be stroked and calmed.

Sabrina held her and murmured softly. After a moment or two a woman in a green paramedic's uniform came over. She asked Lil questions and shone a light in both her eyes. Lil felt dazed. "She'll be all right," said the paramedic. "Mild concussion. She was incredibly lucky."

Her aunt nodded and Lil lay against her again, warm and cozy in her arms, feeling like a little girl again, but there was something . . . niggling at her . . . something she had to do. It all came back to her at once—the burning building, her sister trapped.

She snapped upright, out of Sabrina's arms, causing a red-hot poker of pain in her skull. "Mella!" she cried.

"It's okay," Sabrina said. "Lil, it's okay. She's okay."

"She is?" Relief, disbelief, worry tumbled through Lil, along with a million other emotions she couldn't name; one rose to the top, shining like a bright penny. *Happiness.* "She's okay," Lil said. "She survived. That's . . . it's . . ."

"Amazing. A miracle, I know."

Not a miracle: the Light. Lil didn't know where the thought had come from, but it felt true. "She's all right," Lil said again. Then fear gripped her. "Really this time?

Because I couldn't, not again, like at the hospital."

"Really this time, I saw her." Sabrina wiped a tear off Lil's cheek. She hadn't even realized she was crying.

Lil was exhausted. Her whole body felt heavy; it was an effort to keep sitting. She wanted to sink to the floor, a boneless heap, and sleep for a century. Happiness flashed through her like a rainbow, colors radiating through her and healing that small, dark, broken place inside her. She couldn't take it all in, to process all of this. That would come later. First: "Where is she? I want to see her."

Sabrina hesitated. "It was a miracle they found her when they did. It all happened so fast. I was coming to tell you when you were knocked out. They went back in, the firefighters. One last time, and headed even farther in. And they found her! But . . . there was a lot of smoke, and the fire was strong. They took her straight to hospital in the ambulance. They . . . they couldn't wait."

"But you said she was okay!"

"She is. She's going to be." She didn't add, *I hope.* She didn't need to. Lil's throat burned with tears. "Your mum's waiting for her at the hospital, sweet pea. She'll text updates, but we'll know more when we get there."

"I want to see her."

"I know you do, and you can as soon as—" Sabrina broke off as someone shouted her name. A police officer on the other side of the driveway. "Will you be all right for a bit?" Sabrina asked Lil. "I don't like to leave you, but . . ."

"It's okay, go. But is everyone . . . ?" Lil hesitated. "Did everyone make it?"

"Oh, Lil," Sabrina said.

"Who?"

Sabrina sighed. "Two died. Moon, their high priestess. Their leader. You saw." Sabrina closed her eyes briefly, and Lil knew that moment would haunt her aunt forever too. "And another woman. We haven't been able to identify her yet. There was so much smoke and damage that the firefighters didn't make it to her in time. Mella had hidden in some kind of anteroom, a large closet I guess. It saved her from the worst of the fire." Sabrina passed a hand over her eyes. "A couple of the women are in a serious condition. They're on their way to hospital now. We're waiting for more ambulances for the others."

The police officer called again, and Sabrina waved to say she was coming. She stood up.

"I'm sorry," Lil said quickly, before her aunt left. "I shouldn't have come here. It was stupid and irresponsible. I don't know what I was thinking."

"It was both of those things." Sabrina tried and failed to look stern. "But, Lil, if it weren't for you, we'd never have come in time."

Lil looked up. "What do you mean?"

"After she saw you in the parking lot, Gwen"—the vicar's wife—"came to find me. She said you'd driven off in my car. She doubted that I'd given you permission to go driving in a flood," Sabrina said wryly, "so thought something was amiss. I knew immediately where you'd gone. Officer Burnley and I headed up here right away in her car, hoping to catch you before you arrived. We saw the fire from about a mile away and called the fire brigade. They met us here."

"So . . . so," Lil said falteringly, "we helped? We helped save Mella and the others."

"It was an incredibly reckless thing you did, Lil, but"—and she gave a small smile—"very, very brave, and yes, these women are alive because of you."

"Oh," Lil said. "Oh." It was too much. To go from despair at her stupidity to hero in such a short space of time. "I helped bring Mella back to us," she said, and burst into tears; she didn't know why she was crying, because it was all she'd wanted every second of every day for the last four months.

Sabrina smiled. "You're an incredible young woman, Lil, and I'm so proud of you. Also very angry. You stole my car!" She smiled. "But I love you and I'm too worried about you to stay mad at the moment. We'll talk more about this later, okay?" The police officer shouted again, gesturing wildly at one of the sisters. "Stay right here. Let me deal with this. I'll be back as soon as I can."

Lil nodded. "Wait. Kiran!" she said. "Where's Kiran? He went for help. He—"

"He's fine. We ran into him on the driveway, literally almost. Officer Burnley drove him back to Old Porthpridd in her car. He's all right. Rest now. We'll talk more later, and I'll get you to Mella as soon as I can."

Lil lay back on the blanket. Her sister was alive but seriously injured. She wanted to rush to the hospital immediately, to be with her, but she knew she had to be patient.

And lying down wasn't so bad right then. She was so tired. The muscles inside her muscles hurt.

The sky was darker. Lil reckoned it must be about eight o'clock. The fire was just about out in the house, or what was left of it. No one would be living there for a while, if ever. The gravel driveway in front of it was crammed with people; a lot of them had oxygen masks and bandages.

Where was Seven? Lil couldn't believe she'd forgotten to ask Sabrina about her. Lil looked about. After a moment she stood up, wincing at the pain in her body, not just her head but everywhere: a general soreness. She began to walk slowly between the groups of people— sisters, paramedics, firefighters, and police, looking for Seven. Sabrina had told her to stay put, but Lil had disregarded her orders so much today she doubted one more time would make much difference. She would probably be grounded for the rest of her natural life anyway when her mum found out what had happened.

At first Lil couldn't find Seven, and then she spotted her on a clump of grass, a little farther off. She was with the woman she'd called Luster.

Seven stood up as Lil approached. She hugged Lil tightly. "The Light bless you," she said. "Are you all right? When the window fell . . ."

"I'm okay," Lil said, "really."

"Some of the others are injured. Your sister . . ." Seven's eyes filled with tears.

"Sabrina says she'll be all right." Lil could hear the

fragile desperation in her voice, almost as if saying it would make it true.

"I will ask the Light to mend her," Seven said.

"Thank you," Lil replied, and she meant it. So many strange coincidences had happened over the last few days that Lil was almost ready to believe. Besides, she would ask help from anything that might make her sister well. The image of that burning building would replay in her mind for the rest of her life. She couldn't bear to think of what her sister must have experienced inside, or the extent of her injuries.

"Sit with us?" Seven said.

"For a bit. My aunt might be looking for me. I don't want her to worry."

Seven led her to the blanket and introduced her to Luster, who took Lil's hands in hers. "Thank you for caring for our sister."

Lil blushed. "I didn't do anything that anyone else wouldn't have done."

Luster patted the back of her hand and smiled. "You did much more. You showed her there is Light in the world, and that is a lesson we all needed to remember." She smiled, warmth glowing in her dark eyes. Lil liked her, which was a surprise, given everything that both Mella and Seven had suffered at the Sisterhood. She guessed the rest of the women were just as much victims as Mella and Seven had been. Luster seemed just like someone's elderly great-aunt or even grandmother.

"How is your sister?" Luster asked.

"She's okay. I mean . . . she's on the way to the hospital, but I hope she's okay."

"The Light takes care of Her own. She will be well, I am sure of it."

"I hope you're right," Lil said.

Luster nodded as if it was certain fact, and Lil liked her even more.

"You are as lovely as your sister said you were," Luster said.

Lil colored again. Even after the way she'd spoken to Mella on that last day, the way she'd let her down, Mella still loved her. She even spoke nicely of her. "I'm just glad we were able to get here in time."

Seven shuffled unhappily. "If I'd spoken sooner, we may have prevented the sisters' injuries. I was foolish to be so afeard of the outside. I was stupid to believe that my absconding would save you all."

"The directing of life's path is not in our gift, however much we may hope and fool ourselves that it is," Luster said. She seemed so calm and so knowledgeable. Her presence was reassuring. It made Lil rethink many of her views of the Sisterhood, but it also made her understand the place even less.

"Sabrina said we did help," Lil told Seven. "If it hadn't been for us coming when we did, they'd never have gotten here in time to stop the fire."

"Is that true?" Seven's eyes widened.

Lil nodded.

Seven's brow furrowed in thought, but she said nothing.

"It didn't save us all," Luster said, eyes downcast, and Lil knew she was thinking of Moon and the other woman who had died. "Perhaps Moon and Evanescence are together, which is all Evanescence ever wanted. To protect our high priestess, to guard her." She gave a long sigh. "Forty years I have been a sister. Cloistered up inside a compound. What will happen to me now? We can't come back here, that's for sure." They all turned to look at the house. The fire had torn right through it, like an enormous beast had eaten it.

Lil felt an intense sadness wash over her. What would happen to these women now? What would happen to Seven? Would she end up in care? She still knew so little of the world; she needed so much help and support. Although perhaps, and the thought was the sun breaking through heavy clouds, perhaps she would find her mum.

"What will you do? Where will you go?" Lil asked Luster.

"After the police have finished their questioning? I don't know. There were more of us, but they escaped before the fire. Maybe we can find them. Maybe we can regroup and find a new home. A new way to venerate the Light."

"And it doesn't need to be secret this time," Seven cut in, eyes shining. "You said that us being here helped to save my sisters? Brought them through the flames?"

Lil nodded.

"Do you not see? I *did* lead my sisters from the Darkness. I did forge a path for them through the flames and lead them into the Brightness. To here. This world. This place beyond the compound, where we can be free in the Light. *This* Light is everywhere, not contained within our boundaries, but all around us. Don't you see? It was here all along, in me, in you. In here." She patted her chest where her heart was. "That's all it is, I think. The Light. It's love. That's all it's ever been, and we can take it with us, wherever we go. We have a responsibility to do so, because it's special and precious, and when you find it, you must cling to it and never ever let it go."

Lil smiled; so did Luster, a gentle, indulgent smile. It was a sweet idea but . . . well, whatever made it easier for Seven was not a bad thing, and what did Lil know of the Light and the Sisterhood, anyway? Besides, it was nice to know that not everything had been lost tonight. That there was still hope. And love.

Lil heard Sabrina calling her. It was time to go. She stood up. "Will I see you again?" she asked Seven.

Seven grinned. "I hope so."

"So do I." They hugged, and then Lil gave Luster a squeeze too.

"I hope Sister Brilliance . . . Mella is well soon," Seven said. "I should like to see her again."

"You will," Lil said.

Seven hesitated. "Do not forget what I said about the Light. It's inside you, when you need it. Right here." She pressed her heart again.

"Okay," Lil said, smiling, if not really understanding.

Seven hugged her again. "Thank you," she whispered, "for everything."

CHAPTER TWENTY-SIX

Sabrina pulled up in front of the hospital and took Lil's arm to steady her as she climbed out. As they entered the double doors of the brightly lit emergency room, a tall boy stood up.

Kiran.

Wonderful, brilliant Kiran.

Here he was, waiting for her in the hospital. Without thinking, Lil threw her arms around him. She tried to put everything she felt about him into that hug. How amazing he was. How funny and kind and gorgeous. How she loved him. It was a lot to ask of one hug, but she could sense in the way Kiran's hands tightened around her that she'd managed to convey at least a little of it.

They held each other for a long time. When she did pull back, it was only so that she could press her lips to his. She didn't say anything. Sometimes there was nothing to say; sometimes words just got in the way.

Lil kissed Kiran with everything she'd wanted to say for

months, if she'd only let herself realize it. She didn't care that her aunt was right there, with half the constabulary and the emergency room staff looking on. Kiran kissed her back, his hands circling her. Her hands were in his hair, and his lips were so soft, and he tasted like lemonade and sherbet and sunshine and all the very best things in the world. As they kissed, a warm, tingling feeling spread out from her heart and down through her veins, to her hands, her fingers.

When she drew away, she was smiling and so was Kiran—wide, happy-crazy smiles—and Lil wanted to kiss him again and again and again. She never wanted to stop kissing him, but right now she had to go because her sister was waiting. Sadness pinged her chest, and she wondered how sadness could come so quickly on the back of all that happiness, but then as clearly as anything, she realized that was just how life was.

"I . . . I . . . had to . . . do that," she stammered. "Sorry, I should have asked permission or something."

Kiran waggled an eyebrow. "You know what? You never have to ask permission to do that." He paused. "So long as it's just with me."

Lil smiled her shiny happy smile again: the one that seemed to suck all the light in the room, in the world, inside her. "I have to see Mella now, but . . . will you . . . will you wait for me?" Was it too much to ask? Lil hoped not.

Kiran grinned. "Are you going to kiss me again?"

"Maybe."

The tips of Kiran's ears glowed. "Then I'll wait."

Mum met Lil at the nurses' station in the ICU. She looked tired, but she gave a warm smile and pulled Lil into a hug. "They'll only let us in one at a time," her mum said. "She's pretty weak. There's a room down the hall. I'll wait there. They'll come and get me if you need me, all right?"

Lil squeezed her mum's hand. "How . . . is she?"

"She's okay." Her mum clasped Lil's hand suddenly. "She's home! Lil, she's home!" A small portion of the bleak weariness fell away, and Lil saw a glimpse of how her mum had looked before this all started. It reminded Lil of the X-ray Mella had shown her of a painting by van Gogh that revealed hidden details of a previous painting buried under layers of paint. This experience had irrevocably changed them all, but who they were still lurked underneath. Maybe what was created on top was better, stronger, more lasting.

Lil needed to wash her hands and put on a gown before she was allowed in to see Mella. She scrubbed her hands thoroughly in the metal sink by the door to her ward, squelching the soap in between her fingers and right under her nails. She let the tap run for a long time, making sure the water was scalding hot. She wanted to make sure her hands were clean. She didn't want to risk giving her sister an infection. She was also nervous about seeing Mella. What would she say?

Finally she couldn't put it off any longer, and, heart thudding, she slid into Mella's room. It was darker than Lil expected. They'd closed the blinds, and a soft gray hung over everything. There were various machines around the bed, making whirring, clicking noises. Mella looked tiny beside them—even smaller than Lil remembered. The oxygen mask over her nose and mouth almost covered her whole face. Her eyes were closed and Lil felt a moment's relief. She didn't want to disturb Mella; she'd come back later. Then Mella's eyes flickered, opened, and focused on Lil. She struggled to pull the mask off and sit up, so Lil darted forward.

As she helped her sister to sit up, she accidentally bashed her elbow into Mella's ribs. Lil drew back. "Sorry," she said. "Sorry, sorry." For a second she thought Mella was crying, and then she realized that Mella's wheezing sound was laughter.

With her mouth free of the oxygen mask, Mella said in a husky whisper, "Always so clumsy, Mouse."

Lil rolled her eyes. The incident Mella was referring to had been ten years ago! When she was about six, Lil managed to knock an ornament off a shelf in a shop, and as she turned around to apologize, she knocked two more off. Ever since, her family had called her clumsy.

Mella wheeze-laughed again, and Lil did too. For a second it was like before, like nothing had ever happened. Then Mella began to cough and the sensation was gone. The laughter died in Lil's throat. What should she say? Mella was silent too. She pulled the oxygen mask down again and was breathing steadily through it. Lil's own lungs burned in sympathy. "Want me to get a nurse?" she asked.

Mella shook her head and continued to breathe calmly.

After a minute or two she lifted the mask again and said, "Stay?" After a beat she said, "Missed you. So . . . much."

I missed you, too, Lil thought, but the words stuck in her throat. Instead she said, "You didn't call. Or text. Or anything."

"Couldn't . . ."

"The Sisterhood wouldn't let you?"

Mella nodded and then shook her head. "Not just them. Once you're gone . . . it's hard to . . . come back."

You should have tried, Lil thought, but deep down she understood what Mella was saying. Pride, guilt, embarrassment, doubt that they wanted her home: all those feelings would have clouded Mella's decision, until ultimately it was easier not to face them, easier to stay gone. Lil wasn't ready to admit that, though, not out loud. The last four months had been too painful.

"We looked everywhere for you," she said. "I thought I'd go crazy. I thought we'd never see you again." Lil hadn't meant to say all these things, but they just came pouring out, and once she'd started talking, she found she couldn't stop. "I'm sorry I didn't try harder. I didn't realize things were so bad."

Mella had tears in her own eyes. She put her hand out to Lil, fingers clasping hers tight. Eyes intense, she said in a breathy whisper, "Not your fault, Mouse. Not . . . your fault."

"I missed you," Lil said.

Mella squeezed her hand like she was never going to let go; Lil wouldn't want her to. "I'm so sorry."

Lil shook her head. "It doesn't matter. You're here now." She wiped her face with the back of her hand. "It's okay."

"Does . . . matter," Mella said.

And it did and it didn't, because everything was different now, but also everything was the same, because Mella was back, and while Lil could hold her and talk to her and laugh with her, the anger and pain of when she was gone didn't feel so important. But, like an undertow, it was there, silent and invisible and threatening to rip them apart again at any moment. There was so much they didn't know and would need to talk about. Not just her time at the Sisterhood, but also before. Both were an indelible part of Mella, forever shaping her identity, and Lil wanted to understand her sister better. She wanted to be there for her in a way she hadn't before, but for now she just wanted to enjoy Mella being back.

Still holding Mella's hand, she sat down on the bed. Mella looked exhausted. Her eyes kept flicking closed. Lil didn't say anything else, just stroked her sister's wrist. Mella's breathing steadied and settled. She was asleep.

There was a long gash down the side of Mella's head. It had been sewn together with butterfly stitches, but it would probably scar, another sign that her experiences at the Sisterhood would never leave her.

Mella gasped and her eyes flew open.

"Are you all right?" Lil said, panicked. "What's happened?"

Mella's eyes settled on Lil's face and she smiled. "You're . . . still here."

"Yeah," Lil said.

"Then . . . I'm . . . all right," Mella said, and closed her eyes again.

After a while Lil stood up and drew open the blind just a little bit, so that the last of the day's sun could creep across the bed as Mella slept, her breathing steady and even. Then Lil sat back down next to her sister. She counted each one of Mella's breaths until she got to a hundred, and then she started again. It was wonderful. She had thought she'd never hear Mella breathe again.

The weak sun crept up the bed slowly, carefully, to Mella's face. As it caught Mella in its beam, Lil thought Mella looked . . . happy . . . peaceful in a way Lil never remembered seeing her before. A warmth spread over Lil that came not from the gentle sun, but from somewhere inside, and Lil realized what it was. Love.

"It's special and precious," Seven had said, "and when you find it, you must cling to it and never ever let it go."

Lil leaned over and took her sister's hand. The warmth—the Light—spread between them. Whether it was her imagination or not, Lil didn't know or care, because as she watched, a glow rose up over their joined hands, dancing and flickering like a flame.

ACKNOWLEDGMENTS

✴

Thank you to my agents, Jane Finigan and Juliet Mahony, at Lutyens & Rubinstein for championing this book from the very beginning. Thank you also to my wonderful editors, past and present: Christian Trimmer, Krista Vitola, and Catherine Laudone in the States; and in the UK, Rachel Mann and Lucy Rogers. (You know it's taken a while to write a book when you've gone through three editors!) Biggest thanks must go to Lucy, for her endless patience and incredibly astute comments. The Sisterhood section is what I always wanted it to be, and that is mostly down to her wonderful insight. I'm very grateful to the rest of the teams at Simon & Schuster UK and US for their support too, including Krista Vossen, for the gorgeous US cover. It's hauntingly beautiful, and I love it.

Thank you also to Jon Arrenberg for so kindly looking over the fire scene for me, and for not laughing too audibly at how outlandish it was. His feedback was invaluable, and any mistakes are very much my own!

A huge thank-you to my family and friends, especially my mum.

And the biggest thanks of all, of course, go to my own mini family: my husband, Adam, and my wonderfully funny, smart, and loving daughter.